D1374818

Please return or renew this item before the latest date shown below

Renewals can be made
by internet
in person
by phone

Thank you for using your library

GIRL GENIUS

AGATHA H AND THE AIRSHIP CITY

PHIL & KAJA FOGLIO

TITAN BOOKS

Girl Genius: Agatha H and the Airship City
Print edition ISBN: 9781781166475
E-book edition ISBN: 9781781166482

Published by Titan Books
A division of Titan Publishing Group Ltd
144 Southwark Street, London SE1 0UP

First edition: January 2013
1 3 5 7 9 10 8 6 4 2

Printed and bound in Great Britain by CPI Group Ltd.

Did you enjoy this book? We love to hear from our readers.
Please email us at readerfeedback@titanemail.com or write to us at
Reader Feedback at the above address.

To receive advance information, news, competitions, and exclusive offers
online, please sign up for the Titan newsletter on our website:
www.titanbooks.com

GIRL GENIUS

AGATHA H AND THE AIRSHIP CITY

PROLOGUE

SIXTEEN YEARS AGO

I n a small clearing, an intricate device of glass and metal tubes scanned the night skies. The stars glittered. Barry Heterodyne sat back and rubbed his eyes. Nothing. Around him the nighttime sounds of frogs and insects filled the marsh air. He glanced over at the campsite. Bill sat in front of the black flames, endlessly cleaning his weapons.

Barry sighed. His worry about the state of his brother's mind was steadily increasing. It had been three years since the explosions had ripped through Castle Heterodyne, killing Bill's infant son and covering the escape of his wife's abductors. Three years without a clue to the identity of the perpetrators, a ransom note, or indeed, any information at all.

Barry pulled out a pocket watch and flipped open the cover to check its glowing numerals. He then pulled out a pad of foolscap covered with equations and, for the hundredth time, checked his calculations. He sighed again. It all balanced out. If this was another blind alley—

The device quietly chirped. Suddenly Bill was at his side. Barry swallowed. Whatever deterioration was taking place in his brother's head, there was no effect upon his abilities. If anything, Bill was getting faster.

Barry fitted his eyes to the scopes. Yes! There was a new set of stars in the crosshairs. Two more flickered on as he watched.

Unthinkingly, he gave his brother the old "thumbs up" signal, and then realized with a start that it was the first time he had done so since that terrible night in Mechanicsburg.

The destruction of their castle had only been the first such attack upon the Sparks of Europa. Six months later the attacks had begun in earnest, and in the subsequent two and a half years, thirty-eight of the most powerful Sparks of Europa had been snuffed out.

The most frustrating thing had been the lack of information. There had been no demands, no manifestos, no ultimatums. Just a single-minded effort to destroy as many Sparks as possible.

Of course, in the beginning, accusations had flown between the Great Houses, usually accompanied by wind-up starfish ninjas or giant glass crabs. But as time went on, all the obvious suspects were wiped out in turn, and soon there were few left. Eventually they just started calling the mysterious antagonist "The Other."

Barry switched off the scope and stared up into the sky. The new stars could be seen with the naked eye now and rapidly were getting brighter. This attack looked like it was following the traditional pattern, but this time, they were ready. He handed Bill a pair of bulky goggles and donned a pair himself. Now when he looked, the objects hurtling towards the ground were greatly magnified. Then, they seemed to fall apart and vanish. Barry whipped a hand up to the goggles and flipped a switch. The quality of the light changed and the sky was now orange. He looked about frantically. His brother growled, "Down. Left. At 7:37." It was the most Bill had spoken this week. Barry shifted his head as instructed and—there! Three small shapes in freefall. There was a fourth and—

Without warning the shapes seemed to burst apart yet again, and each one sprouted a huge mushroom-like growth—Barry blinked. It was a da Vinci parachute. But it must be enormous. On the other hand, they certainly seemed to be working, as the objects, now clearly discernable as spheres, were noticeably slowing.

Bill tapped his shoulder, and the two dashed back to the swamp strider, which Barry had left ticking over. Bill maintained observation of the falling spheres, while Barry maneuvered the craft through the pools and bogs.

All too soon they broke through a wall of brush in time to see all ten spheres gently plow into the spongy ground and roll to a stop. The great parachutes fell to earth and were draped over the landscape.

The spheres themselves were six meters in diameter, constructed of glass and metal. As Barry watched, he saw the last of what looked for all the world like bread crust flaking off the spheres and falling to the ground. Possibly some sort of insulator, he mused.

The spheres were hot. They could feel the heat from where they stood. Barry tugged his thick leather gloves out of his belt and pulled them on. Then he hopped down beside his brother who had already begun unloading the swamp strider's cargo pod, and the two of them got to work.

Barely an hour later, as the sky was beginning to lighten, there was a sudden change. Lights began to bloom across the spheres, and machinery could be heard activating. Pumps began to whirr, and pipes sucked and gurgled.

When a Spark was attacked, those who were not crushed by the initial bombardment suddenly found themselves attacked by large, insect-like creatures that would appear, seemingly from nowhere, and overrun the area. While people were battling them, smaller wasp-like creatures would also appear, burrowing into anyone they could find. Many died outright. Those that didn't were infected by parasitic organisms that forced them to obey the orders of the insect army, while physically distorting their bodies in unmentionable ways. These doomed souls came to be called "Revenants." While they were slow and easy to spot, they were fearless and many a despairing band of fighters had been overwhelmed by sheer weight of numbers. The transformation took place quickly enough that, often, newly infected revenants helped overrun their own towns, killing all non-human creatures and converting as many people as they could into monsters like themselves. Once they were finished, they lurched off, without a backward glance, led by their insect masters towards the next target. There was no cure.

Again and again this pattern repeated itself. The governments of Europa were powerless, and many quickly fell into ruin as the Sparks propping them up were exterminated.

Both varieties of Slaver Wasp, for so they were labeled, were examined, but even the greatest Sparks couldn't determine if these creatures were natural or constructs, let alone how to prevent their depredations.

With a hiss, the spheres began to split open. First to emerge were waves of the all-too-familiar soldier wasps; they tottered weakly out of the spheres, and immediately began to feed upon the remains of the parachutes. Barry nodded. No wonder they'd never seen any evidence of them.

Then, from the heart of the burst spheres, reared enormous slug-like grubs, themselves laced with pipes and valves. They stretched upwards, opened their surprisingly small mouths and began droning an eerie call. When the soldiers had finished devouring the last remnants of the parachutes, they gathered around the base of the spheres and waved their claws in time to the song. More and more of the monstrous creatures began to sing in the predawn light. Barry had to fight the urge to clap his hands over his ears. In desperation, he began to hum the comforting atonal drone that helped him to think clearly. Beside him, Bill was already humming in familiar counterpoint.

All of the grubs were singing now. A ripple of color spread over the first, and it opened its mouth even wider and began to spit out a swarm of the feared Slaver wasps.

That was good enough for Bill; he twisted the control lever in his hand, igniting the string of phosphorus grenades that the boys had festooned the spheres with as they lay cooling.

Almost a hectare of swamp fiercely burned with a white-hot glare for several minutes. Within the inferno, Barry could hear the screaming of the great slug monsters and the crackling of the soldiers. Several of the latter attempted to break free of the conflagration, but they were easily cut down by the boys.

Half an hour later, Barry sat down, exhausted. The nature of the swamp had prevented the fire from spreading, but the great heat had ignited enough trees that they'd had to move quickly to escape. But the danger was behind them now, and the fire was already dying down.

Scarcely five kilometers away loomed the gutta-percha citadel of Lord Womak, "The Lightning Eater." Barry had to admit that he felt a small, unworthy bit of satisfaction as the first of the flaming boulders smashed into His Lordship's castle. They had tried to warn Womak, but he had merely laughed and released a pack of flying badgers against them.

A total of ten boulders impacted. Two of them directly upon the main castle. In Barry's opinion, the rest were quite superfluous, as the devastation caused by the first two left no doubt in his mind that the Lightning Eater was pulverized along with everything within the castle walls.

The remaining eight missiles were obviously meant to soften up the town and the surrounding countryside for the subsequent attack by the Slaver wasps.

Womak had situated his castle on a crag outside the nearest town, so the town had only suffered minimally from the impacts that had destroyed the castle. The remaining boulders rained down in a precise geometric pattern surrounding the town, and culminated with the last falling directly into the town center.

Barry forced himself to watch as each boulder impacted. It was as he'd suspected. When they had first viewed a bombarded town, the general consensus had been that the missiles must have contained explosives. But Bill had never been able to find any chemical residue for analysis. Watching now, Barry could see that there were no additional explosions, the devastation was caused by the terrible kinetic force of the impacts themselves. That was the final confirmation of his unthinkable hypothesis.

The Other had tipped his hand. Barry knew where to find him, and once there—

But there was time enough to deal with that later. The townspeople would need help, but for the first time, one of the Other's attacks had been predicted and curtailed.

He could be beaten.

ONE

"In conclusion, the evidence shows that there has not been a legitimate sighting of either William or Barry Heterodyne since they assisted in the cleanup of Woggleburg after the destruction of Lord Womak's castle sixteen years ago. All such reported sightings have proved to be either fraudulent Heterodynes or simple cases of mistaken identity. However, amongst the general populace, the belief that they are still 'out there' fighting the good fight remains unshakable, as is the conviction that someday, they will return. This belief remains despite the fact that their castle is in ruins, their lands are overrun, their servants are scattered and indeed nothing remains but their name."

—SUMMARY OF A REPORT TO THE BARON ON AN
UPSURGE IN FALSE HETERODYNE SIGHTINGS

Agatha dreamed...

Mathematical formulae and gear ratios wound through her head and took shape with a feeling of inevitability that terrified her as much as it excited her. With a groan, the vast machine lurched to life, gears meshing together in a jewel-toned mechanical ballet. As more and more of the machine coalesced, Agatha noticed that the great engine was pulsing at the same rate as her heart, sending waves of energy through her like waves being dashed upon a rocky shore.

This was the answer, ringing in Agatha's ears like a chorus of clockwork angels. Impatiently she reached forward, trying to grasp the shifting, glittering thing before her. Something clicked into place in her mind. She began to recognize the patterns forming before her. She realized that all of the surrounding space was beginning to react to the shining thing before her. Of course. The principles involved could be expanded infinitely outwards, therefore—

A vise slammed shut on her mind. A dark tunnel closed in on her perceptions and squeezed the glittering pattern down, down, down to a speck so small she couldn't see it except as a twinkling mote of light just out of reach. With a sob of desperation Agatha lunged forward to grab it, and—

With a *SMACK*, her hand struck the wall.

The pain snapped her fully awake. She was gasping as if she had run all the way to the University and back, and covered in a sheen of sweat that had soaked her bedding. Her head was a throbbing ball of pain. Gamely she tried to swing out of bed, and almost crashed to the floor. Belatedly she noticed that her muscles were stiff and cramped, and that her blankets were knotted and wrapped around her in a way that told her she must have spun like a top in her sleep. As she began to unwind herself, the headache began to subside. Agatha was a connoisseur of headaches, and was relieved at the transitory nature of this one.

Once free of the bedclothes, Agatha snatched her spectacles from a small shelf and slipped the brass loops over her ears. The world clicked into focus and she was soon at her desk ripping bits off of a small machine, hastily adding others, bending wires and shuffling gears in a frantic attempt to capture the quickly fading memory within the structure of the device.

On an overloaded bookshelf in the corner, a painted metal woodsman struck a golden wolf repeatedly with a miniscule axe. First clock. An enameled couple wearing tiny crowns struck up a mazurka while a chime counted time to their bouncing feet. Second clock. Agatha began to work even more frantically. The beat of the mazurka insinuated itself into the last memories of the dream machine's song, tangling them up and then sweeping them away in three-eighths time.

Agatha growled in frustration and sat back onto her chair with a thump. She blew an errant lock of blonde hair out of her face. Gone. She touched the golden trilobite locket at her throat and sighed.

Getting to her feet, she stripped off the damp nightshirt and stretched in the early morning light that came in through her attic window, past several plants and what appeared to be a small mechanical spider. A variety of prisms caught the light and scattered it throughout the small room. Flashes of bright color glowed against her hair.

On a shelf by the window crammed with devices constructed from wire and fish bones, a small brass mushroom chimed as a cheerful mechanical centipede clog-danced around the stalk. That was the third clock, which meant that it really was time to go. She would have to skip breakfast again.

She poured a dollop of water out of the blue ceramic pitcher into her washbowl and quickly washed up. Her skin pebbled in the cold air as she considered the meager contents of her closet. A white linen shirt, and her green tweed skirt and vest. These last had been a birthday present from her parents, and were Agatha's current favorites. Long striped woolen stockings and a stout pair of boots completed her outfit. Quickly she stripped the sheets from her bed and hung them from the pole that held the bed drape. Then it was down the stairs, grab the large military greatcoat and cap that hung from her hook in the boot room, and through the door of the smithy to the outside world. The device she had cobbled together banging against her thigh through the pocket as she ran down the steps to the street.

She breathed deeply of the crisp cold air and blew out a great cloud of vapor. The sun had barely cleared the city walls and the lamplighters could be seen striding above the cobblestoned street, their stilt suits clacking as they hurried to douse the last few streetlights. It was evident that the city gates had been opened for the day, as the streets of Beetleburg were already full. Carts piled high with everything from produce to machine parts were pulled by horses, oxen and the occasional mechanical construct as they rumbled through the center of the street. On either side, the shops had opened and exposed their wares. The small fried pastries of several different cultures were hawked next to dried fruits and vegetables. Ovens unloaded aromatic platters of fresh bread. Several hundred different types of sausage and an equal number of cheeses were grabbed from hooks and shelves and consumed before the purchaser had gone three meters. Schools of smoked fish and eels hung near sellers of hot beverages, and everywhere there was a bewildering variety of unclassifiable foodstuffs that were served on sticks.

The people consuming this bounty were a varied group. The great university drew students from all over the known world. Most were garbed against the March cold in what were obviously scrounged military uniforms. The garish colors added a festive note to the cold gray streets. Many were workers, trudging to or from the Tyrant's factories. Occasionally men from different shifts would meet and stop briefly to pass along news or laugh at a humorous incident. Clumps of students headed towards the great gates of the University. Some groups were engaged in serious debate, others looked like they'd had a bit too much to drink last night.

Agatha was surprised to see a lone Jägermonster strolling casually down the street. People looked at it nervously out of the corner of their eyes, but were determined to act casual... which the monster soldier seemed to find quite amusing, but then, apparently, Jägermonsters found everything amusing. Except when people tried to beg for mercy. That they found downright hilarious.

This one still retained most of its humanity, as far as Agatha could see. Its frame still fit into an obviously scrounged uniform, although its arms were disturbingly long. The face was covered in what appeared to be small spikes, but that didn't keep it from sporting a large, disturbing grin.

These days the Jägermonsters served Baron Wulfenbach, whose rule currently stretched across most of Europa, but it was unusual to see any forces of the Empire here. Relations between the Tyrant of Beetleburg and the House of Wulfenbach had been cordial ever since the city had been peacefully annexed into the *Pax Transylvania* over a decade ago. In spite of this, Beetleburg continued to be patrolled by the Tyrant's own mechanical forces. Even now, one quick-stepped around the corner, jogged to the center of the block, stopped, and swiveled twice around its axis, looking for trouble. It registered the Jäger, and with a snap, extruded a pair of guns as it skipped towards it. Agatha always thought the watchmen clanks looked like indignant wind-up toys. Everyone did, really, until they started shooting.

The Jäger went still. The clank stopped three meters away from the monster soldier. There was a hiss, and then a scratchy voice asked the Jäger to slowly and clearly state its business. This should be amusing, thought Agatha. The Jägermonsters carefully cultivated and maintained their original Mechanicsburg accent. There had been numerous instances where clanks or other devices that relied on verbal instructions had, upon hearing it, simply opened fire. This was especially disconcerting when said devices were otherwise harmless household appliances.

Agatha was again surprised, as the soldier fumbled at its belt, and pulled out a crumpled bit of paper. It nervously scrutinized it for a minute, turned it upside down, checked it again and then laboriously stated, "I am comingk to... the mar-ket to..." The Jäger was visibly sweating now. "To *buy*, not *schteal*... a piece of... ham." He looked up expectantly. The entire street had gone still, and Agatha could hear the clacking as wax disks shuffled about inside the steel watchman.

The voicebox crackled to life. "Please move this horse. I believe it is dead." With that the mechanical soldier swiveled about, and continued on down the street and bobbled around the next corner.

The Jäger blew out a huge sigh of relief, saw Agatha looking at him and gave her a cocky "thumbs up," before tucking the paper back into the pouch at his belt and strolling on.

As the Jäger passed, the rumble and buzz of the town resumed. Hausfraus resumed their dickering over soup bones, peddlers hawked candied fruits and insects, and swarms of children flowed through the crowds shrieking and looking for dropped treasures.

Agatha frowned. It wasn't the first time that the Tyrant's clockwork soldiers had made a harmless error, but she had been noticing them more often. Discussing it with the Tyrant, however, had proved fruitless. He frequently avowed that the Clockwork Army that had successfully defended Beetleburg for over thirty years had been declared the finest fighting force in Europa by the Baron himself, and thus wasting time and resources on them was unnecessary. Still, Agatha had heard stories about the battle clanks that the Baron's armies used, and more and more she had found herself thinking about ways Beetleburg's defenders could be improved—until a quick, sharp blossom of pain behind her eyes ended the chain of thought. It never failed.

Massaging her brow, Agatha found her progress was suddenly slowed by a crowd of people clustered in front of her. Focusing, she saw that she was in front of the familiar windows of the local bookseller. The display inside explained the crowd, a new Heterodyne Boys novel had arrived, and people were in line waiting for the shop to open. A card in the window displayed the title: *The Heterodyne Boys and the Mystery of the Cast Iron Glacier.* That sounded promising. Agatha made a mental note to put her name down on the request list at the university library. Agatha's parents disliked the Heterodyne Boys novels, and refused to permit them in the house.

People in the bookstore line were eagerly discussing the book, analyzing the cover art, or just reminiscing about the actual Heterodyne Boys themselves.

Passions were easily aroused by this, even though the Heterodyne Boys had vanished over fifteen years ago. Things were a lot quieter now, the older people constantly reminded the younger generation, but before the Baron had imposed the Pax Transylvania, all of Europa had been a crazy quilt of kingdoms ruled by Sparks, embattled royalty, or any number of improbable and unstable combinations thereof. If a mad scientist wasn't at war with at least two of his neighbors, it was because he had his back to the sea, and even then he had to watch out for an invasion of intelligent sea urchins. The populace at large was used mostly as soldiers, laborers, bargaining chips, or in some of the worst cases, monster chow. Into this nightmare world had come the Heterodynes, a pair of Sparks who had taken on the Sisyphean task of stopping the more malignant despots, a task which seemed to involve battling an endless stream of monsters, clanks, armies of various species, and the insane madmen who'd created them.

Now there was a legitimate school of thought that held that the Heterodynes did not actually accomplish all that much. They were, when all was said and done, just two men, two incredibly gifted Sparks accompanied by an ever-changing coterie of friends, assistants and fellow adventurers to be sure, but they could only do so much. The world produced a never-ending supply of dangerous creatures, as well as the scientists who had spawned them. But the point wasn't that they had taken down the diabolical Doctor Doomfrenzy and his giant moss-bees, it was that there was someone actively out there, in the world, trying to make said world a better place, and in some small, measurable way, succeeding. They gave people hope, when hope was in desperately short supply.

And because of this, people remembered them as heroes. Almost everyone over a certain age could recite an incident that had, in some way, touched them personally. As she moved through the crowd, Agatha heard the old arguments about how the world would be better if the Heterodyne Boys were still around, as well as the fervent assurances that one day, Bill and Barry would return and make everything better, starting with the price of oats.

By the time Agatha cleared the crowd and hit the Street of the Cheesemongers, she had slowed to a walk and was once again deep in the mists of her own thoughts. Her feet followed the route to the University automatically, which brought her near the institution's great bronze gates.

The answer she'd glimpsed in her dream was still there, somewhere in her head. If she concentrated, she could almost visualize the correct assembly that would make her little machine actually work. Almost... and then the order of the parts would muddle and blur, the formulae would lose themselves in the murk of her mind and her head would feel as though it were filled with honey—thick and comforting, but impossible to work through. If she could just filter out all of the distractions... She unconsciously hummed a few notes... trying to sharpen her mental sight and cut through the sticky thoughts...

She was so busy chasing ideas around her own head that she

didn't notice the cries of surprise from the people around her, or the electrical smell on the air. A small arc of blue electricity leaping from the metal rims of her glasses to her nose brought her back to the present and she gave a small yelp.

And then a hole in the sky opened up. A huge silver figure pointed the accusation at her as an unearthly voice rang out: "—LIKE THAT?"

In his long military career, Machinist Second Class Moloch von Zinzer had sampled quite a wide variety of alcoholic concoctions. In good times they were made from potatoes, grapes, or sometimes barley. However, in his experience, decent brews could be wrung from wheat, oats, rye, honey, pears, melons, corn, apples, berries, turnips, seaweed, sorghum, sugar beets, buckwheat, zucchini, rice, yams, sunflowers, artichokes, cattails or giant mushrooms. It was sort of a hobby, and one that made him popular with his fellows.

One used what one was able to scrounge, which meant that the drinks were usually brewed up on spare bits of madboy equipment, so occasionally the stuff was blue, or caused you to grow an extra set of ears, but it usually got the job done. But this—this was a new low. He looked at the crudely printed label on the bottle in his hand. "Beetle Beer" it proclaimed. Fair enough, he thought, I can believe that.

Moloch sighed and took another pull. What made it even worse were the smells that even the dank air of the little back alley couldn't hide. Shops selling all kinds of foodstuffs lined the streets, the rich aromas of cheese, sausages and pastries filled his head. To a soldier who'd seen the outside world, a world filled with shattered towns and endless kilometers of abandoned farms, the sight of shops piled high with food that could be bought directly off the street by anyone with a little money was astonishing. It was like stepping into a world he'd thought lost forever. The bread was the worst. He'd have killed for any one of the fresh loaves he could smell baking.

So what had Omar spent the last of their money on? Beetle Beer. Well, it was sort of like bread, and it was all the breakfast he was going to get. When money failed, philosophy would have to do.

Moloch took a long look at his brother. Of all of the companions that he could have been left with, lost in strange territory, his brother Omar was surely at the bottom of his list. He stood in the middle of the alley, despite his wounded leg, swilling his beer with characteristic nervous energy. Moloch wished that Omar would pull up a crate, relax, and for just once, not be poised to fight. Moloch was well-and-truly tired of fighting. Omar would never get enough. He had laughed off Moloch's protests over the lack of breakfast. He'd find money enough, somewhere. Moloch didn't like to think where.

Out in the street, shouts erupted. A bright electrical light flared, the shouts turned into screams and a girl wearing an overlarge officer's coat ran down the alley toward them. In her panic she tripped on a box and landed sprawling at their feet. Her glasses flew off her nose and skittered out of arm's reach.

Agatha blinked. There were muddy boots a few centimeters from her nose, and she realized that she had just missed plowing into their owner. She looked up. The uniform proclaimed a soldier, its condition implied hard use. Although his face was blurred, she could see that he was smiling, and that it wasn't a nice smile. A bottle dangled from one hand.

Agatha had led a fairly sheltered life, but even she could tell that this person was bad news. Her eyes never left Omar's as her hands franticly patted the ground about her, unsuccessfully searching for her glasses.

"Well! What have we here?" Omar eyed her speculatively. "Obviously our very own angel of mercy, here to help out a couple of poor lost soldiers who are down on their luck."

Moloch could see his brother's habitual nastiness gearing up. His heart sank. Begging and intimidation. So they were reduced to that. He shifted in his seat on a stack of crates. The girl started, she hadn't seen him right away. "Ha. She must know that you just spent our last groat on this swill you call booze. Well, help her up, Omar. Show her we can be friendly." Moloch tried to keep his tone happy. Maybe she wouldn't notice the edge to Omar's voice. Maybe she could be convinced to give them a handout quickly, and go away, before Omar had a chance to get them into trouble. Ho ho, look at us, two jolly soldier boys, just like in the music halls. Except one of us is a murderous bastard who couldn't keep out of trouble in a locked duffel... He smiled at Agatha. "Spare some change, Miss?"

Omar stepped toward Agatha. He had got round her as she stumbled to her feet, and was now between her and the alley mouth. "Oh, no, she can spare more than that, look at that fine locket!"

Agatha abandoned the search for her glasses and backed up, eyes huge. Beetleburg was a safe town, but mothers still passed down stories about what soldiers did to girls who didn't take care. Being mugged was a new experience, and her head was still humming from the shock of the apparition in the street, but Agatha still knew she was in trouble.

"A pretty little townie like this, she'll have a whole box of the stuff at home. She'll never miss a couple of small gifts to the deserving. And then—" Omar's grin grew even larger. "Maybe she'll let us show her just how nice we can be."

While a lot of the advice and instruction that Agatha's parents had passed down had been either tantalizingly vague or dryly academic, certain situations had been discussed in detail, as well as their possible consequences. This was one of them.

As Omar reached out towards her chest, Agatha sidestepped him neatly, grabbed Moloch's bottle and in one fluid motion swung it round to connect with Omar's face. Moloch had to admit that it was a superb shot, but with nowhere near enough force to do anything useful. Agatha looked a bit surprised at what she had done, but gamely swung again, and this time Omar was ready. He stepped within her swing, grabbed her lapel, jerked her off balance and delivered two quick slaps that set Agatha's head ringing. As she slumped, Omar's eyes narrowed and a grin of anticipation crossed his face as he slowly drew his fist back.

Suddenly Moloch's hand gripped his upper arm. "That's enough, Sergeant!" he roared in his best military voice. As he'd hoped, the reference to rank checked Omar's swing.

Omar had endured enough punishment duty that its memory could stop him when appeals to reason failed. "She hit me," he hissed petulantly. "I am not taking that from a lousy civilian!" He tried to shake off Moloch's restraining arm.

"Stop it, you fool! Don't you remember what they do to

26

people in this town? Do you want to wind up in one of those damned jars?"

That stopped Omar, as it stopped a lot of people. The Tyrant of Beetleburg had little patience for those who broke his laws. A popular punishment consisted of simply placing wrongdoers inside large glass jars in the public squares. There they eventually died of thirst or hunger. Their bodies lay undisturbed until a new lawbreaker was put in. Consequently, the locals rarely broke the law.

Omar nodded to his brother, but a smirk twisted his face as he drew a dazed Agatha toward him. "Okay, doll, it's been fun, but we have to leave. To remember these happy times—" with a flick of his wrist, he gripped, twisted, and snapped off the large golden trilobite locket at Agatha's throat, "—I'll just take a little souvenir."

Agatha's eyes bugged, but before she could yell, Omar swung his foot and swept her feet out from under her. She collapsed in a heap on the ground as he took off down the alley with a laugh and a wave. "Thanks for the souvenir!"

Moloch trotted along after him, with both of their duffels under his arm. "You are such an asshole," he hissed. Omar grinned.

Agatha scrambled to get up. She spotted a glint upon the ground, which proved to be her glasses, thankfully undamaged. Her anger finally roared up and gave voice. "BRING BACK MY LOCKET!" she screamed, as she went pounding up the alley in pursuit. She burst out onto the street and was confronted by a milling crowd of soldiers and ordinary citizens. Of the great hole in the sky, there was no sign, as there was no sign of the two thieves.

Agatha felt tears well up in her eyes. "You miserable wretched knaves," she fumed. "I'll inform the Watch on you!" Her voice started to climb in volume, and a wild note entered her voice. People in the vicinity began to regard her with suspicion and then fear, as her voice entered registers that set off alarm bells in their heads. "They'll comb the city, and they'll find you, and when they do, they'll put you in the jars, and I'll come down every day and watch you beg and scream and claw at the glass as you die slowly—like the miserable rats you are!"

She took another deep breath and then to the onlookers it seemed as if an invisible bolt of lightning had struck her in the head. Agatha clutched at her temples and screamed in pain as she collapsed to her knees. Another headache. She always got them when she got worked up, and this one reflected her rage with skull-splitting force. A small crowd formed, but no one approached. When people acted strange, anything could happen. In addition to the pain, Agatha felt a wave of embarrassment flow over her.

Suddenly there was a flurry of activity over to one side, and a tall figure loomed over her. A greenish, hirsute hand offered her a canteen. Agatha looked up into the interested face of a Jägermonster. A different one than the one she'd spotted before. "Hey dere, gorgeous." He smiled a smile with way too many teeth. "Iz you okeh, or iz you gonna change into sum kinda giant ting mit no clothes on?"

The concept caused Agatha to blink in surprise, and wonderfully, her headache began to recede, almost as quickly as it had arrived. That was a rare and welcome occurrence. She climbed unsteadily to her feet while trying desperately to look like she wasn't avoiding the monster's proffered hand. "Um... not this time."

"Oh vell, ken't vin dem all." The canteen disappeared with a gurgle. The main clock in the Market Square began to toll. Agatha's head whipped around. The hands stood at seven. "Oh no! Oh NO! I'm LATE!"

Taking off like a shot, Agatha pelted off down the street. The crowd dispersed and yet another Jägersoldier joined his companion. "So vot hyu say to her, eh? Not de old fang polish line again?"

"I din say notting!" He looked after the retreating girl and a quick smile twisted his upper lip. "Pity doh, she smelt verra nize."

Late! Late! Late! Dr. Merlot would have her boil every bottle in the building before she could go home tonight, and little he'd care for her stolen locket. He was Dr. Beetle's second in command, and while not a Spark himself, was as ruthlessly despotic as one. He drove everyone around him as hard as he drove himself, seemingly trying for a breakthrough by the sheer amount of misery he caused his subordinates. He had been with Dr. Beetle for the last twenty years, and had resented Agatha's presence almost from the moment she had been brought into the lab as an assistant, but Dr. Beetle was The Tyrant, and one did not argue with The Tyrant. There were times Agatha wished that she had been assigned to another lab, but she had to admit that the most interesting work was being done by the Doctor himself.

The thought processes of a major Spark were difficult to follow most of the time, especially with her limited understanding. But Agatha found the work exhilarating in a way she couldn't explain. After a heartbreaking series of setbacks in her own fumbling experiments, it only took a few minutes in the presence of the man to fire her up full of enthusiasm all over again. Indeed, part of Merlot's annoyance with her could be explained by Dr. Beetle's insistence on spending as much time with her as he did. She was to be present for every major experiment, and he always asked her opinion, even when the subject was one that had Merlot or Merlot's Chief Assistant, Dr. Glassvich, thoroughly muddled.

Agatha cleared the last of the shops and angled across the greensward that circled the walls of Transylvania Polygnostic University, and towards the great front gates and the cyclopean figure that guarded them.

Mr. Tock was the largest mechanical construct anyone had ever seen, and was still considered the Tyrant's greatest feat of engineering to date. It towered almost twenty meters high. The great clock in his chest was the timepiece the town set its watches by. As intricately decorated as the smaller clanks that comprised the city Watch, but infinitely deadlier. It appeared to move slowly, but this was an illusion brought about by its great size. Those who had underestimated its fighting ability had done so to their regret. Tock had been known to single-handedly quash several small rebellions, one (admittedly poorly organized) army, and an invasion of giant slugs, an event nobody ever wanted to talk about, especially over dinner.

Each year the various schools within the University vied for the honor of polishing the behemoth for its quarterly parade through and around the town, and as a result, his brass exterior gleamed in the morning sun.

As Agatha approached, the glowing blue eyes swiveled down at her, and a plume of steam puffed out from his upper lip, much like an old man puffing out his moustache before speaking. His great metallic voice tolled out across the grounds: "IDENTIFY YOURSELF." Agatha groaned. Students were expected to be within the gates by a certain time.

"Mr. Tock, it's me! You've seen me every day for eleven years! I'm late and—"

"IDENTIFY OR BE—"

"Agatha Clay! Student 8734195!"

"WORKING…"

"Come on."

"WORKING…"

"Come ON!"

"WORKING…"

"Oh please come on!"

"ACCEPTED. ENTER STUDENT." The great feet began to shuffle aside, and then, maddeningly, paused. "YOU ARE… LATE."

"I KNOW!" Agatha screamed and darted past the giant.

The T.P.U. campus was a large complex, and the building Agatha was aiming for was near its center. Clusters of students talked together, many of them discussing the electrical phenomenon of that morning. Several groups were disrupted by Agatha cannoning through them at full speed, leaving nothing but a barely heard "Late!" fading behind her.

Agatha was a familiar figure on the campus, and many of the students simply rolled their eyes at her retreating back. Agatha would have been astonished, and rather appalled, to know that she was the subject of many a speculation. Most of those who tried to strike up a conversation with her were put off by her odd behavior, the more persistent or outspoken found themselves hauled in and given a quiet talk by university officials. Agatha Clay was the Tyrant's assistant and thus Off Limits. This, of course, only added fuel to the speculative fires.

As she approached the massive stone edifice that was Laboratory Number One, the door-clank swung the great bronze portal open in time for her to dart through. Helpfully, it informed her that she was late, eliciting a howl of despair.

Finally she slammed through the blast doors into the Central Laboratory and clung to a railing and gasped as she caught her breath. Below her, on the main floor, Dr. Hugo Glassvitch turned away from a humming device and mildly remarked, "Mademoiselle Clay? You're late."

"I KNOOOOOWW!"

The doctor picked himself up off the floor in time to find his arms full of a sobbing Agatha. "You're only a little late," he said comfortingly.

"My locket! Oh, Doctor, they stole my locket!" Quickly she filled him in on what had happened that morning. "It had the only pictures I have of my parents and it belonged to my mother and now it's gone!"

Dr. Glassvitch looked surprised. "I didn't know that. You never showed—"

Agatha interrupted. "My uncle gave it to me before he went away. He made me promise to never take it off and now it's gone and he'll be disappointed in me again and he'll... he'll never come back because I'm... I'm stupid and damaged!" To Glassvitch's horror, she slid to her knees and began to sob even louder. "Why? Why can't I do anything right? What's wrong with *meeeee*?"

"Agatha! Mon Dieu!" Agatha only sobbed louder. Glassvitch's

specialty was chemical engineering, which minimized his experience with hysterically sobbing young ladies. Up until now, that had seemed like a perk, but now he realized he had no idea what to do. He cast about desperately and his eye fell upon a bulge in Agatha's greatcoat pocket. "Agatha!" He gently shook her shoulder. "Show me your latest machine!"

Agatha's cries stopped as if a switch had been thrown. She blinked up at Glassvitch through her tears. "My machine?"

"Oui!" Glassvitch patted her pocket. "Your petite clank? Does it work?"

Agatha got to her feet and smoothed down her skirt. "I... I don't know." She pulled the little device out of the pocket. It looked like an excessively large brass pocket watch. She wound the stem at the top as she talked. "I... I wanted to show it to you before I showed it to the Master."

Glassvitch nodded encouragingly. "Ah. Good idea. We don't want to waste his time, eh? Let's see it."

"All right." Agatha smiled nervously at him and placed the device on a lab bench. Her index finger hovered for an instant, and then pushed down the stem with a sudden *click*. Immediately, the sound of gears grinding emanated from within. The device shuddered and a small dome on the face snapped up, revealing a crude eye that jerkily surveyed its surroundings. With a lurch, a pair of legs unfolded from the bottom and it shakily stood, then took an uncertain step forward. Suddenly, the ticking of the gears ended with a *Poink!* A horrible grinding rattle came from the little device and it began to shake uncontrollably. Its single eye rolled up out of sight, the body twisted violently and exploded in a shower of tiny gears and springs that sent half of the body casing shooting past a startled Agatha and Glassvitch

33

and out through a window pane. The remaining small bits showered down throughout the room.

Agatha looked at her shoes and whispered, "Sorry. I… I was so sure…"

Glassvitch shrugged and patted her shoulder. "Well, at least this one actually moved before it blew up. That is improvement, no?"

Agatha looked up at him in surprise. She opened her mouth—

"I should have guessed."

The two flinched and turned. At the door stood the Tyrant's second in command, Dr. Silas Merlot. A small, thin, elderly man who owed his current position not to the Spark, but to procedural brilliance and a dogged perseverance in his work. He was rubbing his head and clutching the piece of Agatha's device that had shot out the window. Agatha groaned mentally. Dr. Merlot hardly needed this additional excuse to cause her trouble.

Dr. Glassvitch smiled. He was one of the few friends the cranky scientist had, and often interceded on Agatha's behalf. "Good Morning, Dr.—"

Merlot interrupted him. "I don't know why you encourage her, Glassvitch, we have enough problems today."

"Problems?"

"Baron Wulfenbach is here."

The smile drained from Glassvitch's face. "WHAT? He's early! Weeks early! We're not ready!"

"He's with the Master, if you'd care to complain."

"No! I meant… What do we do?"

"We've got to remove all traces of the Master's project from the secondary labs. Miss Clay, get this lab cleaned up. You've got half an hour."

Agatha started and looked wildly around the lab. It was a rat's nest of equipment and papers strewn about the room. The Master always demanded that it remain untouched during an ongoing project. "Cleaned up? By myself? In half an hour? This room is a disaster area!"

Merlot narrowed his eyes. "Don't be impertinent with me, Miss Clay. The Master may derive some twisted amusement from your pathetic antics, but if this lab is anything less than spotless, you'll see how patient Baron Wulfenbach is with incompetents. Now move!"

As the two scientists hurried to the secondary lab, Glassvitch frowned. "Silas… there's no need to frighten the girl—"

Merlot cut him off. "Listen. The Master's little pet may actually prove useful for once. With her crashing around, perhaps the Baron will not look too closely at the rest of us, understand?" Glassvitch frowned, but after a moment, reluctantly nodded.

Meanwhile a stunned Agatha surveyed the mountains of equipment. "Half an hour?" she whispered to herself. "How can I possibly—" Her eye was caught by a storage closet. Her jaw firmed, she nodded to herself and rolled up her sleeves.

Twenty-nine minutes later, Merlot and Glassvitch were striding back to the lab, muttering to each other.

"Have we forgotten anything?"

"Ssh. Hugo, we have done the best we can. This whole project was a mistake just waiting to destroy everything we've—"

They turned the final corner and stopped dead in their tracks. Before them was the main lab. Every surface was cleared. Every shelf was tidy. The floor was swept and the instruments had been neatly laid out in geometrically perfect rows. In the exact center of the room, a deeply breathing Agatha stood with her hands clasped behind her back.

Dr. Merlot blinked, opened his mouth once or twice and in a dazed voice said, "Well…" It almost choked him to say it. "Well done, Miss Clay." And, because he was an honest man, "I'm… impressed."

Dr. Glassvitch nonchalantly slid his hands into his pockets and rocked back on his heels with an enormous grin lighting up his face. "Not quite so incompetent after all, hm?"

Agatha smiled demurely, "Thank you, doctors."

Suddenly the main door slammed open and a harsh voice commanded, "No von move! Dis is you only varning!"

The hairy face of a Jägermonster quickly surveyed them and as quickly dismissed them, although his weapon never left them. He made a quick motion with his free hand and, with a crash and a hiss, two large Wulfenbach trooper clanks lumbered into the room. The tops of their shakos barely cleared the doorway and their gigantic machine cannons never stopped moving. Agatha saw at once that everything she'd heard about them was correct. Unlike the Clockwork Army, these clanks moved as smoothly as animals. You knew these machines were dangerous.

Behind them came a group of four people. At the center was Baron Klaus Wulfenbach, the man who currently controlled a significant part of Europa. He loomed above the rest of the group, and his movements were quick and sure. No one knew how old he truly was, the only sign of age was the silver color of his hair. Klaus had been an adventurer in his youth, and indeed had traveled with the Heterodyne Boys. It was known that

Klaus and Bill Heterodyne had both vied for the favors of the beautiful but villainous Lucrezia Mongfish, with Klaus finally losing out to his more heroic rival, who had managed to win her over to the side of the angels when he took her as his bride.

Klaus had vanished before the wedding, off to nurse a broken heart it was said. He reappeared four years later, when Europa was deep in chaos and ruin, with the Heterodynes, as well as most of the other Great Sparks, gone. The final blow came when he found his ancestral castle, as well as the town around it, completely destroyed.

He had reestablished the town, and declared that anyone who attacked it would be mercilessly wiped out and their lands absorbed.

Up until that point Baron Klaus Wulfenbach had been considered a minor Spark adventurer, who had never been taken very seriously, as he had always allowed himself to be overshadowed by his more charismatic companions. His proclamation was considered mere bravado. Nearly fifteen years later, thanks to this simple policy, the Wulfenbach Empire stretched from the great bronze gates of Istanbul almost to the Atlantic Ocean.

Next to him was his son, Gilgamesh, who, though fully grown, had only recently been revealed to the world.

Physically, he resembled his sire. Not quite as tall, nor as broad at the shoulder, perhaps, but impressive none the less. His face was set in lines that seemed too grim for one his age. This was no doubt brought about by the numerous attempts on his life that had occurred since his identity had become known. There were many who had reluctantly knuckled under to the Empire, telling themselves that Klaus was but one man, and thus could be endured. These arguments went out the window with the appearance of an heir. The additional knowledge that he was supposedly possessed of a Spark nearly as strong as his father's just made things worse.

Quietly standing at the Baron's right hand was his secretary, Boris Vasily Konstantin Andrei Myshkin Dolokhov, a man feared throughout the Empire almost as much as the Baron himself. He had started out in life with two arms and an eidetic memory, which had brought him to the attention of the Spark who ruled his homeland. Said Spark had given him enhanced speed, strength, balance, and an additional two arms in an attempt to build the ultimate juggler. Sadly, for Boris, he succeeded.

Boris spent several miserable years as court jester before his master had sent an ill-conceived army of land squids against the Baron. This had resulted in the area quickly being absorbed into the Wulfenbach Empire.

Klaus had a sharp eye for talent, and quickly realized that Boris was not born to the stage. However he *was* a natural secretary, and had quickly risen to become Klaus' second in command.

Buzzing angrily around the Baron was the Tyrant of Beetleburg, the Master of the Unstoppable Army, Owner and Headmaster of Transylvania Polygnostic University, Dr. Tarsus Beetle.

Dr. Beetle was a third-generation Spark whose family had established and run the university and its environs for the last hundred and twenty years, maintaining and defending it against other Sparks and their armies. Like the great city-state of Paris, Beetleburg was considered neutral ground. Thus many of the Great Houses of Europa, and elsewhere, had T.P.U. alumnae on staff. About ten years ago, after a particularly hard winter had strained the resources of the area, Klaus, a former student of the University, had offered to absorb both the University and the surrounding town into his expanding empire and extend it his protection, while the Tyrant retained control. Dr. Beetle accepted. This arrangement had worked out well for all concerned, which was why the apparent anger of the Tyrant toward the Baron was so surprising. Indeed he was yelling nonstop as the group entered the room.

The Baron interrupted him in mid-shout and addressed the Jägermonster: "Thank you, Unit-Commander, stand at ease."

"Jah, Herr Baron." The soldier's weapon never faltered, but he allowed himself to slouch a bit. This, for some reason, merely made him look more dangerous.

Beetle resumed his diatribe. "Blast it, Klaus, you're too early! I told you—"

The Baron effortlessly cut him off and strode over to the group in the middle of the floor. "You've had plenty of time, Doctor. Now who are these people?"

Dr. Beetle swallowed his annoyance, and brusquely nodded to each of the staffers as he introduced them. "Dr. Silas Merlot, my second in command."

As he paused, the Baron broke in, "Ah. I read your latest report with great interest."

Merlot bowed and clicked his heels together. "I am honored, Herr Baron."

"Dr. Hugo Glassvitch, my Chief of Research."

"Welcome, Herr Baron."

"And this is our lab assistant, Miss Clay." As he said this, he turned away dismissively. "Now the machine—" Suddenly he stopped, and with a snap, turned to stare at Agatha. "Miss Clay!" He barked, "Where is your locket?"

Agatha blinked. "It... it was stolen, sir. There was an electrical anomaly of some sort and I was accosted by some soldiers while trying to get away."

The Baron's eyebrows rose at this. Beetle looked shaken. "Accosted? Stolen?" His voice rose, "In my city?" He clutched at his forehead. "Oh no! This is terrible! Terrible!"

Agatha tried to address his obvious distress. "I'm feeling better, sir, I—"

At this Dr. Beetle snapped out of his distracted state and grabbed Agatha by the elbow and began to hustle her towards the door. "Sh! No! You're obviously distraught, my dear. I want you to go home. Yes! Go home and have a nice lie down and I'll have the Watch find your locket as quickly as possible!"

"Wait." The force of the Baron's voice arrested Beetle's movement as if he'd been grasped physically. Agatha looked up to see the Baron studying her with interest. "You actually saw the event in the town?" he asked.

"Yes, Herr Baron, I was right in the middle of it."

The Baron nodded. "Stay. I would like your observations of the event when I am done here."

Beetle went pale. "Klaus, the poor girl has had a terrible shock! You must let her go home!"

Agatha tried to calm the distraught scientist. "Master, please! I'm all right. Really."

Klaus nodded to signal that the affair was closed. "I'm impressed by your concern for your people, Beetle, but the young lady appears stable. Let us get down to business."

He turned to Merlot and Glassvitch. He gestured towards a large, obviously half-finished device that sat in the center of the room. It was a bizarre collection of tubes and coils that bent and twisted back on themselves in a most peculiar manner. "Doctors. My Dihoxulator. Why is it not finished? I'd thought I'd explained the underlying theory rather succinctly."

Merlot took a deep breath. "We do not know, Herr Baron. We were able to construct the machine up to a point, but then we hit a block." Beside him, Glassvitch nodded vigorously. "We cannot reconcile the final linkages with the rest of the assembly," he added. "We just don't know what to do to make it work."

The Baron stared at him steadily for moment. "I see." He raised his voice. "Gilgamesh?"

The young man looked up from the device he was examining. "Yes, Father?"

"These fellows seem to be having some problems. Can you assist them?"

"I can try, Father. If you'd explain the theory?"

The Baron nodded, placed a hand on his shoulder and drew him over toward the device. Beetle followed. "The basic idea is to promote *secondary oxidation*..."

Relieved that they were no longer under the Baron's direct scrutiny, Glassvitch turned to his companion and whispered. "Silas, we're doomed! We've accomplished nothing! They'll ship us to the Waxworks!"

Merlot however, ignored him. He was staring at the Baron as a suspicion was growing in his mind. A very nasty suspicion. "...Of course." He muttered, "The Baron knows we don't have the Spark. We weren't expected to finish this. It's a test!"

Glassvitch looked even more distressed. "Then we're failing!"

Merlot shook his head impatiently. "Not us, Hugo, his son! Gilgamesh Wulfenbach is the Baron's only heir. I've heard rumors that the Baron is testing him, trying to determine if the Spark burns as brightly in him as it does in his sire."

"And if it does not?"

Suddenly the Jägermonster loomed up behind them. "Dis is Baron Wulfenbach, sveethot! He vill break him down for parts and try again!" Having divulged this information, he gave them a sharp-toothed grin and sauntered off.

"Mon Dieu!" A shaken Glassvitch breathed.

Merlot shook himself. "Yes. Rather comforting to know there's someone whose life is more wretched than our own, eh?" It was then that he noticed a peculiar buzzing hum that rose and fell in pitch. A scowl flashed across his features and he whirled around to face a distracted Agatha. "Miss Clay!" he shouted. "For the last time, stop that infernal humming!"

Agatha snapped back to the present and blinked wildly. "Hah? I... I'm sorry, Herr Doctor, but I was listening to the Baron, and something he said isn't right, and—"

"Silence!"

Meanwhile Klaus had finished his explanation. Gilgamesh studied the half-finished device and slowly a frown creased his face. "Well?" Klaus prompted.

"Interesting, Father..." His voice trailed off as he scratched his head. "Hmm, I see what they were trying to do... but that won't work... no... wait... hum... this makes no sense!" Gilgamesh stared at the device as if it had personally offended him. "No... this is all... wrong!" His voice began to rise. "This would work at cross purposes!" He wrenched off an armature and threw it across the room. "This is absurd! What are you fools trying to do? Can't you see what you've done?" He began to rip apart the machine. "This is all wrong! I would expect a first-year student to do better! You have forces canceling each other out throughout the entire structure! Where are your plans?"

Merlot looked around, then quickly turned to Agatha. "The plans, Miss Clay! They were on the main board. Where did you put them?"

Agatha looked surprised. "Oh." She said, "They're in with—" She swung her attention to the storage room door in time to see a rivet pop out of one of the door's straining cross bracers. She swung back and smeared a grin across her face. "A-heh. They're in the files in the storage room, doctors. How about everybody goes and has a nice cup of tea while I dig them out?"

Gil strode forward and pushed her aside. "Bah! I'll get them myself! I'm sure your pitiful filing system will be simple—" He turned the handle of the storage room door and yanked just as Agatha shouted "NOOOOOO!" and with a bang, the door flew open and a tidal wave of lab equipment roared out and over the young man's head, smashing him to the ground and carrying him several meters back.

After the shower of material finished falling, Gil could be seen lying on his back, covered in debris. Clutched in his outstretched hands was a small goldfish bowl along with its grateful occupant. Boris and the Jägermonster quickly clambered over the pile of equipment and began to dig him out and help him up. Agatha, Merlot and Glassvitch began to rush forward as well, and found themselves looking down the giant two-meter-long barrels of the clank's guns, a steely "HOLD" their only warning. They skidded to a halt.

Gilgamesh slowly clambered to his feet. "That's the worst filing system I've ever seen."

Klaus rounded upon the huddled scientists. His voice was cold. "Beetle, this sloppiness is intolerable. Have these people—"

"No, Father, wait." He was interrupted by a smiling Gilgamesh, "The thump to my head has cleared it, I think. I believe your theory is... incorrect."

Klaus looked surprised. "What?"

Gil nodded. "Yes, what you want is possible, but your theoretical structure is flawed. There's no way this machine could ever work."

Klaus' face darkened and he drew himself up. When he spoke his voice was glacial, and his words were measured. "Think carefully, boy. You're saying that I am wrong?"

Gil paused, took a deep breath and squared his shoulders. He clutched the fishbowl to his chest protectively, but his voice was firm. "Yes."

Klaus slowly relaxed and looked at him carefully before he swung his arm onto Gil's shoulder and patted it twice. He smiled. "You are quite correct, my son."

As one Merlot, Glassvitch and Agatha burst out with a loud "WHAT?"

Gil frowned in annoyance. "Another test, Father? I am beginning to find them tiresome."

Klaus twitched an eyebrow. "Ah, it is much like raising children then. But I persevere for the moment." He turned to the three shocked researchers. "Thank you, doctors. You will receive new assignments tomorrow."

At this Agatha could no longer contain herself. "This was all for nothing? But they worked so hard!"

Glassvitch began to nod furiously in assent. "For three months we have toiled on this monstrosity!"

Merlot, who had seemed the most stunned, began to show signs of a growing annoyance. "We were simply… window dressing." His voice gained energy. "I see. I understand."

Glassvitch looked at him in surprise. "What? Silas, you're the one who's always going on about how little time we have for our own work."

"Oh, yes—but now I understand why the great Dr. Beetle couldn't be bothered to work on this oh-so-important assignment." His voice began to break with emotion. "Unlike we mere mortals, he had real work to do."

Dr. Beetle frowned and stepped up to the distraught scientist. "Merlot! I don't like your attitude—"

"Then how do you like this?" With viper-like speed, Merlot spun, and his hand cracked across Beetle's face, spinning the older man halfway around and sending his spectacles flying through the air.

The Jägermonster's machine pistol lazily swung towards Merlot. "Ho!" He grunted, "I tink I bettah—"

A hand dropped onto his arm and Klaus shook his head. "Hold. Gil? You are about to receive an important lesson in employee relations."

Meanwhile Beetle and Merlot had squared off, the aging scientist vibrating with rage. "How dare you! I'll—"

Merlot interrupted him. "Shut up! Shut up! My attitude? How dare you treat us like this? Just because you have the gift you think we're simpletons? I have faithfully served you for twenty years and you waste my time with this garbage? I thought you had finally given us something worthwhile! I am not a student! I am not a construct! I haven't got The Spark, but I am not a fool and I do not have to take this from an arrogant has-been like you! Does the Baron know that his trusted old mentor has defied his strictest orders with his latest experiments? Experiments conducted in the middle of a civilian town?"

With a snarl he strode over to an unobtrusive wall panel, jerked it open and threw the switch inside. "Perhaps he would like to see the important work that has been keeping the Beloved Tyrant of Beetleburg so busy!"

Dr. Beetle screamed, "Merlot! Silas! For the love of God! NO!"

However, this came too late, as the back wall of the lab folded back into itself, revealing a hidden laboratory. Dominating the center of the hidden room was a massive glass and metal sphere, festooned with gauges and pipes. Within its depths swirled a thick roiling fluid. Within the fluid, shapes could only vaguely be seen, but when one slowly drifted close to the glass, what could be seen was extremely disturbing. After one look, the Jägermonster and the clanks independently swung their weapons towards the panicked Dr. Beetle. Dr. Glassvitch pulled Agatha back. The expression on Klaus' face would have frozen nitrogen.

A triumphant Merlot gestured at the sphere. "Slaver wasps, Herr Baron! I wish to report that two weeks ago we found a fully functional, unhatched Hive Engine, which Dr. Beetle insisted upon bringing into the heart of this University!" He turned with a vinegary smirk towards Dr. Beetle. "Now—Master—show me how fast that superior mind of yours works! I want to see you talk your way out of this!"

TWO

"When a monster flattens your home, it doesn't matter who built it."

—PEASANT SAYING

The room froze for a timeless moment. Finally Klaus slowly shook his head, his great hands balled into tight fists. His eyes gleamed with controlled fury. "One rule, Beetle. I made one rule when I left you in charge of this city. 'Report all unusual discoveries. Devices of the Other are to be turned over to me immediately.' You agreed."

The smaller man shook with rage. "A pledge made under duress is worthless, Wulfenbach! You threatened my city, my university—I'd have agreed to anything! You were in control then."

Klaus raised an eyebrow in inquiry. "And now?"

Suddenly from above came a *CRACK*—that shook the

building. A white line appeared near the ceiling and spread, revealing itself to be the open sky, as with a thunderous groan, the roof was lifted open upon monstrous hinges by the towering figure of Mr. Tock. His eyes glowed and steam poured from his moustache as a vast hand reached in and aimed an array of fingertip nozzles at the Baron and his son. A voice like a pipe-organ boomed, "DO NOT MOVE."

Beetle drew himself up and a triumphant grin crossed his features. "Now I am in control!" He followed this statement with a burst of laughter that showed that the owner had done a fair share of gloating in his time, and had the basics down pat. "What do you think of that?"

The Baron and his son stared up at the colossus for a moment, then eyed each other, as if each were embarrassed at the thought of speaking first. Finally the Baron cleared his throat and said, "Yes, Gil, what *do* you think of that?"

Gilgamesh looked furiously at his sire. "Are you joking? This is another test?"

Klaus shook his head. "No, no—He's quite serious. But I am interested in your analysis."

At this Dr. Beetle burst out with a startled "Hey!" which the two politely ignored.

Gil rolled his eyes and shifted the fishbowl to his other hand. The fish grinned. Gil sighed. "Oh very well. If we directly attack him, the clank kills us. But if he kills us, our clanks will finish him. An apparent standoff."

The Tyrant cackled. "Correct! Now—"

Gil wheeled on him in annoyance. "Oh shut up before you embarrass yourself any further!" Beetle sputtered in shock as Gil continued. "Being a short man," he gestured significantly at the looming clank, "he places too much importance on size."

"I'M NOT THAT SHORT," Beetle screamed and futilely attempted to kick Gil in the ankle.

Gil ignored him and continued. "Thus the use of the one, slow, unwieldy, but impressively large clank, instead of surprising us with a squad of the faster but smaller units that are no doubt surrounding the building."

"And excuse me, but I do still have the drop on you." This contribution was also ignored.

"He has thus 'Put all his eggs in one basket,' confident that he could contain our group."

"As I have!" the Tyrant screamed.

Gil looked pityingly at the smaller man. "A viable strategy perhaps. If we had come alone."

An explosion rocked the building and all heads whipped upward in time to see half of Mr. Tock's face explode in a cloud of smoke and metal shards. The giant automaton wobbled slightly, then, like a great brass tree, slowly fell over sideways out of sight, though the sound of his hitting the ground left nothing to the imagination, and the entire building shuddered from the impact. A few seconds later, a rain of metal shards pattered to the floor. In the sky overhead floated a fleet of military airships, all sporting the Wulfenbach crest on their sides.

"Tock!" cried Beetle in an agonized voice.

Klaus outlined the size of the forces overhead: "The Third Airborne, the Seventh Groundnaut Mechanical, and the Jägermonsters. Can we end this now?"

"Guards!" Beetle yelled. The Baron's party rolled their eyes.

The Jägermonster sneered. "Now he calls for de guards?"

Gilgamesh shrugged. "Yes, well... make it quick."

The main doors to the labs crashed open as a squad of Beetleburg's feared Watch marched into the room in perfect step. Each unit raised its left gun arm in perfect unison and they all chanted "Stand!" in four part harmony. They were instantly mowed down by the hail of armor-piercing bullets from the machine cannons of the two Wulfenbach clanks.

As the last bits of metal rained down, the Jägermonster gave the order to cease fire. "Dem," he remarked, "dat vas easy."

Klaus looked disgusted. "They were the best self-contained fighting machines on the planet—When they were new!"

Beetle looked stunned. "My... my Watch!"

"Time marches on, Beetle; you remained behind. Well, by now the city should be secure—"

Beetle snapped back into the present. "This is an invasion? Blast it, Klaus, this is my city!"

The Baron looked contemptuous. "Wrong. It became my city ten years ago. I merely let you administer it."

"But... but..." Beetle gestured, "But why?"

Klaus' eyes narrowed. "Withholding a Hive Engine isn't enough?"

"But that would mean..." Beetle stared at Klaus. "Before Merlot... You already knew!"

Klaus idly looked out the window. Screams and explosions could be heard faintly through the glass. "A field team has a sudden 'communications breakdown' followed by several 'accidents.' The river is cordoned off for a night, the laboratory schedules are suddenly rearranged. If you analyze the last week's chemical requisitions, as well as the dramatic increase of the price of honey in this sector..." He slammed his fist down on the windowsill. "Of course I knew!" For the first time an expression of regret crossed his features. "I had hoped I was wrong, old friend, but…" He sighed, "Ah, well."

Suddenly Agatha appeared at the Baron's elbow. "Please, Herr Baron, don't kill him! We need him!"

Klaus closed his eyes. "Where do they get these ideas?" he muttered. "Beetle, the loyalty of the rest of your people does you credit. They can rest assured that I have no intention of killing you. Indeed, I have use for you."

If this was meant to be reassuring to the smaller man, it had the opposite effect. His eyes went wide and his face paled. "No!" His initial strangled whisper changed to a scream: "I'll never submit to being one of your experimental subjects! Never!" As he said this, his hand grabbed one of the stylized, beetle-shaped cloak clasps on his chest and ripped it off. As it came free, it snapped open into the deadly shape of one of the Tyrant's feared seeker drones. It still resembled a beetle, but this one was sleek, armored, and its' brass needles gleamed. The Jägermonster snarled and tried to bring his weapon up, but before he could, Beetle launched the device towards Gil, Klaus and Agatha, shouting, "You won't get me! You won't get any of us!"

Calmly, Gilgamesh tossed the goldfish bowl up high into the air. Pivoting in place he swept a large wrench off a nearby bench and, continuing the motion, smashed the flying device in midair. Clattering and sparking, it pinwheeled back into Beetle's face.

Gil then dropped the wrench, caught the falling fishbowl, grabbed a startled Agatha and pulled her to the ground while yelling, "Down!"

An explosion rocked the lab and blew those remaining

upright to the ground. Agatha felt herself encircled by strong arms. A tiny part of her mind had time to notice the warm, spicy scent of Gil's hair and to identify an odd sensation as that of a goldfish bowl pressing into her back.

The echoes of the explosion died down amidst the clatter of falling machinery and the tinkling of glass.

First on his feet was the Jägermonster. "Herr Baron?"

The Baron rose and dusted himself off. "Relax, Unit Commander."

He knelt beside the swaying figure of Boris, who was trying to raise himself up and dust himself off simultaneously. "Ah—wha—sir?" the secretary muttered.

Klaus helped him to his feet. "Pull yourself together, Boris, you're fine." He nonchalantly looked over toward his son. "Gil?"

"I'm all right, Father." He looked down at the girl in his arms. "And you, Miss Clay?"

"I... I think so. Where—?" It was then that she saw Dr. Beetle's shattered and smoking spectacles upon the floor. "NO," she shouted, "Dr. Beetle!"

Dr. Glassvitch was already kneeling over a small smoldering corpse. "Dead. He's—"

The Baron interrupted him. "His head! How's his head?"

Glassvitch swallowed. "T—totally destroyed, Herr Baron." Klaus swore.

Gil looked contrite. "I'm sorry..."

Agatha twisted away from him. "Don't touch me! You killed him!"

Klaus nodded. "Permanently. A pity, that."

Gil looked stunned. "What? He threw a bomb at me."

Klaus cocked an eyebrow. "A poor excuse."

"Poor excuse?" A look of annoyance crossed Gil's face. "He threw a bomb at me!"

The Jägermonster wandered up holding an unidentifiable organ in its hand. "Hey, I von't say he vas shtupid, but I hain't findin' a lot uf brains around here!"

Boris gave the monster soldier a look of disgust, but merely added, "Can we leave, Herr Baron? My boots are sticking to the floor."

None of them noticed Agatha bristling in the background until she snarled at them. "How dare you!" The three backed into each other before the furious girl. "How dare you? You murder one of the greatest scientists in Europa and you're treating it like a kitchen accident?"

Gil attempted to explain, "But he threw a bomb—"

But a glare from Agatha shut him up. She went on, her voice beginning to take on the power of conviction. "The people of this city loved him! When they find out how you—"

The headache lanced through her skull like a white-hot bar of iron, causing her to scream and drop to her knees. The listeners blinked and looked towards the Baron, who shrugged.

Dr. Glassvitch hurried over to Agatha's side and helped the quivering girl to her feet. "Forgive her, Herr Baron," he pleaded. "She has these attacks when she gets upset."

The Baron's lip curled. "Pathetic."

Gilgamesh stepped close and quietly murmured, "That doesn't make her wrong, Father."

Klaus looked at him, then at Agatha, then slowly rubbed his great jaw. "Hmm..." he conceded. "The populace is sometimes a problem..."

"Possibly not, Herr Baron." Klaus wheeled about to face Dr. Merlot, who quickly realized that drawing attention to himself at this time was not the wisest of decisions, but having committed to it, chose to push on. "Very few people actually saw Dr. Beetle on a regular—*hurk*!"

This last sound was caused by the Baron grasping the front of Merlot's labcoat and effortlessly hauling him up before his face. "I despise traitors." Klaus informed him. "I consider Dr. Beetle's death to be your fault. Without your theatrics I might have salvaged him. I am very annoyed. So now, I'm going to put you in charge."

Merlot squirmed futilely in the Baron's iron grasp. "I... I don't understand, Herr Baron."

"You'll oversee everything. The city, the college, the lands—everything."

"But..." Klaus shook him once. Merlot's teeth shut with a snap.

"And the first time you make a mistake, I'm shipping you to Castle Heterodyne."

Merlot's face went white. "No! All I wanted—"

Klaus released him and turned away dismissively.

"What you wanted is irrelevant. I want Dr. Beetle lying in state—for viewing—by midnight, with a hero's funeral to be held the day after tomorrow."

Merlot stared at the charred corpse on the floor. "But... my work... I just wanted to... do something important..."

Agatha muttered an aside to the Jägermonster. "He was trying to turn chalk into cheese." The soldier guffawed.

Merlot's head whipped around and found a focus for his displeasure. "Right! At least I shall get to do one useful thing today. Miss Clay—get out! Henceforth you are banned from this university. Forever!"

Agatha looked stunned. "You... you can't do that! I'm a student and—"

Merlot drew himself up. "Of course I can do it! Haven't you heard? I'm in charge now!"

Agatha felt her world collapsing around her. She barely registered Dr. Glassvitch's hand on her shoulder. "It may be for the best, Agatha," he murmured. "Without Dr. Beetle's protection, I doubt you would like it here."

"No!" Agatha shook her head. "How will I...?"

Glassvitch cut her off gently, and began to escort her to the door. "I'll come and see you, I promise. But now, I think, you had better leave."

Klaus watched the two leave. His mouth twitched. "Petty," he muttered.

Glassvitch returned and approached him with a worried look on his face. "Herr Baron, the girl is quite distraught... Are the streets safe?"

Klaus sighed. He turned toward the Jägermonster. "Unit Commander! See the girl home."

The soldier grinned. "Hokay!"

Klaus plowed on, "Then come right back!"

The soldier shrugged. "Oh. Hokay."

Once out on the campus, Agatha could see that things were in disarray. There were few students in evidence, though she could see that almost every window was crowded with anxious observers. Several airships had landed in the quad, and Jägermonsters and the Baron's clanks were everywhere. As Agatha watched, one of the late Tyrant's own clanks rounded the corner and advanced. Agatha had time to directly compare its jerky motion to the deadly fluid movements of the Wulfenbach clanks who spun and mowed it down. Other smoking piles of parts revealed the fate of the "Unstoppable Army." The Baron had been right. Beetle's clanks had become quite obsolete. As Agatha turned the corner, she stopped dead in her tracks. There, looming before her was the burning hulk that had been Mr. Tock. A crew of the Baron's mechanics was already swarming over it, and as Agatha watched, a group of hovering airships began to lower cables to their waiting hands. Agatha suspected that the giant clank would be quickly rebuilt. But it wouldn't be the same. Nothing would.

Agatha skirted the vast remains and felt tears well up as she passed through the vast gateway for the last time. "Goodbye, Mr. Tock," she whispered.

Her mood was shattered by the business end of a machine cannon dropping towards her face, and the amplified voice of the clank behind it roaring, "HALT. ALL CITIZENS ARE TO STAY OFF THE STREETS UNTIL FURTHER NOTICE."

Agatha stepped backwards and bumped into someone. Turning around, she found herself face to face with the grinning Jägersoldier she'd last seen in Dr. Beetle's lab. "Hoy," he called out to the clank, "she's vit me!"

The clank paused. "YES SIR," and with a hiss it resumed its watch position.

The soldier then looked back at Agatha and was nonplussed to see her crying. "Vot's de matta, gurl?"

Agatha stared at him through her tears. "They sent you out to eat me!"

The monster soldier actually looked embarrassed. You could

also tell that this was an unfamiliar emotion. "Hy em not gun eatchu." This did nothing to stop the flow of tears, and after several minutes, the exasperated soldier roared, "Onless dats de only vay to shot hyu op!" Agatha's sobbing stopped instantly , and she stared at him with wide eyes. The Jägersoldier nodded. "Now. Vere hyu liff? Let's get hyu home," and when Agatha continued to stare at him blankly: "MOOF!"

The walk back through the town was markedly different from the one she'd taken this morning. The number of citizens on the street was greatly reduced, and the few left were obviously determined to get home as quickly as possible. Shopkeepers were closing up, frantically pulling stock in off the sidewalks or, when they saw Agatha and her escort, abandoning it altogether and slamming shut doors and window shutters.

The only sign of fighting that Agatha saw was a shattered member of the Watch, which still twitched and feebly ticked against a wall as they passed by. More and more of the giant Wulfenbach clanks and soldiers wearing the Wulfenbach crest were to be seen assuming positions on various street corners, and with chilling silence, a small troop of Jägermonsters swarmed across the rooftops of the buildings across the street and disappeared. Shadows from the overhead fleet glided across the streets, causing the townspeople to involuntarily duck their heads and move even more quickly.

Soon enough they turned on to Forge Street, and the large former stables that housed Clay Mechanical came into sight.

Agatha turned to her companion. For the last several blocks, the Jäger had abandoned its attempts at conversation, and had been sniffing repeatedly, while a look of distracted concentration flowed across its face. "That's it. That's my house. Um… thanks." With that she bolted for the main door. The Jägermonster lazily leaned against the nearest wall and watched her scurry inside. With a sigh, he shook his head and muttered, "Tch. Poor little ting." Again he sniffed deeply, then shrugged irritably and loped off.

Inside the shop, machinist and master blacksmith Adam Clay grasped a thick chain in his massive fists and pulled. The ceiling beam that held the combined pulley system groaned, and the front of the steam tractor the chain was attached to began to slowly rise upwards.

Herr Ketter's tractor had some leaks. Adam was pretty sure he knew where. A small collection of probable replacement parts were neatly laid out on a small bench by his side.

Adam liked this sort of job, as it didn't involve dealing with madboy technology. Whereas Sparks were able to design and construct bizarre, physics-skirting machinery, their devices were never really able to be mass-produced or even reliably duplicated by regular people. Even trained machinists eventually suffered nervous breakdowns if they were forced to try.

One of the Wulfenbach Empire's groundbreaking ideas had been that instead of exterminating rival Sparks after defeating them, Klaus hired them. He kept them happy by keeping them supplied with materials, tools, and food, and a dedicated staff that made sure they ate it. They found themselves free of the petty concerns that had plagued their lives, such as what to actually do with that small country once they had proved that they could conquer it with nothing more than a navy composed of intelligent lobsters. He also gave them challenges, adoring minions, and on a regular basis, a large dinner celebrating their accomplishments along with a beautiful calligraphed award expressing the sincere thanks of the Empire in general and Klaus in particular.

As a result, almost any one of the Sparks Klaus had defeated over the years would have disintegrated you if you had seriously attempted to offer them their freedom, and they gleefully built and repaired the airships and the armies of clanks as well as the other terrifying monstrosities that supported the Pax Transylvania. This easily made up for the tightly guarded warehouses full of devices that made ants run backwards or could remove the rings from Saturn that they occasionally delivered in their free time.

And of course, regular science marched on, if only in self-defense.

The pulley caught. Adam grimaced and gave the chain a sharp tug, and a link snapped with a sound like a gunshot. The tractor slammed back, shaking the entire building.

Adam looked at the broken chain as if it had personally betrayed him, and then he dropped it to the ground. He walked over to the tractor and quickly inspected it to make sure there was no additional damage. Seeing none, he glanced around and, reassured that he was alone, grabbed the front of the tractor in one large hand and slowly lifted it above his head. Satisfied, he hooked a foot around the bench that contained the spare parts, slid it over to his side, selected a wrench from a loop on his belt, and began working on the undercarriage.

Adam was a construct. Whereas the term "construct" encompassed any and all biological creatures created by Sparks,

Adam was an example of a "traditional old-school" construct, i.e., a patchwork collection of body parts that had been revivified by a massive dose of electricity. They were the simplest form of construct to make, and the vast majority of Sparks had started their careers by assembling one. Unfortunately, while reviving the *corpus* was simple enough, the brain remained a tricky thing, and most Patchworks, as they were called, were either dull-witted or homicidally deranged, which meant that a significant number of Sparks had their careers *ended* surprisingly soon after they started.

As a result, there was a well-established tradition of such constructs being viewed with suspicion at best, discriminated against with impunity, and made the butt of jokes in sensationalist novels, such as those chronicling the adventures of the Heterodyne Boys. Their loyal construct companions, Punch and Judy, were portrayed as oafish clowns. Music halls and traveling shows across Europa also embraced this interpretation, and the two were solidly established as the personification of low humor. Constructs tended to avoid popular entertainments.

Refreshingly, the Baron had long let it be known that blatant discrimination against constructs was officially frowned upon within the Empire, and he backed this policy up with force.

But this was a rule that was often ignored in the small towns and rural villages that rarely saw the Baron's forces or polysyllabic words. As a result, constructs moved into the larger, more cosmopolitan towns and cities. There they were reluctantly embraced. Those like Adam and his wife, who, with a bit of effort, could pass as human, tried to do so.

And thus Adam and Lilith lived happily amongst the general

populace of Beetleburg, and were respected members of the community. Adam impressed many with his ability to repair the simpler Spark creations, and did regular piece-work for the Tyrant. Lilith played the piano, giving lessons in music and dance, and provided entertainment at various functions. There were those in town who knew what they were, but usually they were constructs themselves.

Suddenly the door slammed open behind Adam, and before he could react, he found a sobbing Agatha clutching at his chest. "Oh, Adam," she cried, "I've had the most awful day in existence! Dr. Beetle is dead! And I was robbed! And I'm not allowed back in the University! Ever!"

Adam strained to keep his balance, and the arm holding up the tractor began to shake. Agatha continued, "I can't think of anything that could make it worse!" Sweat began to form on Adam's brow as he tried to gently disengage Agatha from his shirt with one hand.

The door to the inner house opened, and Agatha's mother appeared. "What is all the noise out here?" She blinked at the scene before her. "Agatha? You're back? What's wrong child? Come here."

To Adam's great relief, Agatha turned to his wife. "Oh, Lilith, Dr. Beetle is dead!"

Shock crossed Lilith's face. "What? How?"

"He was killed in his lab by Baron Wulfenbach!"

At the sound of Wulfenbach's name, Adam gave a start, dropping the tractor, again shaking the building.

Lilith's eyes widened. "Baron Wulfenbach! Here?"

Agatha looked at her in surprise. "Yes. He's taken the town. You didn't notice?"

Lilith looked embarrassed. "I've been canning all morning—" she looked at Agatha again, "Klaus Wulfenbach. Are you sure?"

"Lilith, I work in the main lab. I was right there. I saw the whole thing!"

Lilith only looked more worried. "Did he see you?"

"Dr. Beetle introduced all of us."

"Yes, of course he did. Why shouldn't he? How did—?" Suddenly a look of horror crossed Lilith's face and she grabbed Agatha and lifted her up before her eyes. "Your locket!" she exclaimed. "Where's your locket?"

Agatha looked surprised at the turn of the conversation. "I was robbed. By two soldiers."

"Wulfenbach soldiers?"

"I... I don't think so. They looked too shabby."

Lilith set Agatha back down and turned to Adam. "We've got to find it!" Adam nodded.

Agatha interrupted. "With everything else that's happened—that's what you think is important?" Adam and Lilith looked at each other, and unspoken communication passed between them.

Lilith's face took on an expression that Agatha knew as "I'll explain this when you're older," a look that at eighteen, she no longer had any patience for. "Your uncle was very clear. You must always wear—"

"Dr. Beetle is dead! Don't you understand?"

"Agatha, when your uncle left you with us, he told us things we'd need to know if—"

"If he didn't come back! Things I needed to know! Well what are you waiting for? It's been eleven years! Maybe... maybe he never meant to come back at all and—"

Adam's vast hand dropped gently onto her shoulder, cutting her off in mid-word. The look in his eyes as he slowly and deliberately shook his head conveyed the message that whatever else, her uncle had never intended to leave for good.

Lilith nodded in agreement. "Agatha, your uncle loves you very much. Almost as much as we do." With a sigh, Agatha allowed herself to be enfolded by the arms of the two constructs. The quiet minute that followed would be one of Agatha's most poignant memories.

It was ended by Lilith straightening up and assuming her no-nonsense voice. "Now. Agatha, Adam and I are going out. There are a few things you must do. We're leaving Beetleburg. Pack everything of importance to you, but it must fit into your green rucksack. No more than two sets of clothes, but take two extra sets of stockings, the thick wool ones, and linens."

Agatha blinked in surprise. "Leaving town? But the shop! Our house! Your canning!"

Lilith nodded. "It can't be helped. If Baron Wulfenbach has taken the town then we have got to leave." Agatha opened her mouth, but Lilith cut her off. "Once we are on the road, I'll answer everything, but now there is no time. Prepare similar packs for Adam and myself, as well as the blue shouldersack that is already packed in our closet and—" she paused, and seemed embarrassed, "Our generator."

Agatha looked somber. "We really are leaving."

Lilith nodded and looked around the cozy room. "Yes. I'm afraid so." While they were talking, Adam strode over to the fireplace. Lifting aside the rag rug, he exposed a stone tile over a meter square set into the floor. In the center was an indentation that proved to be a handle, as Adam grasped it and effortlessly lifted. The tile was revealed to be a cube that easily slid from the hole with the sound of stone on stone. Depositing it to the side, he leaned in and lifted out a thick money belt, as well as several small canvas bundles, before smoothly sliding the block back into place.

Lilith continued. "Then you must clean the house." Agatha opened her mouth, but Lilith raised her hand. "Start a fire in the fireplace. Burn everything in the red cabinet. This is very important, Agatha. When you're done with that, I want you to disassemble our two spare generators and scatter the parts around the shop. Then go through the house and if you find anything that you think would tell someone that the people living here were constructs, get rid of it."

"You're terrified of Baron Wulfenbach finding you."

"Yes. And you should be too." She forestalled Agatha's next outburst. "Tomorrow. Now Adam and I will go and check the pawnshops and jewelers for your locket. If it's not there, we'll talk to Master Vulpen and see if it has made its way onto the Thieves' Market. In any case, if we're not back, make sure all the doors are locked, be in bed by eight o'clock and ready to leave by dawn."

"The Baron has established a curfew," Agatha warned her. "He's using clanks and those creepy Jägermonster things."

Adam and Lilith looked at each other. To her surprise, Agatha saw that they were more relaxed than she had seen them in quite a while. "Really? It'll be like old times then. Now get to work, lock the door, put up the 'Away' sign, and don't let anyone in while we're gone."

"Okay." Agatha headed up the stairs. "Be careful."

Adam and Lilith watched her go. Lilith allowed herself a brief fierce hug with Adam. "Confound the master," she muttered into his vast chest, as he tenderly patted her head. "We're not equipped to deal with this. Eleven years! Where can he *be*?"

Three hours later, Agatha sat wearily on her bed. She had tackled the cleaning of the house first, then the dismantling of the generators. Although she knew that Adam and Lilith were constructs, her parents had never talked about who had created them. Agatha suspected the reason had something to do with the competence of that unknown Spark or, rather, the lack thereof. There were numerous flaws with the pair, such as Adam's inability to speak. The most painful to them was their inability to have children. The most embarrassing was the lack of care that had been taken when assembling them regarding things like uniformity of skin tone, and Lilith's left eye, which was noticeably larger than her right. When she was younger, Agatha had pointed out that the variegated skin revealed that at least their creators had been equal-opportunity exhumers, while Lilith's mismatched eyes were a flaw shared by the famous Heterodyne construct, Judy, and thus no detriment. Lilith's reaction to this statement had always puzzled the youngster. It was only as she got older that she realized that the Heterodyne plays that were performed at fairs and circuses by traveling players consistently portrayed the Heterodyne Boys' construct servants as buffoons, and that none of the constructs that her family knew enjoyed these plays. Agatha had thus realized that constructs were considered second-class citizens, and explained her parents' efforts to keep their status as such hidden.

But the most annoying flaw in their construction was that

they were unable to maintain the charge that gave them life. Periodically, they had to hook each other up to a small hand-cranked generator and re-vitalize themselves. At a young age Agatha had once stumbled upon them during this process and had suffered nightmares for several weeks as a result. The generator was never talked about except when absolutely necessary.

Agatha looked around her room now, and mentally packed the large rucksack at her feet. No matter how she did it, there were things she loved that were going to have to be left behind.

Before Adam and Lilith, she had lived with her Uncle Barry. All she could remember about him was that he was a large, good-natured man who was very good at repairing things, seemed very worried about things he couldn't talk about, and who would, without warning, periodically uproot them from whatever town they had established themselves in and have them travel for days, sometimes for weeks, to another town.

In the beginning Agatha had thought it was fun. But as she got older, she realized that she had no friends. Partially this was caused by their constant travel, and partially by the fuzzy-headedness that began to increase its hold upon her thinking around that time. Upon their arrival in a new location, children could tell that there was something not quite right about the newcomer, and with the casual sadism of the young, proceeded to give her a hard time. After an especially cruel series of pranks, which even her perennially preoccupied uncle had noticed, they had come to Beetleburg, and the Clays, where she had found the loving stability she had so desperately needed.

She remembered the guarded joy she had felt when the Clays had told her that this was her room. For quite a while, she tried to do as little to it as possible, convinced that they would soon leave. It had started out as a simple, bare attic, but as time passed, Agatha had begun to devote a great deal of time to it, and now it was a thing of beauty.

At a young age, Adam had shown her how to carve wood, a skill many machinists honed, as they often had to design and forge their own parts. Her early efforts defaced the bottoms of newel posts and cabinet doors, but eventually she began to develop a grace and geometric precision that allowed a profusion of cunningly interlaced designs to cover many of the wooden surfaces. The ceiling had been painted a dark blue and covered with bright yellow, white and orange stars. Hanging from the ceiling were various objects that Agatha found interesting: a gigantic dried sunflower (which she had been convinced was the result of some Spark's biological tinkering), a stuffed iguana she had discovered in a musty old junk shop, an airship kite that her uncle had built for her long ago, and a Roman sword that Dr. Beetle had discovered while digging the foundation for a new building. Crammed on shelves were her precious books, fossils, unusual bits of madboy tech, clocks, and a small misshapen clay dog that a boy had given her when she was eight.

On the shelf in front of her single window were racks containing pots of plants, some common herbs, some exotic and strange things that she had collected from the spice shops or the Tyrant's Botanical Gardens.

It would all have to be left behind.

Even, and the thought filled her eyes with tears, her work table, a vast swivel-topped affair that Adam had constructed in secret for her one Yuletide several years ago. All that remained on it were her drafting tools, her notebooks, and the remains of the few, painfully few, devices she had constructed that actually worked: the butter clock, the air-driven quill sharpener, the hooting machine, and the wind-up hammer. They had already been dismantled, and that had been the hardest thing to do. With a groan she allowed herself to fall back onto the bed in despair.

They had all lived together happily for several months, and Uncle Barry had made the occasional trip while leaving Agatha in the care of the Clays. Agatha had vague memories of a growing tension amongst the grownups, which culminated in a late night argument she could dimly hear from her bedroom. The next morning, the tension appeared to have cleared and Barry announced that he was going on another trip. A lengthy one, that might take as long as two months. He had written three times: once from Mechanicsburg, the home of the fabled Heterodyne Boys; once from Paris; and over a year later, a much travel-stained letter, full of disquieting and vague ramblings, that was found to have been slid under the Clays' front door while they had been outside the city picking apples.

It was the last they had heard from, or of, him.

The thought of returning to that wandering lifestyle filled her with apprehension and she felt her head begin to throb in a peculiar way that left her feeling dizzy.

"Maybe a short nap," she muttered, and stripped down to her camisole and pantalets before burrowing under the covers. A thought eased its way to the forefront of her mind even as she felt herself begin to slide into sleep: her whole day had started going wrong when that electrical phenomenon had appeared. But bizarre things occurred all the time, such as last week's sudden mimmoth infestation. The tiny pachyderms had been discovered living in the sewers, and an ill-thought-out poisoning scheme had seen the creatures emerging from drains in alarming numbers and establishing themselves in houses all over town.

No, the problems had really begun when those two soldiers had stolen her locket. Agatha's last coherent thought as she succumbed to sleep was "I wish I could get my hands on them."

In a small, cheap rooming house, the objects of Agatha's thoughts were reaping the results of that morning's encounter. Moloch paced back and forth in the tiny room, as a lean man wearing a long white apron over his suit examined Omar. Moloch's brother was stretched out unconscious upon the room's single bed. The doctor removed his stethoscope and leaned back with a hiss of annoyance.

Moloch turned towards him. "Please, Herr Doctor, can't you help him? What's wrong with him?"

The doctor tugged at his small beard in frustration. "I don't know. I've never seen anything like this. This man should be in a hospital."

Moloch shuddered. "Oh no, I saw enough of them in the war."

"I don't mean one of those butcher shop field hospitals. Ours is fully equipped and your brother needs—"

"What? What does he need? What could they do? You don't even know what's wrong with him!"

The doctor opened his mouth, hesitated, and then nodded reluctantly. "Yes. No fever, no chills. No respiratory problems, no sweating, no convulsions—But... it's like he's... shutting down, like..."

"Like a boiler when you've blocked the air intakes."

The doctor looked at him with mild surprise and nodded. "Yes. Well put, young man."

Moloch ignored the compliment and leaned over the unconscious man. "Ach, Omar," he muttered, "you're a jerk, but you're all I have left. Fight it!" He slapped his brother's face but got no response.

Behind his back, the doctor's look of worry increased. "How long has he been like this? Days? Weeks?"

Moloch shook his head. "He started to feel dizzy, um... a little before twelve hundred. He got more and more disoriented and collapsed around fifteen. Towards the end he had trouble talking, and I... I don't even think he knew who I was. He passed out around sundown."

The doctor looked shaken. "That quickly? Dios," he muttered. "How do you feel?"

Moloch looked surprised at the question. "Me? Okay, I guess, why?"

"I'm trying to decide if I should have you moved to the hospital along with your brother."

"What? But I'm not—"

The doctor was paging through a book he had removed from his medical bag. He stopped and looked Moloch in the eye. "Listen, von Zinzer, was it? This could be some sort of plague."

Moloch went white. "Plague?"

The doctor nodded. "The big question is how contagious it is. Aside from hospitalization, my other option is to quarantine the pair of you in this inn. You talk to anyone other than the innkeeper?"

"No, there weren't any customers when we—"

"Praise be for that. Where do you work?"

"Nowhere. I mean, we just hit town this morning."

The doctor made a small grunt of satisfaction at this news and made another checkmark in his book. "Mm. Probably something you picked up outside then. Eat anything unusual? Find anything odd?"

"Odder than Beetle Beer? No, we—" Suddenly Omar convulsed upon the bed. A strangled groan came from his mouth. Moloch and the doctor were at his side instantly.

"Omar?" Omar's head whipped from side to side twice, froze in position, and a deep final breath rattled from him as he sagged back into stillness. Moloch knew he was dead even before the doctor checked his brother's pulse and then drew the sheet over his head. In the silence, the sound of something hitting the floor echoed through the small room with unnatural loudness. In death, Omar's hands, which had been clutched for hours, had relaxed, and Agatha's locket had dropped to the floor.

The doctor reached down, examined it briefly, and handed it over to Moloch. "I'm sure it gave him some comfort." Moloch looked at him blankly, the locket clutched in his hand. The doctor continued, "I myself don't know whether the Heterodyne Boys will actually come back someday, but I do believe that we should live our lives as if they were. People like your brother, who try to make the world a better place, do so by the very act of trying. I'm sure the Heterodynes would have been proud of him."

Moloch looked woodenly at the locket and then back at the doctor, who changed the subject as he donned his hat and greatcoat. "I'm afraid I must be going. Now listen up, soldier. I'm confining you to this room. I'll have a medical disposal team up here before dawn for your brother. You can relax, our Dr.

Beetle doesn't permit unauthorized resurrectionists in this town. You'll be fed and examined for the next week and after that you'll be free to go. So sit tight soldier, and we'll do our best." And with that he slipped out and shut the door behind him.

Moloch grimaced. "Reckon Omar and me have seen your 'best.'" He turned to glare at the sheet-covered form. "You idiot! Your last act on earth is to steal from a townie and leave me stuck holding the evidence waiting for her to report me. That's making the world a better place, huh? Leaving me stuck like a sitting duck!" In his fury he threw the locket against the wall where it smashed open with a bright blue flare and the sounds of gears scattering. A smell of ozone filled the room and brought Moloch up short. "What the...?"

He bent down and gingerly picked up a few bits of the locket. It had contained a pair of portraits, a handsome-looking man and woman. But hidden behind the portraits were the smashed remains of delicate machinery. Machinery that Moloch was totally unfamiliar with.

He muttered as he gathered together the bits from the floor. "Too complicated to be a watch. Not a music box. I've never seen anything like this..." A chill swept over him. "This is madboy stuff." He examined it again. "But what did it do?" He raised his eyes and found himself looking at Omar's body.

With a cry he leapt back, scattering bits of locket across the floor. After a moment, he gingerly picked up the larger pieces and examined them again, to ascertain that it was indeed broken. Of this there could be no doubt.

"This is what killed Omar," he muttered. "He started acting strange right after he stole it from that girl..." A new thought emerged. "The girl! She was wearing it and it wasn't killing *her*.

72

She must have… turned it on, somehow. She knew it'd do him, the black-hearted—wait! Wasn't there a note?"

He turned the locket over and indeed there was lettering engraved upon the back:

IF FOUND, PLEASE RETURN TO
AGATHA CLAY
CLAY MECHANICAL
FORGE STREET, BEETLEBURG.
REWARD

Moloch grabbed his greatcoat and slung it on as he left the room. "A reward, huh? I'll give her a reward a'right, and she'll be making no reports when I'm done with her either."

Agatha was very small. She ran into a large room filled with tools and machines and things that she didn't understand, but knew were full of magic, mystery and excitement. At the center of this collection sat the master of the magic, her uncle Barry. He was a large shadowy figure hunched over a workbench, where something full of gears and springs grew under his tools. "Hey, Uncle Barry," Agatha cried as she entered. "I learned a trick!"

The large man paused and slowly turned to look at her. Even now his face was in shadow. A small set of spectacles glinted in the light from his bench. "A trick?" he enquired.

Agatha nodded, and jumped up and down in place with excitement. "Yeah! You know how when you're tryin' to think and there's noise and stuff botherin' you? Well I found out I can make other noises in my head and it makes the botherin' noise stop! And then I can think real good! Listen!" With that she stopped jumping, serenely folded her hands and began to hum, no, to whistle? To buzz? No... It was all of these and yet none of them, a soft melodic sound that you couldn't call music, but...

The effect of this performance upon Uncle Barry was electric. He stiffened in shock and the handle of the screwdriver clutched in his hand cracked. His voice was strained. "You... no! It can't be!" Agatha hummed on obliviously. "You're only five years old! You're too young! You've got to stop!" His large hands shot out and grabbed her shoulders and began to shake her. Agatha kept on humming. She could no longer stop, even as her uncle cried, "I don't know what to do! I don't know what to do! I don't—"

A particularly violent jerk snapped Agatha awake. She was slumped over a table—another jerk—someone was grabbing her hair!

She twisted around enough to see that her assailant was one of the soldiers who had accosted her this morning! Without thinking she swung her left hand and the large spanner she was grasping connected with Moloch's jaw and sent him crashing to the ground.

Agatha blinked in surprise and examined the tool in her hand. "Where did this come from?" she muttered, and then noticed that the hand holding it was black with grease and dirt. With a cry, she saw that both of her hands were dirty up to the elbow, as was her underwear—

Her underwear? But she was in the middle of Adam's shop

floor! A wild look around showed her that tools were scattered and parts were littered across the floor. Heat still radiated from the great welding torch and, most astonishing, the tall double doors to the street were wide open.

As Agatha hurried to close them, she saw that outside, in the first light of dawn, a small crowd had gathered to help the ironmonger across the way right his wagon, which appeared to have been overturned in the night.

Slamming the doors closed and surveying the disheveled workshop and the unconscious soldier, Agatha could only mutter to herself, "What's happened?"

THREE

"When lightning hits the keep the wise man does not sleep."

—TRADITIONAL FOLK SAYING

I n the early dawn light, the streets of Beetleburg were quiet. Most of the populace peered out through shuttered windows or from behind curtains. Beetleburg was a town under occupation, the Tyrant was dead, and no one was sure what the future held.

A few brave shops were open, carters still moved necessary supplies through the streets under the watchful eyes of Wulfenbach forces, but the heart of the town, the University, was closed. Crowds of students and teachers filled coffee shops and taverns discussing the events of the previous day. These conversations fell silent whenever the tall brass clanks of Baron Wulfenbach passed by outside. Their machine cannons constantly moved from side to side as they slowly strode down the center of the streets.

Human officers patrolled the area as well, identifiable by the flying castle badge they wore. They regulated traffic, politely answered questions and put a human face upon the occupation.

The inhuman face was supplied by the Jägermonsters, who had, during the night, stopped several bands of looters, seized fourteen people who had attempted to leave the city under cover of darkness, and apparently captured a large saurian that had been prowling through the city's sewers for some time. Several of these (including the saurian) were on display in the Square of the Tyrant.

The most talked about incident had occurred when a small band of Jägers had blithely walked into the Thieves' Market. Instead of closing it down, they wound up dickering furiously with Blind Otto for some hats. After they left, it was discovered that they had managed to steal the boots off of Otto's feet. Blind Otto was said to be, grudgingly, impressed.

The death of the Tyrant had stunned the populace. There was a great deal of confusion as to which event, the Master's death or the town's occupation, had come first. So far there was little anger. Dr. Merlot had been correct in his assessment that for the populace at large, the presence of the Master had been more of a reassuring concept than a day-to-day experience. The actual takeover of the town had been quick, and the hand of its new master lay lightly so far. Civic leaders had been honored with an audience with the Baron himself, and the ones who survived the experience moved with a new purpose.

The greatest disturbance had appeared, unexpectedly, in the western part of town. The Baron, his son Gil, Boris, several clanks, a very brave and opportunistic doughnut seller, and a squad of Jägermonsters stood in the center of the street and watched with interest as a large, crude clank, belching black smoke and moving with a ponderous slow step, lurched around the corner. To the trained eye, it was obvious that the device had been built out of a large steam tractor, with the addition of a pair of large solid legs. A single manipulator claw was folded up beneath the prow. At each step, the device paused and swung its front end from side to side.

The Baron, his hands clasped behind him, observed the device with genuine pleasure. "Well well well." He murmured, "*This* is interesting. Boris?"

His secretary, who was munching on a doughnut, took a sip of coffee, delicately wiped his lips and gestured in the direction of the machine simultaneously. "Not one of ours, Herr Baron. Nor is it from outside the town. It has caused some minor damage, but I believe that to be unintentional." The Baron nodded.

The clank was now halfway down the street, and appeared to register their presence. The whistle perched upon its top gave a brief hoot, and it began to advance steadily towards them.

"Purpose?"

"It *appears* to be looking for someone."

"Indeed?"

"Allow me to demonstrate." Boris turned to a Jägermonster standing nearby who was gnawing on a sausage. "Sergeant? Go up to it."

The soldier spit out a chunk of sausage in surprise. "Vat? *Me?*"

Boris nodded. "Yes, you. Go up to it."

The soldier glowered at the shorter man. "I don' take schtupid orders from you."

"I don't *give* them. Now go do something *useful*."

The Jäger grinned. "Ho! So I can *sqvish* you den, hey, bugman?"

Boris and the Jägermonsters despised each other. Boris, a naturally fussy man, found their permanently disheveled lifestyles an affront to everything he believed in. The Jägers thought him a self-important, officious prat. Boris had yet to give any Jäger an order that was not automatically questioned. This had escalated until the famous incident where a Jägermonster who was on fire had to be ordered several times, in writing, to put himself out, after which Klaus had stepped in. There were still arguments, but now there was a time limit.

This morning Klaus intervened early. "Boris, is it safe?"

"I honestly believe so, Herr Baron."

"Good. Sergeant? Carry on."

"Jah, Herr Baron." With a theatrical sigh, the soldier tossed his weapon to Boris, who managed to catch it without spilling his coffee, and stomped over to the machine, which had advanced to meet him in the middle of the street. When he was within range, the arm quickly unfolded from underneath and grabbed him. "Oh, help," he muttered in a disgusted tone of voice, "I hef been captured by a clenk. Help. Help."

The machine raised him up to what appeared to be an array of crude sensors on its front. "Hokay," the Jäger muttered, "get *on* vit it."

Several of the sensor lens flared into blue-white brightness and swept over the captive soldier, who flinched at the glare. After several seconds of stillness, the device casually tossed the Jägersoldier onto the ground and again began to advance.

Boris smiled serenely and bit into a fresh doughnut. "You

see, Herr Baron, entertaining, but harmless."

The furious sergeant strode up, while brushing off his hat. "You *is* schtupid! Dat ting could be lookink for *hennybody*! And ven it *finds* dem, *den* you gots *trouble*!"

Klaus nodded. "You are correct, Sergeant, but this is also a priceless opportunity."

Boris looked stricken. "I don't understand, Herr Baron."

The now grinning Jägermonster poked him in the back of the head. "Dots because *hyu* ain't the schmot guy."

The Baron turned to his son, who quickly finished his own doughnut. "Gil?"

"Well, Father, I've thought of four ways to stop it, depending on whether you want it destroyed, shut down, contained, or immobilized."

The Baron sighed. "Actually, I want it *distracted*."

A look of annoyance flashed across Gilgamesh's face. "Of *course* you do." It was replaced by a mischievous look and with a "Consider it done!" he bounded forward, ignoring his father's cry of alarm.

Striding up to the machine he jauntily addressed it. "Hullo, Herr Clank! Are you looking for *me*?"

Again the metal arm whipped out and grabbed, but all it brought up to its sensors was an empty greatcoat. Several yards away, from atop a stack of barrels, Gilgamesh gaily called out, "Ho! You'll have to do better than *that*!"

Instantly the giant device launched itself towards him, displaying an unsuspected turn of speed. The ground shook under the impacts of its massive feet. Gil stood, apparently unconcerned as the device thundered towards him, until the last second, when as the great hand smashed into the barrel where he'd been, he leapt onto the shaft of the arm, and with a bounce, latched onto the case containing the sensor array, blocking it with his body.

The device stopped dead for several seconds. Its arm swung up, but could not reach Gil. It then began a twisting, gyrating series of movements to try and throw him off. Clinging grimly, Gil called out, "Any *time,* Father!"

Klaus, after his first display of agitation, had gone still, as he intensely studied the movements of the control unit at the rear of the clank. It was a small bullet-shaped mechanism equipped with several flexible arms which furiously operated the levers and wheels that actually drove the main engine. After a minute or so, a grim smile crossed his features and he reached into his coat, pulling out a small grappling gun. In a single motion he aimed and fired, and the automatic grapple closed upon the lever he desired. A sharp tug, and the switch was thrown. With a massive hiss of escaping steam, the clank pitched forward onto its knees, inert. Gil released himself at the last moment and landed lightly upon his feet. Nonchalantly dusting himself off, Gil remarked, "Well *done,* Father."

Klaus wheeled at him and roared, "*LACKWIT!* How *dare* you put yourself at risk! You or I may very well *be* this device's quarry! I needed a *distraction*, not a *sacrifice*! *That* is what the Jägermonsters are for!"

Boris looked askance at the sergeant. "A pity we can't use them *all.*"

The Jäger dismissed him with a good-natured wave of his hand. "Ah—go kees an *hoctopoos*. Oh vait, you mama already *did*!"

His point made, Klaus began to examine the motionless

device. The monster soldier sidled up to a silently fuming Gil and murmured. "Hey, keed." Gil blinked as a large hairy hand descended on his shoulder. "Hyu deed pritty goot dere, hen don be fooled. You papa doz crazy schtupid stoff like dot *hall de time*. Hokay?"

Gil nodded. "Hokay. Ah—I mean okay. Thanks."

At that moment the Baron yelled, "Everybody *back*!" as he leapt from the rear of the clank, which, with much hissing and squealing, was pulling itself back up onto its feet. Once there, it spun around several times, and whistle blowing, strode off down the street by which it had come. Klaus nodded in satisfaction. "Sergeant," he roared, "prepare some 'C' bombs! First patrol—Follow that clank!"

Six Jägers roared, "Jah! Herr Baron, ve *hunt*!" and pelted off down the street.

Gil turned to his father who was shrugging off his greatcoat. Even beneath his shirt and vest, muscles could be discerned, shifting and moving. "What did you do, Father?"

"The device was programmed to *find* someone and then bring them 'home.' I simply reversed the device's task order." He flung his coat at a startled Boris. "Now let's *run*!"

As one, the two men sped off down the road, to the astonishment of the observing townspeople. As they ran, Klaus called out, "Tell me what we'll find!"

A look of exasperation crossed Gil's face. "Everything does *not* have to be a *test*!"

Klaus laughed and effortlessly cleared a cartload of barrels that had been knocked down by the passing clank. "*Life* is a test! Now *answer*!"

Gil concentrated for a moment as he ran, then spoke as they

leapt down a set of stone steps. "It's not one of Beetle's—it's too crude. Maybe a student, or a younger professor."

The streets were beginning to fill now, people were staring after the clank that had rumbled through the streets and the Jägermonsters that had pursued it, but the way was still clear enough that the two men were able to run unhindered.

Klaus shook his head. "No. Anyone at the University would have had access to better materials. The construction *screams* inexperience, and since there have been no new Sparks in this area for several *years,* I believe this to be a *breakthrough*! A *new* Spark, and I want him!"

"Maybe Beetle was hiding him?"

"No. The preliminary stages of a breakthrough are extremely difficult to disguise. *Remember?*" Gil nodded. His own breakthrough had had to be explained as a venting explosion in the main labs, and everyone else had just assumed that the pools of raspberry jelly were a bizarre side effect. Klaus continued, "Beetle couldn't even hide a *Hive Engine*. A new Spark would have been *impossible*."

Gil looked and saw that the street up ahead had completely filled with curious bystanders. Without a word the two men swerved, and leapt atop a wall that ran along the street, upon which they dashed past the astonished crowd. "Unless, Father, he'd *known* that this particular person would break through, and had isolated them beforehand."

Klaus frowned. "Unlikely. We keep records on the families of all established Sparks, and there are none unaccounted for. As for detecting a potential breakthrough amongst the general populace, even *I* have yet to develop a sure test for *that*. What *else* can you tell me?"

Gil thought for a moment while leaping from the wall. "It wasn't constructed at the University. So a foundry or a machine shop off-campus. Only they'd have the necessary tools. But if he's a newcomer to town—"

Klaus interrupted: "Shops can be rented. What about the man himself?"

A series of overturned carts, shouting peddlers, and items strewn about the streets indicated they were entering a market district. Gil vaulted over a load of spring onions. "He's been *wronged* by someone. Someone he can't touch through normal channels." He grimaced. "Most likely *us*."

Klaus nodded grimly. "Yes, the timing is *perfect*. Beetle is dead at our hands—"

"He threw a *bomb* at me."

"Someone here is *very* upset." They raced through Beetle Fountain Square, with its spitting statues. Pigeons clattered upwards around them, the birds' clockwork mechanisms almost inaudible over the sound of their wings. Suddenly one of the birds froze and dropped to the ground, where, Gil suddenly noted, dozens more lay. Obviously the events of the last day had interfered with the pensioners whose daily job it was to wind them. "Many people are going to be upset, Father."

"Beetle was loved by the populace," Klaus admitted. "But more in the abstract. He did not interact with the general populace on a day-to-day basis. Therefore our question is who would be *so* upset that it would trigger a *breakthrough*?" He grinned wolfishly. "*That* is the mystery, and soon enough we shall know the answer!"

* * *

Adam and Lilith hurried through the meager crowd in front of the shops along Market Street. Their dark clothing, while a bit somber, did not stand out as much as their size. However, people in the district were used to the oversized couple, and no longer gave them much thought. Adam looked glum. Lilith, being able to give voice to her annoyance, was more animated in her displeasure. "Fruitless!" she grumbled. "We've wasted a good part of yesterday and an entire night thanks to those stupid Jägerkin and no one knew *anything* about the locket *or* the thieves." She looked at the dawn sky with trepidation. "We must leave the city at *once* and get as far away as possible. I'm guessing that we have a week at *best* before…"

A subtle change of the pressure on her arm caused her to look at her husband in annoyance. "Adam, you're not listening to a word I'm—"

This was all too true, as Adam's head had snapped back at a booming noise that was getting closer. Effortlessly he swept up the startled Lilith and hurled them both to one side just as the clank, its smokestack pouring forth clouds of black smoke, thundered past them. Raising themselves up, they were just in time to see a squad of Jägermonsters fly past, howling. Purely by chance, Adam's eyes locked with that of an older Jäger, who grinned widely at them before running on.

Sweat started out on Adam's forehead. Lilith pulled herself up, her eyes wide with realization. "Was that… That was Herr Ketter's *tractor*!" The full ramifications of what they had seen caused her face to go white. "*Agatha!*" she cried.

* * *

Agatha was furiously scrubbing her hands in the big zinc tub when a pained groan came from the figure on the floor. She was a bit unsure about what she should do. Normally, of course, she'd have summoned the Watch, but as the only law enforcement lay in the hands of the Wulfenbachs, she'd decided that it would be easiest to wait for Adam and Lilith to return. She had hoped they would do so before the man had revived, but obviously it was not to be. She decided to go on the offensive. "Finally waking up, eh?"

Moloch rolled over and tried to move his arms, but found them tied behind him. He sagged in despair. "Ow. My face. Ow."

Agatha came over and grasped his chin and examined the lump there. "It's not broken. You'll live." She hefted the wrench she held in her other hand menacingly. "But I'll smack you *again* unless you tell me what you *did* here."

Moloch looked at her ruefully. "I woke you up. Not really a morning person, are you?"

"No, I mean, why did you bring me down to the shop? Why did you *trash* the place?"

Moloch looked genuinely surprised. "I did *not*! You were already here asleep on that bench and the place looked like this when I *got* here. Even the door was open."

Agatha frowned. "Then who—?" At that moment the great doors swung open and the doorway was filled by an enormous clank that stepped within the forge and paused. Agatha dropped her wrench. Moloch tried to scramble away, but got tangled in the coil of rope, and he tumbled backwards. A small part of Agatha's brain noted with alarm that Moloch had managed to surreptitiously slip his bonds.

Before he could disentangle himself, the clank's arm snapped out and the metal hand snatched the soldier up, kicking and squealing. It swung him up towards its sensors and a bright flash filled the gloomy shop accompanied by Moloch's scream of terror. Several seconds of whirring and clicking within the depths of the machine suddenly resulted in an array of green lights blooming across its front. A small bell rang and the arm gently swung Moloch down and offered him to a bewildered Agatha, who backed away. As she did so, the machine followed her, jogging its hand encouragingly. Agatha shook her head. "What? What do you want?"

Moloch caught her attention. It was obvious that he was being squeezed rather tightly, if the way his eyes were bugging out was any indication. "Help," he whispered.

Agatha blinked. "I... ah... down! Put him *down*."

Gently the device deposited a shaken Moloch onto the floor of the shop, dinged twice, and ceased all movement. Agatha and Moloch stared at it for a moment, but it did nothing else. Moloch turned towards Agatha. "What *is* this thing?"

Agatha shrugged. "I don't know." Suddenly her eyes narrowed as she examined the device. The core was certainly familiar though, wasn't that Herr Ketter's—?

The sound of breaking glass caused both of them to turn. Agatha saw the small hole in the west window. Moloch saw the small metal container that landed on the floor and spun about on its weighted base, a small windup key ticking gently. As Agatha murmured "What in the world—" Moloch yelled in his loudest battlefield voice, "*C-GAS!*"

Agatha just had time to look up and ask, "What's—" Before a cloud of gas exploded upwards, filling the room and enveloping them both.

* * *

Five minutes later, a Jägermonster stuck a furry face around the open front door and sniffed the air. Satisfied, he stepped forward. "C-Gas has dispersed, Herr Baron. C'mon in."

Several Jägermonsters and the Wulfenbachs entered the shop. Outside, two of the tall brass clanks flanked the doorway. At a silent signal from the elder soldier, a runner was sent off to check on the Jägers that had encircled the building.

The Baron and his son moved towards the two crumpled figures on the floor. Klaus turned towards the senior Jägersoldier. "Check the rest of the building. Bring anyone you find. Unharmed."

"Jah, Herr Baron." With quick motions of his hands, he sent half of the squad into the main house.

Gil turned about and examined the layout of the shop. His brows rose at several of the heavier pieces of machinery. "Nice set up." He gestured at the quiescent clank. "This could easily have been built here."

Klaus had knelt down and turned Moloch over onto his back. He smiled in satisfaction. "So *this* is our new Spark."

"It *could* be the girl, Father."

Klaus sniffed. "Hmf. Don't you recognize her?"

With a feeling of embarrassment, Gil glanced at the scantily clad girl. She was tall, and full-figured, and her long reddish-blonde hair covered her face. Suddenly his eyes narrowed and he knelt by her side. He gently brushed the hair from her face. There was a smear of grease across her small nose. "The student assistant in Beetle's lab! Miss... Clay." He glanced at a delivery wagon which had "CLAY MECHANICAL" neatly painted along the side. "I see."

Klaus nodded. "Yes, decorative, but evidently damaged. Held in contempt by those she worked with. Obviously *not* what we are looking for." An unexpected movement caught Klaus attention. Gil was removing his waistcoat. "What are you doing?"

Gil nodded towards the unconscious girl. "I was just going to cover her up."

Klaus nodded approvingly. "Commendable, but your waistcoat will do little. Here." Effortlessly he lifted Moloch, stripped off his greatcoat and handed it over. "I'm sure they'll not mind."

Gil looked up as he tucked the coat over Agatha. "Oh?"

Klaus stood up. "Yes, it all falls into place. The girl was truly upset at Beetle's death. Her soldier lover had recently returned home and her agitation was enough to trigger a breakthrough, and he built this clank for her."

Gil arched an eyebrow. "Lover?"

Klaus frowned at Gil. "You don't find the fact that the girl is running about in a machine shop in her underwear to be *unusual*? Red *Fire*, boy, what sort of laboratory did you maintain at school?"

Gil blushed. The Jägersoldiers guffawed. "Father! *Please!*"

The faintest hint of a smile twitched at the edge of Klaus' mouth. "Very well. What would you do now?"

Gil gratefully turned to the question. He gestured to the two figures on the floor. "Ideally? Talk to them, but what with the C-Gas, we must assume that they'll be out for at least thirty-six hours. So…" He thought for a second and then wheeled about to face the silent clank. "Examine the device?"

Klaus sighed. "No, no *no*! You must get your priorities straight. Examining the clank *is* important, but it can wait." He gestured to the room at large. "What is *missing* here?" He pointed to Moloch. "*This* fellow is still travel-stained. The shop is not run by the girl…"

Gil nodded. "The owner! Her parents, the Clays. Where are they?"

One of the Jägermonsters who had been sent to search the house stepped forward. "Dere ain't nobody else in de house, Herr Baron."

Klaus nodded. "They'll tell you much, when you find them." Klaus had turned away and was examining the workbench with professional interest.

Gil frowned. "Well that should be easy enough."

Klaus had found a set of micrometers and was evidently impressed by the workmanship. "Yes, no doubt," he said absently. He found the case and turned it over until he found the maker's mark, and Gil knew that he was memorizing the information. The Empire always needed good toolmakers. If he was any judge of workmanship, the Clays would find themselves hired as well. Gil sensed there was something different about his father now, but was unsure as to what it was. One would never use the word "slumped" when thinking about Klaus Wulfenbach, but the energy he had exhibited earlier in the morning seemed diminished.

Gil continued. "The clank will be transported to the University and your new Spark—"

Klaus had carefully replaced the tools on the workbench and turned back to his son. "*Both* of them will return with us to Castle Wulfenbach."

Gil blinked. "The girl as well?"

"Yes. If they are indeed lovers, she'll be an additional lever. If she is merely an exhibitionist, we'll send her back."

"Her parents might not *like* that."

Klaus walked outside and surveyed the neighborhood. "They'll take her back anyway."

Gil followed him outside. "That's *not* what I meant. Father, what's *wrong*? You seem... disappointed."

Klaus nodded. "I am. I was hoping for something... *interesting*. All we have here is a sordid little tale of revenge and manipulation, set up and solved." He took a deep breath and stretched, then clapped his son on the back, to the surprise of all present. "But it was a good bit of morning exercise and he *is* a new Spark, and those are always useful. However, while it is fortuitous, it is hardly urgent." He then dropped his hand and began to stride down the street. He called back over his shoulder, "*I* must finish consolidating our takeover of the town. I'm sure you can finish up here on your own."

Caught by surprise, several of the Jägers who had been stationed outside pelted up alongside the Baron, the eldest said, "I vill assign you two—"

Klaus waved him off. "I will go by myself. Let the people see that I *can*."

The Jägers stopped and watched as the Baron strode around the corner and out of sight. The senior Jäger muttered, "Hokey, fine, diz iz vun a dose moods, izit?" He turned to two of the soldiers with him. "Dey make great coffee back vhere der Baron is going. Go get me some. Und dun let him see hyu."

The two monstermen looked offended, slung their weapons over their shoulders and, faster then one would think possible, scaled the building across the street and were silently leaping across the rooftops. Shaking his head, the officer returned to a fuming Gilgamesh.

"Oh thank you, sir. Yes I'm sure that even *I* can deal with *this*." Gil sighed. "Well, let's get started."

Gil and the senior Jäger entered the building. As the elder soldier got his first whiff of the interior, he started, and looked around in surprise. Gil noticed. "Something wrong, Günther?"

The Jägermonster looked at him blankly. One of the younger soldiers piped up. "D'pipple who liff here. Dey schmell fonny."

Almost faster than Gil could follow, Günther scooped up a chunk of lead pipe and threw it at the younger soldier, catching him between the eyes. He blinked. "Ow. Vat for hyu—?"

Günther roared at him, stunning him into silence. "Hey! Hyu iz in schombodies howz! Iz not goot manners to say dey schmells fonny!" The rest of the Jägersoldiers gawped at the elder monster in astonishment. This was a new one.

Gil bore down on the younger soldier. "'Funny'? Like how?"

Günther glared at the younger monster over Gil's shoulder. The recipient of this glare was nonplussed. Lying was easy, but it was always good to know what you were lying about. "Um... ahh... like... like machines or someting?"

Günther nodded in satisfaction and spoke up. "Vell, dey *iz* mechanics, you dumbkoff!"

Gil looked unconvinced. He pointed to Agatha. "Does *she* smell 'funny'?"

The Jägers clustered around and leaned forward. "She schmells *goot*."

Gil nodded. "All right, I—"

Another Jäger interrupted him. "She schmells *really* goot."

The others joined in. "Really *really* goot."

Gil flushed and turned away. "Yes, yes, that's *quite* enough! Now get that wagon ready."

Reluctantly, the soldiers began unloading machinery from the Clays' wagon. Gil failed to notice Günther still kneeling by Agatha's side, a stunned look on his hirsute face as he remembered a large familiar face he had seen on his way here. Absently, his hand clutched at a small object on a chain around his neck...

Quickly, he snapped back to attention and approached Gil. "Hey. Hyu vants me to get schome of her clothing und schtuff? Or ve gun let her run around the kessel in her undervear?" The accompanying leer suggested that this last would be a fine idea.

Again Gil reddened and turned away. "Yes. I mean, yes, as in go get her some clothing." He looked over at Moloch. "And see if there's anything of his lying around as well."

Since he was looking elsewhere, he missed the look of satisfaction that crossed Günther's face. "Hokay, your loss, boss."

Meanwhile, others were preparing to load Agatha and Moloch into the wagon. "Don't drop him on his head, he's a schmott guy." A loud thump followed. "Vell, at least dat vasn't *his* head."

An argument broke out over Agatha. "I vant to pick op de gurl."

"No! Hyu vay too clumsy. *I* peek op de gurl."

"Me!"

"Me!"

"Me!"

"*ME!*"

Gil stepped into the middle and roared. "*Shut up! I'll* do it!" The Jägermonsters looked abashed. "Vell hyu dun gotta get *cranky* over it," one muttered. Gil knelt down and gently picked Agatha up.

Instantly, the tractor clank lurched to life and the great metal hand flashed out towards an astonished Gil, who felt himself jerked backwards as a Jägersoldier swept him away. The hand plowed into the monster soldier, throwing him back against the far wall, where he slumped to the floor. Gil managed to keep both his balance and Agatha in his arms as he hit the floor. The smoking device wheeled towards him. "Clanks!" He yelled, "Contain it!"

The two tall Wulfenbach clanks rushed in through the doorway and plowed into the side of the engine, slamming it against the wall. But after a second the greater weight of the more primitive engine allowed it to gain better traction, and it slowly began to force itself back up despite the best efforts of the two other machines. Gil circled around, heading for the rear of the rogue engine. "If I can get to the control unit—"

Then one of the Jägers yelled, "Stend beck!" Gil glanced back and froze in horror. Three of the Jägermonsters had manhandled one of the Wulfenbach clank's massive three-meter machine cannons into firing position. "I alvays *vanted* to try dis," one shouted.

"NOOOO!!" screamed Gil, even as he dived for the floor, desperately trying to shield Agatha. With a roar that was only magnified by the enclosed space, a stream of shells poured forth. The first few indeed hit the struggling clank, but the rest sprayed wildly around the room. The stream of fire stabilized only long enough to completely demolish one of the Wulfenbach clanks before the shooting stopped.

Gil dared to look up and saw that the recoil of the cannon

had smashed the Jäger manning the trigger, as well as the last quarter of the gun itself, into the wall. The other two, their clothing on fire and their hats in tatters, looked sheepish. "Ho! Leedle recoil problem dere, sir." One of the standing soldiers grinned. "Pretty neat though, jah?"

Meanwhile, the iron clank had thrown its lighter opponent into a pile of debris. As the Wulfenbach clank struggled to regain its feet, the tractor-clank swiveled about and despite a shattered leg joint, again headed for the two humans. "The control unit on the back," Gil yelled, "you must be sure to—"

The other remaining Jäger grabbed his gun. "Hoy! Got'cha!" Circling around behind the crippled machine, he scrambled atop some boxes and launched himself over the stumbling clank. The zenith of his arc carried him over the bullet-shaped control mechanism and as he passed he pointed his weapon downward and fired a charge into it at point-blank range. The resulting explosion completely obliterated Gil's plaintive, "— Not destroy it... never mind."

The clank and the soldier hit the ground at the same moment, the one to twitch and vent gouts of steam, the other to pose dramatically, to the approbation of his fellows.

The lone note of disapproval came from Gil, but this was turned upon himself. "Stupid. Stupid. *Stupid!* My father is going to—"

The leaping Jägermonster looked offended. "Vot did ve do *now?*"

"Not you, *me!*"

"Hah?"

Gil kicked at the cooling clank at his feet. "The clank activated to protect its master! Why wasn't I ready—"

The Jägersoldier interrupted. "But ve got *him* into de vagon mit no problem. It didn't move until—ow!" The "ow" was caused by a flying wrench smashing into his nose, thrown by Günther, who had re-entered the room, clutching a large valise.

"What for you hit me in the nose?"

"Cause you all de time yakking like an eediot!" Günther pointed towards the corner, where the Wulfenbach clank was still foundering awkwardly amidst the debris. "Get dat clenk op, hyu fools, or do *hyu* vanna pull de vagon tro de strits?" That caused the rest of the monsters to quickly begin hauling the great clank back to its feet.

Gil ignored this interplay, as he was struck motionless by the thoughts triggered by the logic of the Jägermonster's words. With a quick shake of his head, he dismissed the idea. His father had said—

"Hey, hyu gun carry dat gurl all day?"

With a start Gil realized that he was clutching the unconscious girl tightly in his arms. He looked up into the leering face of Günther. Awkwardly, he handed her over and, lost in his thoughts, failed to notice the excessive care with which the old soldier placed her in the wagon and covered her up with Moloch's coat. "Ve's ready to go, sir," he announced.

Gil looked up. "Pick one of you to wait here for the owners and the crews to collect the clanks." He glanced over at the steaming ruin. "We might still be able to learn *something*. When the owners get here, have them lock the place up and bring them to me. Assure them we'll pay for any damages."

After the inevitable game of sock-paper-scissors, the Jäger who had allowed himself to be socked slouched against the doorway rubbing his nose as the wagon began to roll out.

Gil suddenly yelled, "Stop!" The Jägers looked at him in surprise as he scrambled aboard the wagon and bent over the two unconscious figures. Gently he lifted Agatha's hands and examined them closely. Though she had scrubbed them, there were still ample amounts of grease and oil under her fingernails and embedded within the lines of her palms.

A similar inspection of Moloch's hands revealed grime, yes, but no evidence that the owner had recently worked with heavy machinery.

Thoughtfully, Gil climbed back out of the wagon. After a moment he indicated that it was to move on without him. Günther protested, "Hyu poppa vould skeen us alife! Und I dun meen dat in a goot vay."

"What would he do if he found out you'd assigned him guards after he told you *not* to?" The two appraised each other. Gil waved his hand. "I'm just going to walk a bit behind. You can keep an eye on me." Günther nodded reluctantly and the wagon started off.

As they pulled ahead of Gil, Günther whispered fiercely to the others, "Dun mention *notting* about dis mawnink. Not de fonny schmells, not the clenk schtarting op, *notting*! Dis iz schtoff for de generals."

The others looked surprised. "Hokay." they agreed. Günther nodded in satisfaction and looked at the young man following the wagon, a look of concentration on his features. The young master was going to be trouble enough.

FOUR

Hide the women! Hide the beer!
The Baron's great big thing is here!
It's huge and fat and long and round
And you can see it from the ground.
It flies way high up in the air
He rides it here, he rides it there.
And every mad boy lives in fear
That Klaus will stick it in his ear.

—POPULAR TAVERN SONG

Agatha blinked and stretched. Her mouth tasted metal-lic. She opened her eyes fully and stared at the ceiling. Something was different. The light—

Suddenly a hand roughly clasped itself over her mouth. Her eyes jerked around and saw that the hand belonged to the soldier who had appeared in her father's shop. A sudden surge of memories, as well as the current situation, made her twist and flail about.

Moloch dropped forward, pinning her arms to the bed. "Quiet!" he hissed. "*Quiet!* I'm not gonna hurt you unless I *gotta*—but I *will* if you act *stupid*!" With this, he tightened his grip upon Agatha's face. Having little choice, she froze, and then sagged. Her eyes stared at Moloch like those of a frightened animal. The hand relaxed slightly. He continued. "Now I'm gonna take my hand away. I'm giving you *one* chance. *Don't Blow It.*"

After a second, he released her face. Agatha licked her lips, but said nothing. Moloch relaxed slightly, but still pinned her arms. Agatha noted that he had been cleaned up, his beard trimmed, and an attempt had been made on his hair, but it was the sort of hair that defeated anything but an all out tonsorial assault.

He was dressed in a large sturdy labcoat, which Agatha realized she had seen on Wulfenbach staffers who had visited the late Dr. Beetle's lab.

When she still did nothing, Moloch continued. "Good. Now *listen*. We've been taken prisoner by Baron Wulfenbach."

Agatha frowned. "Why?"

Encouraged by this response, Moloch sat back, allowing Agatha to sit up on the bed and rub her arms. "Because of that clank I'm supposed to have built back in Beetleburg."

"*You* built that clank?"

Moloch snorted. "Of course not! But the Baron *thinks* I did, and I'm not going to tell *Baron Wulfenbach* that *he* made a mistake. So I'm his madboy until I can make a break for it."

Agatha saw the wisdom in this, but—"What does he want you to do?"

Moloch looked up at her with grim humor in his eyes. "He wants me to build him some more clanks. He wants to see what I can do in a *real* lab with *proper* materials."

Agatha cocked an eyebrow and her mouth twitched upwards. "Ho. You *do* have a problem."

Moloch observed the smirk and he leaned forward in satisfaction. "*We* have a problem, sweetheart. He *also* thinks you're my little assistant."

"*What!*" There was no way Agatha wanted to get involved in anything like this. She leapt up and threw open the door. "Forget it! You can just get out and—"

It was a soft "woo!" from the outer room that brought her up short. Turning her head, she saw that the door opened out into a large common room. Easily two dozen people, mostly children, along with a sprinkling of young adults, were casually gathered around several long tables which were set for a meal. All eyes were riveted upon Agatha. A sudden cool breeze dragged her eyes downward to reveal to her that she was dressed in naught but her underclothes. With a squeak, she slammed the door closed and, blushing furiously, turned upon a grinning Moloch.

Grabbing a blanket off of the bed she fumbled with it awkwardly. "Do... do those people know you're in here alone with me in my *underwear*?"

Moloch made soothing motions with his hands. "Don't worry about your reputation."

Agatha drew herself up. "I most certainly *will*. I have *never*—"

Moloch cut her off. "They *already* think we're lovers." The blanket dropped from Agatha's hands as she swayed in shock.

Moloch took the opportunity to survey her critically. "You're not really my type…" he sighed. "But I guess I'll just have to fake it."

"Why should I let *anyone* think—"

"Because *I* didn't build that clank!" Moloch leaned in and whispered triumphantly, "Your *father* did, didn't he?"

Agatha rocked back. "My father?"

Moloch nodded. "That was his shop, wasn't it? Before I woke you up, I saw the wheels he'd taken off the tractor, and when you told it to put me down, it *did* it. It followed your orders." He paused for a second as an idea hit him: "Did *you* build it?"

Automatically Agatha answered honestly, "No, but, Adam—"

"No buts. Unless you want me to inform the Baron where he can get a *real* madboy to take my place… ?"

Agatha looked into his face. "You *wouldn't*."

"I *will*. Unless we got a deal."

Agatha stared at him with loathing in her face, but could see no way out. It explained so much. Adam and Lilith had been scared to death of encountering the Baron. Everyone knew that Klaus collected Sparks, when he wasn't defeating them. The longer she gave them to get away from Beetleburg… "Yes."

Moloch closed his eyes and took a deep breath. "Good." At that moment Agatha realized how tightly he'd been keeping his fear in check. She felt a flash of sympathy for him. There were numerous stories of innocent people who had come to the attention of those with the Spark. None of them ended well.

Moloch continued, "So, the way the Baron figures it, I'm your boyfriend and I built you that clank because you were mad about the Baron killing this Dr. Beetle guy. You see any loose ends?"

Agatha slipped her glasses on. "Hm. Yes. You had a friend."

The reaction this statement got astonished her.

Moloch wheeled furiously and looked as if he would strike her, but with great effort he held himself in check. "My *brother*," he said menacingly. "And we don't have to worry about him, *you* saw to *that*!"

Agatha found herself pressing up against the wall as Moloch advanced towards her. As he talked, he fished around in his pocket. "And if you've got any hopes about *me* going the same way, you can just *forget* it." Triumphantly he pulled forth Agatha's battered locket. "It's been *deactivated*!"

"My locket!" Agatha reached for the locket, only to have it snatched away and stuffed back inside Moloch's coat. "Give it back, you thief!"

Moloch smiled coldly. "Oh no, sister, that's my *ace*. You'll get it back when I leave here *safely*."

"What do you *mean*, it's been—"

Moloch interrupted her. "Omar was my *brother*, but he *did* steal from you and hit you. I'll admit that. You help me get outta here and we're square. Mess with me and I'll have company at the Waxworks, I *promise* you." He turned towards the door. "I gotta get going. I'm not even supposed to be here, so…" He thought for a second with his hand on the door handle. He glanced at Agatha and a mischievous smile came to his face. He opened the door and spoke loudly. "Okay, that's enough kissing for *now*, doll. I'm glad you're okay, but give me a chance to rest up and we'll celebrate properly *later*!"

With eel-like swiftness he was out of the room and had the door shut before Agatha could reach him. Furious, she yanked open the door and almost collided with a tall, reserved-looking man who had obviously been just about to knock. A raised eyebrow was his only comment as to her attire. Quickly she scooted back behind the door and peeked out.

"Miss Agatha Clay?" he enquired with an upper-class British accent. Agatha nodded.

"Good morning. My name is Ardsley Wooster. I have the honor of being Master Gilgamesh Wulfenbach's man. Now that you are awake, he requests your presence in his laboratory immediately."

Agatha looked at him with trepidation. "Gilgamesh Wulfenbach? Wants to see me?"

"Yes, Miss. Immediately."

Agatha looked back into the room and then down at her outfit. "I'm not going out like this. I'm not... not dressed."

Wooster smiled. "Of course not, Miss. There should be a package containing clothing and toilet articles from your home on the dresser. I shall wait until you are ready."

Agatha glanced at the dresser. There was nothing there. She quickly surveyed the room. It was about six meters square, and contained two beds, separated by a nightstand, two tall armoires and two dressers. The side she had awoken in was bare, but the other had obvious signs of an occupant. Portraits of aristocratic-looking people and an impressive castle adorned one wall. A rack of fencing foils were hung with a display of awards. An ornate family crest was displayed over the bed, which was covered with a sumptuous quilt. The other dresser was covered with a tasteful array of books and knickknacks.

She turned back towards Wooster. "There's no package there. I don't see it anywhere."

A mild look of consternation flitted across Ardsley's face. "If I may, Miss?"

Agatha pulled back the door and hid behind it as the man stepped into the room. He quickly scanned the room, stepped around the bed, and opened the armoire. Empty. He bent down and looked under the beds. Nothing. With obvious reluctance, he opened the other armoire. It was neatly stacked with clothing and other items, but nothing that could be called a package, and he closed the door without disturbing anything within.

"My apologies, Miss Clay, it appears that your clothing has been... temporarily misplaced. If you will excuse me." With that he backed out, closing the door as he went.

Less then a minute later there was a soft knock and a redheaded girl poked her head in. She spoke with a faint Irish accent. "Hello. I'm Sleipnir O'Hara. Mr. Wooster here says that you be needing some clothes."

She stepped into the room. She was wearing a mechanic's work suit, with a toolbelt around her waist; kneepads, wristbands and a pair of goggles pulled up onto her head completed her outfit. She had an embroidered Chinese robe over her arm. "Your Mr. Wooster reckons that we're about the same size, so you can borrow something of mine."

Agatha smiled. "That would be very kind. I'm Agatha Clay."

As Sleipnir and Agatha shook hands, Sleipnir's nose wrinkled. "Hm. I'm thinking before we get you dressed, a trip to the showers."

Agatha looked blank. "What's a 'showers'?"

"It's a kind of bathing system, but without a tub."

"Oh." Agatha looked down at herself and flushed with embarrassment. "Need one, do I?"

Sleipnir waved her hand before her nose. "Oh yes." She handed Agatha the robe. "Here. We're not all as relaxed about being in our unmentionables as you are. Are you from England, then?"

Agatha reddened down to her chest. "No! I—"

Sleipnir interrupted her. "Whatever you do, don't let the Von Pinn see you like that."

"The who?" The two headed out the door, and Agatha's question went unanswered as a swarm of young children, ranging in age from six to twelve swarmed around her.

"Hey! It's the new girl! She's awake!"

"Hello, new girl!"

"She's stinky."

"She's the one who came out *naked* and you *missed* it!"

"You're lying!"

The room itself was long, lined with doors leading to, Agatha assumed, apartments similar to the one she had awoken in. The walls between the rooms were covered in bulletin boards filled with drawings, letters, strange looking objects such as leaves, insects or bizarre tribal masks.

Dividing the room was a large sunken area, which contained the long tables she had seen earlier. Several dark-clothed servants were quietly clearing the plates, aided by what appeared to be older children.

Sleipnir made shooing motions. "Oy! Clear off, you rigger rats! And I'd better not see any of you hanging around the showers or I'll—" The threat was left unsaid, but the smaller children nodded seriously, except for a slightly older boy who spoke up defiantly. "Or you'll *what*? Feed us to the gargoyles?"

Sleipnir leaned in close to him. "Or I'll tell the Von Pinn that you were peeking into the showers, you dirty little sod."

Instantly, the boy went pale and bolted from the room.

Agatha and Sleipnir went down the hall and into a locker room.

"What's with all the kids?" Agatha asked as she undressed.

Sleipnir leaned against a locker. "They're students." Agatha raised an eyebrow. "Hostages, really. You're one too, you know. We're mostly the children of the various Great Houses in the Baron's territory. We're all *supposed* to be learning about science and how to administer properly and such. Of course we all know we're *really* here to keep our folks in line. So your fella won't be doing anything stupid because himself's got *you* safe and snug."

Agatha paused and considered how much concerns for her safety would be likely to check... at this point Agatha realized that she didn't even know the man's name. "That's a great comfort." She reached for the robe, but Sleipnir stopped her. "You'll not be needing that yet. Now come on."

Sleipnir ushered Agatha into a large, tiled room. A complex brass boiler system hissed quietly in the corner. Agatha felt exposed, and vainly tried to cover herself with her hands while Sleipnir threw a switch and turned a large wheel valve. She then gently pushed Agatha under a large sunflower-shaped nozzle in the ceiling. "Brace yourself," she warned, and pulled a hanging cord. A cascade of water poured from the nozzle. Agatha screamed in shock as the water hit her, then realized, to her amazement, that the water was warm! To a person who had lived her whole life boiling bathwater on the kitchen stove, this was luxury indeed.

Sleipnir chuckled at her reaction. "When you're done, I should have some clothing for you," and she exited.

For several minutes Agatha forgot her predicament and just let the water cascade over her. After a moment she noticed a small metal table in the middle of the room. On it were racks containing bottles, which were labeled as containing shampoo and various hair oils, as well as bars of soap. Agatha selected one and examined it. Even the soap here was different, transparent, and it smelled like oranges. A far cry indeed from the stuff that Agatha helped Lilith boil up out of ashes, lye and lard from the rendering plant. The very oddity of the mundane object in her hand helped Agatha begin to think clearly. She began to lather up her hair.

When Agatha emerged, her skin glowing red, vigorously toweling herself off, Sleipnir was rummaging around inside a locker. Turning around with a few outfits hung over her arm, she critically eyed Agatha and frowned.

"I was afraid of that. I may be the closest match to you sizewise, but you're a bit larger than me, especially in the chest."

Agatha sighed. Sleipnir's next words surprised her. "I wish I looked as good as you." She turned back and rooted deeper within the locker and turned back while holding up a red leather overall. "There's a few things we can adjust a bit when we've got the time, but for now, it's this or nothing." She shook out the outfit. "Luckily this has always been a bit loose on me."

It was not loose on Agatha. Indeed in several places it took a bit of shoehorning to get all of her inside it, but eventually they got the final buttons buttoned.

"It's... tight."

Sleipnir nodded. "It most certainly is that. The good news is that as it's leather, it'll stretch out a bit once you get moving."

"At the moment, I'm more worried about breathing."

"Overrated."

Agatha caught sight of herself in a large mirror. Her face

went as red as her outfit. "I can't wear this!" She turned and looked at her backside, which the outfit revealed all too well. "I mean—*look* at this!"

Sleipnir shrugged. "it's a bit tight, but I *said* it'll stretch—" A realization struck her. "Have you ever *worn* trousers before?"

"Well... no."

Sleipnir nodded. "You'll get used to it. Here no one expects you to be daft enough to work inside the big engines in a dress, that's a good way to get yourself mangled. The Baron scandalized everyone when he said women wouldn't wear them. The boys'll stare a bit, but they stare at everything. Call 'em on it and they'll go red as a brick. You'll see. It's fun."

Agatha took another look at herself in the mirror. The outfit looked like it had been sprayed on. "Fun."

Sleipnir grinned. "Oh, yeah. Now c'mon, if you're done admiring yourself, there's people waiting for you. Who *is* this Mister Wooster anyway? He's a bit of a codfish, isn't he?"

Agatha was taken aback at Sleipnir's language, but gamely ignored it. "All I know is that his name is Ardsley Wooster. He's come to take me to Gilgamesh Wulfenbach."

Sleipnir stopped dead. "Gil? He's here?"

"I guess. Why? Do you know him?"

Sleipnir looked sad. "Sure, and I used to. I thought I did. He was raised here with us, but no one knew who he was, of course. Once he left for school in Paris, he never even answered our letters, and no one has seen him since he got back." They walked for a moment. "I really miss him, he told the funniest stories."

Agatha tried to reconcile this image with the serious young man she had seen in Beetle's lab "Funny stories. Gilgamesh *Wulfenbach*."

Sleipnir sighed. "I expect he's changed quite a bit. We've read—" She shook her head, cutting herself off, and looked to Agatha. "When you see him, tell him I said 'welcome back.' At least I can say I did the right thing there."

"Okay."

As they exited the shower room, Ardsley Wooster glided up from where he'd been standing. Sleipnir waved goodbye, and the two of them exited into the bustling corridor. "So what does Master Wulfenbach want to see me for?"

"I'm afraid that is not my place to say, Miss Clay."

This seemed to shut down any hope of conversation, so Agatha took the opportunity to look around. The corridor she found herself in was quite large, easily ten meters wide and the ceiling was almost as high. The only unusual thing was that instead of wood or stone, it appeared to be constructed of metal. This oddity extended right down to the floor, which Agatha noted, wasn't solid but was some sort of grate. To Agatha's disappointment, there didn't seem to be any windows, but the view before her was fascinating enough without one.

Growing up in Beetleburg, Agatha had considered herself to be fairly cosmopolitan, but the crowd here made her feel like a small-town girl on her first trip to the big city. A surprisingly large number of the people moving purposefully along seemed to be Wulfenbach airship personnel, but perhaps that was because their bright red-and-white-striped shirts caused them to stand out. The other armed forces were certainly represented; their brightly colored uniforms, in every possible variation, were a treat for the eyes. Black clad domestics kept to the sides of the large paneled corridors, carrying bundles and pushing carts. People from all over the Baron's wide-flung empire could be seen, as well as visitors from outside its borders. Fairly regularly, there would be a goose-like honking, and a young child in a blue uniform, astride a tall golden unicycle, would expertly weave through the crowd like it was standing still, leather messenger bags slung over the cyclist's shoulders. A procession of silk-garbed Chinese moved sedately down the center of the corridor. The procession was preceded and followed by a squad of sleek, ornately coated footmen, whose gait caused Agatha to study them intently. There was something not quite right... One of the footmen looked directly at her. Large, luminous green eyes with thin, vertical pupils examined her and then swung away. Agatha shuddered and moved a bit closer to Mr. Wooster, allowing the procession ample space in which to pass. She noticed that hers was not an unusual reaction, as everyone seemed eager to give the inhuman footmen plenty of space. As the Chinese passed, Agatha noticed that they all held themselves quite rigid, their faces expressionless, except for one of the junior clerks bringing up the rear. He was obviously terrified of the creatures escorting him. A faint odor of lilac reached her as they passed. A quick glance at her companion revealed that he observed the procession until it was out of sight before continuing on their way.

He noticed Agatha's look. "The creatures in the purple coats are known as the Lackya. The Baron employees them for many tasks, but it is wise to steer clear of them." With that he turned about and moved on.

There were other non-human creatures in the crowd. A squad of huge bulky men passed by in single file. Perched upon each of their shoulders was a small woman who appeared to have a glass dome set upon her head. As Agatha looked closer, she saw, with a shudder, that the men had no heads, but instead, similar, larger glass domes where a head should be, and within their crystalline depths, machinery gleamed with an odd purple light.

Clanks there were in abundance, not just the now-familiar soldiers who, Agatha noted, carried much smaller weapons than the immense machine cannons she had seen in Beetleburg, but others in a bewildering variety of shapes that lurched or rolled along on mysterious errands.

And sprinkled throughout the throng were odd, unclassifiable creatures whose differences ranged from the blatantly obvious, such as the octopus with spectacles who operated its own rolling aquarium, to the disquietingly subtle, such as the charming young lady who, only as she was walking away from Agatha, revealed a cow-like tail that swayed in mesmerizing counterpoint to her hips.

Eventually, after a bewildering maze of such passages, and several sets of metal stairs, they found themselves in front of a massive steel blast door. Ardsley broke the silence. "We have arrived, Miss." With that he discreetly knocked twice, spun the large metal wheel in the center of the door, pushed, and it slowly swung inwards.

They entered atop a metal catwalk that surrounded a large open workshop. Agatha's practiced eye saw an impressive array of lathes, mills, disintegrators, presses and shapers. An efficient-looking forge took up one wall, and tables and benches were covered with racks of tools, vats of chemicals, piles of humming, crackling electrical devices, or often some intriguing combination of all three. Clouds of steam rose from several large boilers, and the smell of machine oil and ozone filled the air. Overhead, a bank of arc lamps lit the scene with a harsh blue light.

In the center of the room was a large sunken bay, which was filled with a sleek green machine. To Agatha it appeared to be some sort of motorized carriage, although the aerodynamic effect was spoiled by some sort of large, multi-layer fender attached to each side. Bent over a large motor located amidships was Gilgamesh Wulfenbach, clad in a blue work shirt and a leather work apron. Agatha's eye was caught by a sudden movement. From under the machine came a bizarre little creature. She couldn't really tell *what* it was, as it was concealed within a large greatcoat several sizes too large, and an enormous felt hat. The only clues as to its species were the bright blue claws that extended from the sleeves as it dragged a large mallet along the ground, and a pair of long, blue, articulated antennae that poked out through two holes that had been cut into its hat. It moved with a manic energy that belied its diminutive size.

Wooster coughed. "Miss Agatha Clay, sir."

Both the man and the creature looked upwards. Agatha noticed that the creature possessed but a single eye.

Young Wulfenbach smiled and tossed the wrench he was holding into a bin resting on the cowl of the machine. "Ah, Miss Clay. Glad to see you on your feet." He waved his hand towards one of the benches on the side of the room. "If you would be so kind as to bring me a left-leaning Lurning wrench on your way over? Wooster? You may go."

The butler paused slightly, but bowed and silently backed out of the room, shutting the great door as he did so. Gil turned to the creature who continued to stare at Agatha. "Zoing? Bring

Miss Clay some tea, please." The creature dropped the mallet and scuttled off to another bench while making high-pitched squealing noises. Gilgamesh turned back to his engine.

After several seconds, Agatha swallowed and climbed down the metal ladder and went to the indicated bench. Seeing the young man had sent a peculiar feeling through her, one she attributed to her conviction that he was responsible for Dr. Beetle's death. She reflected upon this while searching through the tools. To her immense surprise, she saw the goldfish that had been kept by Dr. Beetle. For some reason this upset her more than ever, and by the time she had located the correct wrench and climbed down into the work pit, she was building up to a fine temper. There was a small step-ladder leaning against the machine, and Agatha climbed up to the cockpit with a murderous gleam in her eye.

Gilgamesh was now elbow-deep in the motor cavity, and with a grunt of satisfaction, pulled out a small hairy mimmoth. These pests, the result of some unknown madboy's tampering, had infested most of the known world, and frequently fouled machinery. It honked at him. He spoke without looking at her. "I hope you found your quarters comfortable, I—"

A wrench was thrust into his face with a commanding "Here."

Startled, he turned and saw a sullen Agatha regarding him, the wrench in one hand, the other hand upon her hip. A look of annoyance settled upon his face. He briskly tossed the mimmoth into a container and stripped off his work gloves. "Right. So much for small talk. Let us have this out right now. Sit down."

"There's nothing—"

Gil's head swiveled towards her and he fixed her with an icy stare. "Sit. *Down*," he commanded.

With a thump, Agatha found herself sitting upon a small bench seat.

Gil regarded her warily. For the first time, he seemed to notice her outfit. Agatha saw the direction of his gaze and squirmed in embarrassment. Her outfit creaked in protest.

Gil realized his mouth was open slightly and shut it with a snap, then shook his head and spoke calmly. "Miss Clay, I'm *really* sorry about Dr. Beetle. I know he was important to you, and I agree that his death was a complete waste, but—"

Agatha looked away and interrupted coldly, "But he threw a bomb at you. Yes, you've said."

"*NO!*" Gil's fist crashed down and a startled Agatha saw him staring at her intently. "*I* think he threw a bomb at *you!*"

After the first shock, Agatha felt herself getting angry. "Dr. Beetle *loved* me! He wouldn't—"

Gil ignored her. "He wanted you out of that lab. In retrospect I can see that he was *terrified* of you being there. Why? What is it about you that could have gotten him in even *more* trouble with my father than his hiding a *Hive Engine*?"

"*Nothing!* There's *nothing* about me!"

Gil leaned back and regarded her seriously. "Then what about your parents, the Clays?"

Agatha's sudden start caused a tight smile of satisfaction to flash across his face. "Yes, *that* hit a nerve."

Agatha rallied. "*Wrong.* My parents are simple, normal people."

Gil nodded agreeably. "Did you know that you have been asleep for around thirty-six hours?"

Agatha felt off-balance at the change in conversation. "What does that have to do with—?"

"I can't *find* these 'simple, normal people' of yours."

A small smile curved Agatha's lips. "Oh, really?"

Gil leaned forward. "And that doesn't surprise you. It certainly surprises *me*. We had the town sealed and they *still* got out. How did they do that? More important, *why* did they do that? At the very least, one would think that they would inquire about you, their only daughter, but they never even returned to their home. Should we be worried about *them*?"

Agatha bit her lip. These were legitimate questions. The idea that Adam and Lilith could actually be in a situation where they needed assistance was a foreign one, but there was always the possibility. "I don't know."

Gil studied her for a moment longer and nodded. "I see." He smiled. "Now let's talk about Herr von Zinzer."

Agatha looked blankly at him. "Who?"

Gil's smile widened. "Moloch von Zinzer?"

"I'm afraid I don't—"

Gil continued, "The man you help build clanks with? While in your *underwear*? Your boyfriend? Your *lover*? The reason you're *here*? Ring a bell?" he asked innocently.

Agatha flushed. "I *never*! He's n—" Too late she caught Gil's look of satisfaction. She quickly shifted mental gears. "He's... nnnice!"

Gil looked at her askance. "Nice?"

Agatha nodded inanely, scarcely believing the drivel pouring out of her mouth. "That's what I call him. Herr Nice. I don't even *think* of him as... as..."

"Von Zinzer."

"Von Zinzer. Yes."

Gil raised an eyebrow. "Ah. Well then, you'll both be happy

to know that you'll be assisting... Herr... Nice, with his next clank."

"Oh. But... Good," she finished weakly.

Gil smiled. "And I'm sure you'll be relieved to know that we have a *very* relaxed dress code in the labs."

Agatha stiffened. "You know, as much as I'd miss Mowgli—"

"Moloch?"

"*Herr Nice,* I'd rather just go home and help look for my parents."

Gil got serious. "I assure you, Miss Clay, we're doing everything we can to find them. Unless you can think of somewhere in particular we should look?"

Reluctantly, Agatha shook her head. A sudden *clink* made her look around. A small blue claw appeared over the side of the machine, holding a delicate delftware teacup. Agatha reached out and took it. The tea within smelled delicious. "Thank you," she murmured.

The claw then grabbed onto a protruding ring-bolt and Zoing hauled himself upwards. Up close, Agatha still couldn't penetrate the gloom under the little creature's hat. Feeling her eyes upon it, Zoing looked back briefly, then reached inside a wide sleeve and pulled out a sugar bowl, which it offered graciously. Agatha declined. Zoing shrugged, and deftly extracted several sugarcubes and popped them inside its coat. Satisfied crunching noises followed.

Gil's voice brought her back to the conversation. "Anyway, I'm afraid my father won't allow you to leave just yet, he considers you his guarantee to Herr von Zinzer's good behavior."

Agatha felt an uncharacteristic flare of temper. "You can't just keep me here."

Gil had the grace to look slightly embarrassed, but he shrugged. "We *can* actually. It's not like you could walk out the front door, you know."

"Why not?"

"We don't *have* one." His face brightened. "You don't know where you *are,* do you?"

Agatha blinked. Gil grabbed a control box that was attached to a long cable that went up into the ceiling. He grinned and stabbed at a button. "Let me *show* you!"

Agatha heard a squeal of alarm from Zoing, and then with a great *CLANG!* the floor split into two massive panels that swung downward, and the machine they were sitting in dropped. A quick look over the side caused Agatha to think she'd gone mad, as the ground was easily several thousand meters below them. A few farms nestled beside a river, and a vast forest covered much of the land. "What have you *done?*" she screamed against the uprushing wind.

Gil was busily manipulating the controls of the machine. He grinned again. "Ha! Watch *this*!"

He threw a large switch, and the motor behind them coughed twice and then stopped. Silence surrounded them as they fell. Agatha crossed her arms. "Oh. It's a Falling Machine. I'm *so* impressed."

Gil looked annoyed. "Weird. It worked perfectly on paper…" Simultaneously the both of them swarmed over the engine.

"How's it work?"

"Fuel here. Spark here. Main shaft. Boosters."

"Interesting. Should this be loose?"

"Yes, it's a balance arm."

Agatha glared at him. "A balance arm? You're wasting

117

space in a flying machine with a *balance arm*?"

"Well... *yes,* you still need—"

Agatha pushed him aside and reached into the engine compartment. A quick wrench and the small device was flung out into space, where it hung in front of Gil's face.

"And *this*!" Another part was ripped loose. "This is a *heat pump*! Superfluous!"

Gil eyed the slowly spinning device with regret. "Nicely designed though, eh?"

Agatha reached back, grabbed his shirt front and hauled him beside her. "Look—" she commanded. "With more room you can enlarge this flywheel and *it* will act as a balance! Add coolant lines here and *here* and then it will also act as a *heat dump*!"

The light dawned on Gil's face. "I *see*! Then we can also get rid of these here if we add more vents!"

The two of them grinned in accord and began ripping various pieces of engine out and tossing them over the side. A gleam came into Gil's eye, and his voice began to match Agatha's in intensity. "That'll fix our heat problem *and* tighten up these linkages! I see! Yes! There's a whole *bunch* of stuff we can get rid of!" He grabbed a large wrench. "Help me unbolt the engine!"

At this Agatha heard a strangled noise from behind, and felt an urgent tapping on her shoulder. Turning, she saw Zoing hanging upside down from the steering wheel. The small creature looked at her beseechingly and pointed over the side. A glance downward revealed the ground rushing upwards at an alarming rate. She in turn tapped Gil on the shoulder. "Um... of course, we *are* still falling."

Gil looked at her blankly for a second. Then he rolled his

eyes. "Oh, *that*." He reached into the engine compartment. "This wire was loose. Let's try it now."

So saying, he turned to the controls, and threw a lever. Instantly the engine caught with a roar. The odd fenders unfolded with a snap to reveal themselves as a pair of large green wings, and with a massive jolt, the machine's fall turned into a graceful dive that swung forward, and the machine gently began to climb back up into the sky, barely clearing several of the taller treetops.

With a squeak, Zoing toppled forward onto the floor and twitched. Agatha decided not to disturb him. She looked around, but failed to see any buildings at all, let alone one tall enough to have fallen from.

"So," she asked, "How did we get so high in the first place?"

Gil grinned. "We started higher. Look up."

Agatha did so and gasped.

"We started from Castle Wulfenbach."

And indeed, above them loomed the greatest symbol of the Baron's authority. Castle Wulfenbach was a vast dirigible, almost a kilometer in length. The surface was encrusted with engines, viewpoints, and complex structures that would have dwarfed entire earthbound castles. Massive gun turrets bristled along its length. A row of windmills turned slowly along its keel. Perched atop its spine, minarets, domes and towers filled every square meter. Gardens were visible, as were the three great smokestacks venting steam.

Surrounding it on every side, above and below, was an armada of hundreds of smaller airships, although, Agatha realized with a shock, several of these "smaller" ships were themselves dreadnoughts in the Baron's fleet, made small only by the presence of the larger ship they escorted. Even at a glance, one could see an order in the seeming chaos, as ships arrived and departed to and from the wide-spread empire.

The Baron had begun construction of the giant airship almost sixteen years ago, and had continually enlarged it until it had reached its current size. As his base of operations, it was unique as the only capital that was able to patrol its own empire. Onboard was the bureaucracy that allowed the Baron's Empire to function, and many a local warlord had awoken to discover that the master's crack teams of accountants and inspectors had landed in the night and were anxious to question him about irregularities in the books or that peculiar smell coming from the hidden laboratory. Its support crew numbered in the thousands, and rumor had it that vast numbers of them had not touched the earth in years. Many things were whispered about what went on aboard the gigantic airship, but surprisingly few townsfolk had been there. Sightings always caused the local population to pour out into the streets to stare until it had passed by. The panic started when it stopped overhead.

Agatha sat down as she stared upwards. She had traveled with Dr. Beetle several times on airships. They had been cramped, utilitarian vehicles. "I didn't know... it didn't feel like we were aboard a..."

"Really? I wouldn't know. I grew up there."

This brought Agatha back. "Oh yes. Sleipnir O'Hara said to say 'Welcome back.'"

Gil's face hardened. "Oh, she did, did she? Nice of her to *remember* me."

Agatha was surprised at his reaction. "She seemed very fond of you, actually."

"She has a funny way of showing it. I never heard from her, or *any* of the others once I left for Paris." It was obvious, despite his light tone, that this was something that bothered Gil quite a bit.

Agatha frowned. "Now wait a minute. She said that *you* never responded to any of *their* letters."

"I never *got* any letters, and they never bothered to come see me when I returned."

"Did you try to see them?"

"No," Gil said coldly, "I thought they'd made their feelings clear enough—"

"Guess they felt the same way."

"But I didn't—" Gil paused. His eyes narrowed. He continued slowly, "Or rather, I had been led to believe…"

The engine gave a sudden cough and both of them looked at it. It hiccoughed and then roared back to full power. Gil nodded. "You had some interesting ideas regarding the engine." He paused. "Build many?"

Agatha slumped down into her seat. "None that work. I can't *concentrate*. Nothing I do *ever* works. It's so *frustrating*! I can *see* it in my head, but everything I build explodes or falls apart."

The engine burped again. A worried look flitted across Gil's face. "Um… Maybe I'd better check that engine again…"

Agatha ignored him. "And when I *do* try to concentrate, I get these *terrible* headaches that prevent me from doing *anything*! It's so—"

Gil broke in. "You were working pretty intensely a minute ago and you didn't get a headache then."

Agatha looked at him owlishly. "Why, you're *right*." She thought, "Maybe it was because I was interrupted by your…"

She looked at the little construct who had been waving at her frantically, but gave up, "Zoing?"

Gil studied her. "But if you've never been able to concentrate, how could you have—?" At this point Zoing grabbed the front of Gil's coverall and began to furiously shake it. Annoyed, Gil turned. "What *is* it, Zoing? I—"

It was then that they saw the enormous gallery of windows set into the side of Castle Wulfenbach looming scant yards before them. All three had time to see the reflection of their stricken faces before they plowed straight through them in an explosion of glass and metal. Agatha found herself clutching Gil for dear life as the flyer burst into a causeway and continued through the walls on the opposite side. Wood paneling and various weapons flew about. The machine crashed to the ground and began to skid upon an ornate oriental carpet as debris bounced through the room, smashing furniture and knocking what appeared to be hunting trophies to the floor. In an enormous chair in the center of the room, a large creature looked up, startled at the intrusion. He had a large ornate teacup halfway to his mouth, and a book clumsily held in his oversized hand. They were heading straight for him when the creature calmly dropped his book, stuck out his arm, and with no apparent effort, halted the skidding machine dead.

Agatha, Gil and Zoing were thrown forward. Agatha flew through the air and suddenly found herself gently cradled in the crook of an enormous arm, while a pair of curious eyes beneath furry white eyebrows peered down at her. A wreath of white hair encircled the monster's brow, and a fearsome set of tusks protruded from his mouth. The lower set had been elegantly capped in gold. The rest of the creature was dressed in an elaborate red military uniform, encrusted with medals and festooned with gold lace and buttons. The sharp-toothed mouth gaped wide. "Iz hyu hokay dere, sveethot?"

Agatha blinked. The dialect was unmistakable. This was a Jägermonster, but unlike any she had ever seen or heard of. "I... I think so," she said.

"Goot!" He turned to Gil, who clambered out from behind the remains of the steering wheel. "Howzabout hyu, kiddo?"

Gil tried to stand, and wound up sitting instead. He looked at the enormous creature sitting calmly before him, and looked at the front of the little flyer. The image of a gigantic clawed hand was deeply imprinted in the machine's nose. "General Khrizhan! Are *you* all right?"

The Jägergeneral snorted in amusement. "Ho! Uv caurze, a leedle machine like dot? Pliz!"

At this point, Agatha realized that the monster soldier had not put her down. "Excuse me?" she ventured. The general looked at her with surprise, and with evident reluctance, gently set her to her feet.

He looked at the damage to his room, and seemed to find it genuinely amusing. He turned to Gil. "If hyu vaz tryink to zuprize hyu poppa, hyu vaz a leedle off. He iz not due for hour meetink for anodder—" he twisted his head to look at the face of an ornate clock that was smashed onto its side "— fife meenutes."

Gil went pale. "My *father*? My father is coming *here*?"

"Ho yez."

Gil clutched at his head. "Was I just thinking that this day couldn't get any *worse*?"

Agatha spoke up from next to the mangled flyer. "I think

the engine is still salvageable. We could—"

The change that came over Gilgamesh was astonishing. Instantly he became the grim, efficient creature that Agatha had seen in Dr. Beetle's lab. He pointed towards the door. "*GO!*" he barked.

Agatha looked stunned. "What?"

"Go! I've got to deal with my father and I do *not* want him to—" He seemed at a loss. "Just go!"

General Khrizhan broke in. "Ho dun be like dat. Hyu poppa vould understand. Vy the tings hive dun to impress a pretty gorl make dis luke like nodding! Some tea end—"

Gil forcibly picked Agatha up, carried her to the door and thrust her outside. "Zoing!" he yelled.

The little creature scuttled out from under the general's chair clutching a tea biscuit. "Take her back to the dorm level. *Now!*" And with that he slammed the door behind them.

The general shrugged and raised a hand to his face to hide a grin, and totally failed to do so. "A peety." He rumbled, "She seemed verra—" He stopped suddenly. He sniffed at his hand deeply. He paused. "Master Wulfenbach," he asked casually, "who vas dot gorl?"

Gil kicked a flyer part off of the remains of the carpet. "She's just a lab assistant." He looked closely at the Jägergeneral. "Why?"

Khrizhan grinned toothily. "She smells… verra nize."

Embarrassed, Gil turned away. "Oh, please, what is it with you people? She does *not* smell 'nice'!"

Unfortunately, this last statement was delivered with enough force that it was clearly audible to the people standing outside the door. In addition to Agatha and Zoing, there was a crowd of Jägermonsters as well as a growing number of airship personnel, many of them obviously prepared to deal with fire or some other disaster.

As Gil's pronouncement rang through the air, everyone turned to Agatha, who reddened, and radiating fury, stalked off with Zoing scrabbling to keep up. One of the Jägermonsters called out to her. "He dun know vat hees talkink about, sveethot! Hyu schmell vunderful!"

At this point it was hard to tell where Agatha's skin began, and the red coverall ended, but she managed to turn the corner with her head held high. Her attitude was evident enough that the onrushing crowd parted around her, until the familiar figure of Ardsley Wooster rushed up. "Miss Clay," he cried. "Where is Master Gilgamesh?"

Agatha glared at him icily. "Your swinish employer is in with a General Khrizhan. He's better than he deserves to be."

Ardsley blinked, but wisely realized that these were waters best avoided. "Ah—thank you," he said, and dashed off.

Agatha watched him go. She looked down at Zoing. "Are *you* okay?"

Zoing bobbled affirmatively and offered her a nibbled tea biscuit.

Agatha suddenly realized that she was starving. Enough so that she seriously considered the offered biscuit. "No thank you. Let's go."

Almost half an hour later, the enormity of Castle Wulfenbach had been firmly established, and Agatha was feeling a bit overwhelmed.

Eventually they reached a set of doors labeled "Student Dormitory," which were guarded by a pair of bored-looking soldiers. They asked Agatha her name, checked her off against a list, and waved her through. Once they stepped over the sill, Zoing stopped, tipped his hat and skittered back the way they'd come. Agatha sighed and pushed open the inner door and found herself in the long common room. Cries erupted from the apparently ever-present swarm of children.

"There she is!"

"Master Gilgamesh really took you on a *flying machine*?"

"We saw you out the windows!"

"You were flyin'!"

"Were you in your underwear?"

"Did you really crash into the Castle?"

"We all felt it!"

Sleipnir pushed through the crowd of chattering children. Agatha was surprised at how happy she was to see a friendly face, and impulsively hugged the redhead, who smiled, and hugged her tightly in return.

"Are you okay?" Sleipnir asked. "You were really flying with Gil?"

Agatha nodded. "I'm okay. No one was hurt, but it was a real mess."

One of the little boys piped up in a singsong voice, "Your boyfriend is gonna be *jealous*."

A hissing voice filled the room, freezing all the children into immobility. "No, he won't—"

Agatha started to turn, but a sudden blur turned into a black claw that grabbed the front of her outfit and swung her around as it hoisted her into the air. Agatha found herself staring into the face of a furious woman, her blonde hair pulled back into a painfully tight bun, a ruby-red monocle was screwed into her left eye and her mouth filled with sharp, pointy teeth. Her tight black leather outfit was fastened with a variety of buckles and straps that creaked and clinked whenever she moved, which she did with an inhuman quickness. Effortlessly she brought Agatha up to her face with one hand and snarled, "He will be in *mourning*!"

FIVE

Monsters and machines blotting out the sun
Fighting in a war that never can be won.
The men in the castles are having lots of fun
And all we can do is run, run, run.

—TRADITIONAL CHILDREN'S SONG

"I am Von Pinn," the ominous figure continued, "I am in charge here. You—" she gave the dangling Agatha a sharp shake, "are Agatha Clay. I have not heard good things about you." She indicated the children who were frozen into immobility around the room. "I take the safety of these children *very seriously,* and I have just witnessed an example of your reckless behavior."

Agatha tried to break in. "The flying machine? But I didn't—urk"

Von Pinn loosened the grip that had cut Agatha off.

"Understand that you are here to keep a minor Spark in line. Nothing more. I will not permit you to place any of my charges in danger."

"I wouldn't—gurk!"

Von Pinn's voice became even more ominous. "I have also heard reports of your tendency towards *indecency*. Your upbringing has obviously been *shockingly* lax. This is no doubt the fault of your parents."

A small switch in Agatha's head clicked over from "scared" to "angry." "Oh, now hold on! My parents—"

She was jerked to within inches of Von Pinn's face. "*Silence!* I am aware of the swinish behavior of the *lower classes*."

Agatha's eyes bulged. "You... I... If..."

"While you are in my care you will conduct yourself in a more seemly fashion. And despite any pathetic dreams you may have about 'bettering your position,' I assure you that Master Gilgamesh, in particular, will not be taken by your slatternly ways."

Agatha grasped Von Pinn's arm and glared at her in fury. "I wouldn't have your Master Gilgamesh if you stripped him naked and dipped him in *cheese*!"

Everyone watching gasped. Von Pinn's face froze. Slowly she brought Agatha's face to within an inch of her own. "And what," she asked dangerously, "is wrong with Master Gilgamesh?"

Rage filled Agatha and exploded outwards. "PUT ME DOWN YOU WRETCHED *CONSTRUCT*!"

Instantly, Von Pinn's hand snapped open and Agatha fell to the floor. A look of shock and horror crossed Von Pinn's face as she stared at her open hand. That look changed to fury and she turned to face a dazed Agatha, her hands forming into claws, when suddenly, a soft chiming sound came from her waist. Faster then the eye could follow, a hand dipped into a hidden pocket and extracted a small gold pocket watch. Von Pinn glanced at it and snapped the cover shut. When she looked at Agatha, she was once again in control.

"I have a class in three minutes. I am never late. I will deal with you later."

Agatha stood up. "*Deal* with me by *listening* to me. I—" A puff of displaced air and the slamming of the door at the end of the room announced Von Pinn's departure.

Agatha blinked. "Wow. That was *fast*. How does she—?" It was then that she noticed the circle of open-mouthed faces staring at her in astonishment. The tableaux continued for several seconds before Agatha broke it with a sharp "What?" This was the signal for all of the children under six to begin crying at the top of their lungs.

"What did I do?" Agatha asked Sleipnir, as she held a sobbing four-year-old.

"You got Von Pinn riled up." A boy who appeared to be about twelve, with a small silver clock imbedded in his forehead, started tossing a little girl up into the air. "Sleipnir said you were friendly. She neglected to mention that you were *suicidal*."

A tall, dark-skinned, young man with sleek black hair pulled back into a short ponytail emerged from one of the apartments. He took in the situation, stepped up to the railing and his voice boomed out. "Hey! Who wants to hear a Heterodyne story?"

Startled, the children stared at him and then began clamoring in assent, their fear forgotten. The young man settled down at the top of the steps and made a great show of scratching his chin in thought. "Well now, what's a good one?" The children clustered about his feet and made suggestions.

One boy stood slightly apart from the rest and crossed his arms defiantly. "Aw, the Heterodyne Boys weren't real people." This caused the children to gasp in surprise.

The young man turned to him. "Of course they were, Olaf. The Baron used to work with them. My Aunt Lucrezia *married* one of them. They're real people all right."

"Then where *are* they?"

"Ah, now that's a good story! It's called *The Heterodyne Boys and the Dragon From Mars*!" All of the children, even Olaf, leaned forward in expectation.

Off to the side, the older children relaxed. Agatha nudged Sleipnir and indicated the storyteller. "Who's that?"

"Theopholous DuMedd. He's head boy."

"Head boy?"

Sleipnir looked slightly embarrassed. "There's a... pecking order here. There's some that take it more seriously than others. It factors in family lineage, Sparkiness and some other nonsense. Theo's related to the Heterodynes by marriage, and he's got a touch of the Spark to him."

"Really? Wow."

Suddenly, Theo jumped up, stretched out his arms and intoned, "And the revenants saw them and they *RAN*!" Which was apparently the signal for all of the young children to run squealing about the room, a lumbering Theo in pursuit.

Sleipnir smiled. "He's a great storyteller."

They paused as a swarm of children fled past. Theo followed stiff-leggedly. He nodded to the girls as he passed. "*RHaah*," he said conversationally.

"And he knows how to talk to a lady, he does." Sleipnir looked over at Agatha and "tsked." "I see you'll be needing a change of clothes. The Von Pinn's a rough one." Agatha glanced down and saw that where the construct had grasped her, her outfit was sliced and torn. "Come on, I got you some stuff from crew supplies. It'll probably fit you a bit better too."

Inside Sleipnir's room, Agatha tried on several outfits. They did fit better, and Agatha felt more herself once she was back in a proper, ankle-length skirt. But Sleipnir did insist on including a few pairs of mechanics trousers in the wardrobe they assembled. "You'll get used to 'em," she promised. Agatha doubted it.

"So, this Von Pinn. What is she?"

"She's the nanny. She's in charge of the children." Agatha stopped and looked at Sleipnir closely, but as far as she could tell, the redhead was serious.

"You've got to be kidding. That vicious lunatic is in charge of *children*?"

"Oh, aye. I've been raised by her for the last ten years. It's very comforting, really. She's never hurt any of the children, and you *know* that nothing could get past her to hurt *you*." Sleipnir looked Agatha in the eye, "And on this ship, this close to the Baron, that's worth knowing." Her voice dropped conspiratorially, "They *say* that she was once Lucrezia Heterodyne."

Agatha was surprised. "Really?"

"Oh, aye. The Baron found her in the ruins of Castle Heterodyne after the Other destroyed it and brought her back here."

"That would be a heck of a case of P.R.T."

P.R.T, or Post-Revivification Trauma, was a frequent result when people were brought back from death as constructs. The chief symptom was memory failure, which could range from the temporary blanking of a few hours, up to and including total, permanent identity loss. This latter was the more common result, and was the main reason why more madboys didn't transform themselves into constructs in the first place. It was still tempting, as the basics of construct technology were fairly well understood, as were the steps required to give the standard improvements to speed, strength and lifespan. Many a madboy, impatient with the limitations imposed upon his body by nature, had succumbed to temptation only to awaken with no knowledge of their previous life. Most of these creatures were subsequently destroyed by vengeful citizens or were now working for the Baron. This was because another frequent result was a shift in personality, and many a fulminating madboy now found simple contentment as a researcher or lab assistant. Theoretically, it could also go the other way around, but as the supply of meek, quiet, sensible Sparks was vanishingly low to start with, it had, so far, remained merely a tricky essay question on the "Ethics of Revivification" final exam at Paris' Institut de L'Extraordinaire. These revived Sparks were so useful that the Baron actively encouraged his more hysterical fellow Sparks to "give themselves a makeover."

"That's as may be," said Sleipnir, "though I've heard it whispered that the Lady Heterodyne had quite a temper in her before."

They emerged just at the climax of Theo's story. Agatha was sorry she'd missed the rest, as it apparently involved a gigantic mechanical dragon that was currently being dragged off to Mars via some sort of water portal, pulling the Heterodynes in behind it aboard a rowboat. Suddenly the portal shut with the

SMACK of Theopholous' hands coming together, causing his rapt audience to jump and then squeal in appreciation.

Then one of the boys announced that he was hungry and the others joined in. At this, the dark-clad servants swooped in and began seating the children at the table.

Agatha was forcibly reminded of how hungry she was at this point by her stomach growling loud enough to be heard by Sleipnir, who laughed and showed her where to sit at one of the long tables.

There was a quick round of introductions, but Agatha found herself distracted by a flurry of activity from a small group of children who had not sat down, but had, to Agatha's surprise, produced several odd-looking devices. These proved to be controllers of some sort, as with a crash, several primitive clanks rolled, or in one notable case lurched, into the room from what was obviously an attached kitchen.

First came a tall, spindly device that made sure everyone had knives, forks and spoons. Unfortunately, it delivered them with such speed that, as it swept past, it left a small forest of utensils imbedded into the wooden tabletop, still vibrating. Agatha couldn't help but notice that the tabletops looked brand new, and were held in place by spring-locked brackets for easy replacement. Suddenly, this made a lot of sense.

Next came the lurching clank, which was loaded with a precarious tower of ever-shifting china soup bowls. To everyone's astonishment, it stepped up onto the tabletop itself, and proceeded to spill bowls onto the table in an endless cascade. After the first panic, everyone realized that the bowls wound up undamaged, upright, and perfectly positioned upon the table. Agatha stared at the wildly flailing mechanism and saw how the "falling" bowls were actually skillfully guided down by a series of well-coordinated taps. Everyone understood now, and the table spontaneously erupted in applause right up until the clank strode over the edge of the table and crashed to the floor, sending shattered bowls across half the room. An eight-year-old girl with bluish-black hair and prominent eyebrows dropped her controller and began to cry. A servant knelt to comfort her while several of the others quickly swept up the mess.

The third clank looked like a small tanker car on treads. It lumbered up and a pipe swiveled out. The pipe gurgled and Theo, with a lightning fast move, twitched his bowl under the pipe in time for a stream of hot soup to pour forth. The bowl filled perfectly, and Theo closed his eye and sniffed appreciatively, which is why he failed to see the pipe swing towards his head with a dull *BONK*. A small child with a swarthy complexion swore in Greek and made an adjustment on the controller. The pipe elevated, the clank advanced, and the process repeated. By the time the device had swung around the table and got to Agatha, a fourth clank, held aloft by an ingenious collection of balloons and propellers, had made several trips back and forth delivering baskets of fresh hot bread, racks of condiments and ramekins of fresh butter.

Agatha ducked under the pipe and examined the soup, which smelled incredible. It was a rich chicken soup, filled with an array of finely sliced vegetables, several of which Agatha was unfamiliar with. A bowl of thick yellow spätzle noodles was handed to her by Sleipnir. Agatha took her cue from the others and spooned a ladle full into her soup.

The children were wiping down their clanks and congratulating each other. The girl with the bowl-dispenser clank was still snuffling a bit, but had rallied.

"That was pretty amazing," Agatha said. "Does that sort of thing happen at every meal?"

"Are you joking?" DuMedd muttered sotto voce, "We'd be dead in a week." He twitched a thumb and Agatha noticed several small holes in one of the walls. "You're lucky you missed last Monday's Swedish meatballs."

Agatha thoughtfully turned back to her meal. The soup itself was tangy and delicious and Agatha found that she had emptied half her bowl before she looked up. "You were hungry," Sleipnir allowed, and poured Agatha a large glass of a thick, white liquid from a broad-based pitcher. Agatha sniffed it and a brief taste confirmed that it was tangy, like buttermilk, but sweet.

"That's called lassi," Sleipnir said as she lowered her own half-emptied glass. "It's a fermented milk drink that Theo brought."

Further down the table, DuMedd waved a hand in acknowledgement. "Everyone's expected to provide a few dishes from their homeland. Makes for a nice bit of variety," he explained.

Agatha found herself chewing a spicy vegetable that required the rest of her lassi to quench. She demurely wiped her lips with the heavy linen napkin from her lap. "You know, I'm quite fond of the Heterodyne Boys stories, but I've never heard that one with the dragon before."

Theo grinned and pushed his spectacles up his nose. "I just made it up. You liked it?" He had a deep voice that made Agatha's ears tingle.

Agatha nodded. "*My* favorite story is *The Heterodyne Boys and the Race to the West Pole.*"

A short young man with a noble prow of a nose spoke up. "You have an ear for the truth. That one really happened." He became aware of the rest of the group looking at him. "Well, *mostly*," he added defensively.

Agatha cocked an eyebrow at him. "Right."

"No, no! It is true! My father built the Mechanical Camel!" Agatha blinked. "Your father is—?"

The young man drew himself up proudly. "The *Iron Sheik*. Yes. And I am his son, Zâmî Yahyâ Ahmad ibn Sulimân al-Sinâjî." He smiled. "But you may call me 'Z.'"

Agatha sat back in her chair and regarded him with wide eyes. "Golly. I'm not used to thinking of the Heterodyne Boys and the people in the stories as... as real people."

Zâmî shrugged. "As real as you or I."

At this point, a large dish of various cheeses began to make the rounds. None of them looked familiar, and Sleipnir made a few helpful suggestions. Most of them were delicious, but one of them caused Agatha to choke, as she was convinced that she was eating someone's unwashed foot. The others at the table, who had been watching her surreptitiously, snorted in laughter at her expression. "Give it up, O'Hara," said Sun Ming, a slim Asian girl seated next to DuMedd. "No one else but you likes that stuff."

Sleipnir morosely took the remaining chunk of the offending cheese off of Agatha's plate. "You are all heathens, who wouldn't know the ambrosia of the gods from a cod's head and I pity you all, sure enough." She popped it in her mouth and chewed.

Agatha found herself laughing with the rest. While the circumstances behind her being here were alarming, she found that she enjoyed the company of these people more than she had ever enjoyed the company of the students at the college.

A thought struck her and she looked around. Between the older and younger children, they occupied just two of the vast tables in the common area. There were easily another twenty of these, all unoccupied, except for a cluster of the servants who sat near the younger children, keeping an eye on them while they supped on their own bowls of soup. "I can't help but notice that there aren't a lot of students here," Agatha observed. A few of the others nodded.

"You came at a quiet time," DuMedd explained. "The Baron insists that those with lands that need planting in the spring should help oversee the process personally, and actually assist if they're old enough."

A tall young man with wildly disheveled hair who'd been introduced as Nicodeamus Yurkofsky chimed in. "He says that it gives them a better appreciation of where their power comes from and who's actually keeping them fed."

Agatha thought about some of the members of Royalty that she had seen come through the Tyrant's labs throughout the years. "I'll bet they love that," she said carefully.

"It's the older generation that gets all horrified," DuMedd said with a laugh. "The kids look forward to it all year long. That and the harvest. The fact that it scandalizes their parents? That's usually seen as a bonus."

Agatha looked around at them. "So what about your families?"

DuMedd's face got sober. "I don't have any family." Agatha started to stammer an apology, but he waved it aside. "You couldn't know. My parents died fighting air pirates about twelve years ago."

"Really? Were they Sparks?"

"Yes. My father was more into the theoretical stuff, but my mother was Demonica Mongfish."

The Mongfish name was one that was mentioned prominently in any history of the Spark. From their citadel in Novaya Zemlya, they had periodically terrorized the surrounding area. The latest, Lucifer Mongfish had been a perennial opponent to the Heterodyne Boys, so much so that, eventually, one of his three daughters, Lucrezia Mongfish, actually married Bill Heterodyne. After that, everyone pretty much agreed that fighting in public would be unseemly. Holiday get-togethers, however, were a different matter, and by mutual agreement, every event was held at a different location to reduce the collateral damage.

Most of the others had similar stories. Sleipnir concluded, "There's also a few of the others who are still here, but they're on duty, like your roommate, Zulenna. You'll meet her later."

"Zulenna. That's a pretty name. Is she nice?" The others looked at each other.

"Um... no, not really," Sleipnir admitted. "There's a reason why she's without a roommate at the moment."

Suddenly they became aware of raised voices from the children's table. "No—that's not how they worked!"

"Oh, like *you'd* know!"

"I know enough to do basic research on biomechanics!"

"The only thing that's basic around here is your grasp of the theories behind mechanical forces!"

"Oooh! You take that back!"

Agatha found this discussion a bit disconcerting, partly because it was delivered by a pair of twelve-year-olds, and partly because it sounded exactly like an argument she'd heard last week in the teacher's lounge at the University.

"Make me, stupid head!"

"Ooh! I'm telling!"

Yep. Exactly.

Theo reached in and pulled the two apart. "Now what is this all about?"

A small, wiry boy sporting a large pair of goggles spoke up. "The bugs—"

The other boy, the freckled redhead with a small silver clock set into his forehead, interrupted. "Duh—Slaver wasps."

"Get wound. You can't just suck them out of people like in Theo's story, can you?"

Theo nodded somberly. "That's correct, Itto. Nothing can cure a revenant."

"But the story said—"

"Stories are for *fun*. Do not mistake them for *facts*."

Another child spoke up. "My father said that the wasps came out of *machines*."

"That is correct. They're called *Hive Engines*."

A little girl piped up. "Oh *that*. We saw one of those."

"What?" Sleipnir exclaimed. "Where?"

"We were playing on the dirigible deck and the footmen said we had to go. But we hid and we saw them unloading this big thing they called a Hive Engine." She pointed towards Agatha. "They unloaded *her* too. She and her *booooyyyfriend* were on stretchers."

Everyone looked at Agatha expectantly. She nodded. "There was a Hive Engine in Dr. Beetle's lab. I guess they brought it here."

Zâmî looked upset. "A Hive Engine? In the middle of a *town*? What was this Dr. Beetle *thinking*?"

One of the black-clad servants suddenly appeared at his elbow. "Such talk is *not* for younger ears. Off with you." To the obvious disappointment of the younger children, the older group moved off down the hall.

"I... I don't know *what* he was thinking," Agatha admitted. "About *anything*."

Sleipnir broke in, "What is the *Baron* thinking bringing it *here*?"

Nicodeamus proclaimed, "The Baron can handle *anything*." The others looked at him. He shrugged. "Mostly."

Meanwhile Theo had gotten a faraway look in his eyes. "So—*Where* would this Hive Engine be, do you think?"

Sleipnir looked at him askance. "The Large Dangerous Mechanical Lab would be my guess. Why?"

"Well... I've never *seen* a Hive Engine, now *have* I?"

Sleipnir wheeled around and prodded his chest with a finger. "You want to go sneaking into one of the Baron's labs? Even after what happened to you the *last* time?"

Theo looked at her blankly. "Well... Yeah."

Sleipnir did a quick jig. "*Sweet!* Let's go!"

"What exactly *did* happen to you the last time?" Agatha asked.

"Oh never you mind that, Agatha," said Sleipnir. "Come on, it'll be fun!"

"Plus," pointed out Nicodeamus, "she's the only one who knows what this thing looks like."

Agatha felt a sudden tug at her skirt. Looking down, she saw Itto standing defiantly. "I want to come too," he announced.

Theo shook his head. "Forget it, Itto. You're too young. Von Pinn would *kill* me."

"I won't *tell* her!"

"*No!* You stay here."

With that, the group moved off. Agatha's last view of Itto was of the youngster sullenly kicking a table leg. Once around the corner, she hurried to catch up to Sleipnir. "You can't tell me that we can just waltz into one of the Baron's labs."

Sleipnir winked. "You'd be surprised. Most of the labs aren't that well guarded."

Zâmî nodded. "The Baron is most careful about who gets onto the Castle in the first place."

"And getting off is even harder," Nicodeamus added.

"Besides," Theo pointed out, "we're not going to walk in through the front door. There's *lots* of ways—" He was interrupted by Agatha, who had stopped dead and put a finger to her lips. The others stopped and, a second later, a small figure slipped around the corner they had just turned and ran straight into Agatha's waiting hands.

"*ITTO!*" Frantically, the boy tried to break free from Agatha. Theo's hand descended onto his shoulder. "You were told not to come."

Agatha looked slightly relieved. "I'll just take him back—"

Sleipnir shook her head. "Oh no, he's coming with us now."

Itto punched the air. "Yes!"

"BUT—" Sleipnir continued to the boy, "if you get infected by a Slaver wasp, we'll have to kill you."

Itto's eyes got huge behind his goggles. "What?"

Sleipnir looked sad. "Sure, and I'd hate to do it. So whatever you do, *don't open your mouth*. Understand?"

Itto nodded frantically and clapped a hand over his mouth.

They moved off in silence, twisting and turning through

corridors until Theo stopped before an unobtrusive door. Reaching into his vest, he pulled out a large bunch of keys. He flipped through them, selected one and delicately probed the lock. A quick twist, a muffled *thunk,* and the door swung open. With a flourish, he bowed them into a small antechamber lined with maintenance lockers. Against the far wall was a metal ladder that ascended into the darkness. He lightly grasped the ladder to feel for the vibrations that would indicate that it was in use, and felt nothing. He nodded in satisfaction and turned to the others, his face serious. "This is an access ladder to one of the lighting maintenance platforms. Once we get up there, move slowly and gently, they're not made to take a lot of extra weight." He looked directly at Itto. "And above all, keep quiet."

From behind his hand, Itto grunted an acknowledgement.

When Agatha's turn came, she stepped onto the ladder, and with a sigh of resignation, began climbing. Eventually she joined the others on a small metal platform dominated by an enormous arc-light. The air was sweltering, as the great light put out heat like a furnace, and the platform shivered unnervingly whenever anyone stepped too heavily. It looked out upon a large cavernous room, lined with workbenches and machinery. Agatha noticed, however, that there were also racks of weapons to hand, as well as excessive amounts of firefighting equipment, medical supplies and large mobile barriers. Also standing about the room were some of the large creatures that Agatha had seen in the corridor. The domes that occupied the place where their heads should have been gleamed under the arc-lights.

Sleipnir noticed the direction of Agatha's gaze. "Those

are Radioheads," she whispered. "The Baron acquired them from some madlad he had to put down in Albania a few years ago. He figured if he could build fighters without brains, they wouldn't get scared or feel pain or worry about dyin'. The Baron doesn't use them off the Castle, because they creep people out too much."

"But… If they don't have a brain, how can they do *anything*?" Sleipnir directed Agatha's attention to a group of uniformed women that were on a small balcony on another wall of the vast chamber. All of the women were lined up, peering at the room below them. They seemed relaxed, and Agatha could hear their voices as they idly chatted amongst themselves. A flash of reflection made Agatha realize that they were all wearing a small glass dome atop their heads as well.

Sleipnir continued, "Each one of them controls a Radiohead. Like a puppeteer, except it's permanent."

Agatha shivered. "Those poor girls."

"Don't feel sorry for them. The Baron's offered to free them from the connection, but not one of them took him up on it. They're happy the way things are."

Agatha blinked. She was spared having to reply by Theo touching her arm. "Agatha, is that the Hive Engine?" He whispered. She followed his finger and was startled to see that the device was almost directly below them. Within its thick glass shell, the now-familiar disturbing shapes slowly roiled in the thick green liquid.

"Yes, that's it." A trio of figures emerged from a doorway and approached the sphere. "Isn't that the Baron?"

Everyone else froze. "Yes, it is," whispered Theo in a strangled voice. "Now *shhhh*!"

On the floor below, the Baron walked around the vast sphere, examining it closely. Following him were two of his oldest assistants, Dr. Vg and Mr. Rovainen. Vg was a tall, whipcord-sleek Asian of indeterminate sex. Mr. Rovainen was a short, shambling figure who was swathed in thick bandages, goggles and a voluminous coat. The bits of him that were exposed glistened with a soft nacreous sheen. Mr. Rovainen had not shaken hands with anyone in years.

Klaus stopped and faced them. "So. Your preliminary analysis?"

Mr. Rovainen spoke in a wet, buzzing voice. "It is *definitely* the work of the *Other,* Herr Baron." He slowly rubbed his bandaged hands together. "A viable Hive Engine—after all this time. *Fascinating.*"

Vg broke in angrily. "No, *terrifying*! I *strongly* recommend we put it on a fast ship and drop it into the nearest *volcano.* There is *nothing* we can learn that is worth the risk presented by having this thing aboard the Castle."

Klaus raised an eyebrow. "Really. Then you can *already* tell me whether this device is indeed eighteen years old or *brand new.*"

Shocked, the two scientists glanced at each other and then wheeled about to stare anew at the slumbering engine. Mr. Rovainen coughed wetly. "My apologies, Herr Baron. Not yet."

On the platform, the students were straining to hear what was being said. "It's smaller than I thought," Theo murmured.

"What are they *saying*?" Nicodeamus muttered.

"What if the Slaver wasps escape?" whimpered Itto.

"Then all *we* have to do is run faster than *you*," Sleipnir replied.

Looking slightly ill, Itto backed away from the edge of the platform. Suddenly he noticed a pale lump on an adjoining ledge. The lump rippled. Itto felt his throat close in terror. The lump moaned softly and extended a pale protuberance. Itto backed up until he ran into Sleipnir.

"Wa... wa..." he moaned.

"Itto? What is it?" The lump reared itself upwards and a pair of gleaming eyes opened.

"*WHAAAAASSSPP!*" Itto screamed and scrambled over the others, throwing them into confusion. The large white cat that had been slumbering on the platform bolted off into the darkness. Suddenly there was a loud *CRACK!* and the platform began to move. It tipped forward sharply. Agatha grabbed for the wall and snagged an exposed ring bolt. Her arms twinged as the platform stopped with a jerk, but suddenly everyone screamed as they felt the floor begin to buckle. With a groan, and a snapping of restraining bolts, the great arc-light swayed forward, flared, went out, and with a slow twist, pulled free from its restraints and fell over the side.

Agatha and the others watched in horror as the plummeting light smashed into the Hive Engine, knocking it off of its pedestal. The massive sphere hit the ground and began to roll directly towards the three startled scientists. Dr. Vg and Mr. Rovainen stared at the looming engine, spun and ran shrieking. Klaus sighed and sidestepped the great sphere while scanning the upper reaches of the room.

"Who's up there?" he yelled. "Are you all right?"

Above him, Theo pulled Sleipnir off of the swaying platform. "We are so dead," the girl moaned.

"Only if they *catch* us," Theo reminded her. "Now come *on!*"

All of the others were already scrambling down the ladder.

The door to the lab burst open and a group of Lackya flowed in and surveyed the situation.

On the floor, a squad of Radioheads had rushed forward and brought the great sphere to a stop. A swath of crushed lab equipment showed its path through the room. In the corner where they'd trapped themselves, Vg and Rovainen realized that they were clutching at each other and hastily disengaged.

One of the footmen appeared next to the Baron. "Is it an *emergency,* Herr Baron?"

"No, no, the engine hadn't been activated." He pointed upwards. "There are some students on that light platform. Bring them to me."

In another corridor, the students were moving as quickly as they could without attracting suspicion. Theo was in the lead. "If we can just get out of this sector—"

"WAIT!" Agatha's shout brought them all up short. She pointed at a small figure running back the way they'd come. "It's *Itto*! He's running the wrong way! We've got to get him!"

Sleipnir caught hold of Agatha's sleeve. "Not to worry! The footmen will catch him and they'll bring him back to the dorm unharmed. Von Pinn would *destroy* anyone who hurt him."

Agatha looked confused. "Then... why are *we* running?"

Theo put a hand on both girls' shoulders and pushed them along. "Itto is too young. *We,* on the other hand, will be put on grease trap duty for life. *Again.*"

"That's *bad,* is it?"

"RUN!"

* * *

Back in the lab, the Baron looked up from a pile of debris to see a squad of footmen approaching. They stepped aside to reveal the terrified figure of Itto in their midst. The Baron looked askance at the leader. "*This* is all you caught?"

"So far, Herr Baron. Though he *does* say that he was alone."

Klaus scowled. "Yes, that's what I would *expect* the son of Jurgen Wheelwright to say."

The boy spoke up. "It... It was all *my* fault, Herr Baron."

"I expect it was. Why were you here?"

"I wanted to see a Hive Engine, sir. Everyone knows the story about how you defeated a dragon from Mars that captured Lucrezia Mongfish and spit out Slaver wasps and turned her into Von Pinn and I wanted to see what could *do* that."

Klaus' jaw snapped shut. His massive hand thoughtfully rubbed his nose, incidentally concealing a smile. "I'd have given a lot to see that myself," he conceded. He turned serious and leaned down until his face was inches from Itto's. "You will never mention to Mistress Von Pinn how she used to be Lucrezia Mongfish. She wouldn't *like* it. She wouldn't like it at *all*. Do you understand?"

"Yes, Herr Baron," the boy whispered.

"Good." The Baron straightened up. "You will now assist me in sorting out this mess." Itto looked astonished, then quickly snapped to attention. "Yes *sir*, Herr Baron!"

Klaus nodded. "And while you're working, tell me this story." Itto took a deep breath, but Klaus held up his hand and turned to the waiting footmen. "Katz? Tell the Blue Level

Kitchen Master that young DuMedd is on grease trap duty until further notice."

The footman smirked and bowed slightly. "Yes, Herr Baron."

Klaus' voice caught him broadside as he straightened up. "As is your entire squad if you fail to catch him and his companions!"

Katz gave a strangled "glurk!" and he and his squad swirled out of the room and were gone.

"Theo? I hear people running."

Sleipnir slumped against a wall, panting. "I think we're goin' down, boyo."

"What we need is a place to *hide*." They rounded a corner. Theo brightened. "Wait! I know where we are! That's an empty lab! Come on!"

"What if someone is *in* it?" Agatha asked.

"Relax!" Theo said as he pulled out his keys. "We'll use the old 'Mimmoth Catcher' routine. It works every time!"

The keys proved unnecessary, as the door was unlocked. Theo straightened his outfit, ran a hand through his hair, and briskly knocked three times before quickly opening the door. "Excuse us," he sang out, "mimmoth exterminators. Don't let us disturb—" He stopped dead.

Gilgamesh Wulfenbach, who had been hauling the twisted remains of his flying machine up onto a massive workbench, paused, hanging onto the pulley chain with a nostalgic look upon his face. "Wow. Does *that* ever take me back." He eyed the frozen Theo. "You're in trouble. You need a place to hide. Probably from my father." His lip curled. "I should have *known* none of you would talk to me unless you *needed* something."

Theo glared. "Well if you hadn't told Von Pinn that you were too *busy* to see anyone—"

Gil looked surprised. "What?"

Theo plowed on: "You're obviously *far* too important to associate with *us* anymore, so we'll just—" As he turned away, Gil grabbed Theo's arm. Theo tried to shrug him off and found instead that he couldn't move his arm at all. A startled glance at Gil's face showed the faraway look that meant his brain was racing.

He focused on Theo. "Did you get *any* of my letters?"

Theo blinked. "No," he said slowly. "Did you get any of *ours*?"

He then hissed in pain at the viselike grip on his arm as a look of fury filled Gil's face. "Someone was intercepting them" he growled. "I don't know who, or how, but I will!" Suddenly his face cleared and he noticed Theo's distress. He released his arm. "How many of you are there?"

"Um, five."

"Right! Into the cracking vat, I'll get the rest!"

He swung open the door to reveal the astonished face of Sleipnir. "Gil!"

"Sleipnir! We'll talk later! Everybody into the vat!"

Sleipnir took a step into the lab and then stopped dead. "*Whoof!* What is that *smell*?"

"Ah! There's this girl, a Miss Clay—"

He turned and found himself face to face with a furious Agatha who grabbed his shirtfront and shook him like a terrier shaking a rat. "I have had quite enough of your public opinions about how I *smell*, Herr Wulfenbach!" She snarled, and so saying, she hauled off and smacked him across the face. "I'll face that Von Pinn again before I take any help from *you*!"

Before the stunned young man could say anything, she was off down the corridor at a dead run.

"No! *Wait!*" Gil pulled himself to the doorway. "Because of your redesign of the engine—" She was gone. He turned to Theo, who had an amused look on his face. "Because of her redesign, I can use this *great* new fuel additive, but it really stinks and I—"

Theo patted him on the shoulder. "You still have that *fine* touch with the ladies, I see." The others grinned.

"GET IN THE VAT!" Gil snapped

Agatha stomped along muttering to herself. "—and then we'll see how he likes smelling *that*! Get me to a chemical lab and I'll brew up something that will make that pompous jerk wish he'd never been *born*!"

Having got that off of her chest, Agatha surfaced from her thoughts, took note of her surroundings and stopped dead. She was in a dimly-lit side corridor. A part of her brain had noted that there had been fewer and fewer people in the corridors she had passed through, and for some time now, she had traveled alone. She briefly considered turning around, but rationalized that as she had no idea where she was, retracing her steps could only aid any lingering pursuers.

She pushed on, through long winding corridors lined with sealed and locked hatchways, and the occasional large space filled with enigmatic machinery, which hissed and gurgled as she passed. There were no signs, no labels, and nobody else.

Initially, she would have avoided another person, but now she was actively calling out, trying to find anyone at all. At yet another unlabeled crossway, she stopped and glared at where, logically, a sign should have been.

"This is ridiculous. *Somebody* must come through here." No one, however, conveniently did so.

She passed a series of open storerooms. Dimly lit vaults full of drums and bales. She turned a corner and saw a light wink out from a doorway halfway down the long corridor. Someone was here! Agatha broke into a run and called out, "Hello? Please wait, I'm lost. Hello?" But there was no answer, and indeed, no sign of anyone when she reached the doorway in question.

"I know I saw a light," Agatha muttered to herself. She reached around and found the power switch in the usual place and threw it. There was a snap, and the room filled with the harsh white glare of the overhead lamps. Agatha was taken aback. This light was different from the dimmer, more golden light she'd seen. The room was filled with giant spools containing bolts of the crusty metallic fabric that sheathed Castle Wulfenbach. There was no sound. Agatha felt herself beginning to get annoyed. She stepped in and looked around. The idea that she had been mistaken never entered her head. She came to the end of an aisle of spools, turned, and stared.

Laid out on the floor of the aisle was a collection of debris that was obviously out of place. Such untidiness was doubly shocking after the neatness and order that was rigorously maintained everywhere else aboard the great airship. Agatha was about to go when she noticed that in the middle of the pile was a large ship's lamp. On a hunch, she went over to it and gently touched the metal hood, snatching her hand back at the heat. There *was* someone here!

Quickly she stood and looked about. She took a step and noticed the ringing sound her foot made upon the deck. She'd heard nothing like that as she approached, so unless the mysterious garbage collector was wearing naught but socks upon their feet, there was nowhere else to go but—

Agatha whipped her head upwards, causing the large white cat that was watching her to jump upwards in surprise.

She puffed a lock of hair out of her face in annoyance, and looked back at the objects at her feet. She looked again. Odd. From here, it was obvious that the objects were not haphazardly strewn about. They had been laid out quite deliberately. A book caught her eye. It was an open comb-bound manual. Upon examination, Agatha realized that it was an instruction manual for flying one of Castle Wulfenbach's small inspection airships. Excitement seized her. This was exactly what Agatha needed! She examined the line drawings that showed the airship controls. They looked fairly simple and—

Agatha paused, looked again at the debris on the floor, and then re-examined the drawing in the book. There was no mistake. Someone had meticulously re-created the control panels out of various found objects. The inference was obvious. Someone else was surreptitiously trying to learn how to fly one of the small airships.

Now Agatha felt conflicted. Yes, she desperately needed to get off of the airship, but here was evidence that someone else had the same need. Who knew what their reasons were. She thought fiercely for a moment, hugging the book to her chest. Then she spoke up. "I need to get off of this airship," she said loudly. Her voice echoed through the vast room. She listened intently, but heard nothing. "My parents need me, and the Baron won't let me help find them. This book, the airship instruction manual, will help me get off of this ship, so I'm taking it."

Silence. Agatha noticed that the cat, which had been watching her all this time, was lashing its tail in an agitated manner. "Sorry, kitty," she said, "I'll be out of here shortly." The cat hissed at her.

Agatha again called out, "If you still need this book, speak up now, and we can work together. My companion and I just need to get down to the ground safely. Your reasons are your own."

Again there was nothing.

"Okay. I've done my best." However she still had a twinge of guilt as she tucked the book within her jacket. Looking around, half expecting someone to appear at any moment, she exited the room, switching off the light as she did so, and continued down the hallway. Atop the stack of fabric, the cat stared balefully at the doorway and, with a savage swipe of its claws, tore a great rent in the fabric at its feet.

Buoyed by her discovery, Agatha quickly realized that her immediate situation hadn't really improved. This was driven home by her arrival at yet another desolate, uninformative intersection. She sighed. "I guess I'll just keep going until I meet somebody or run out of dirigible."

This decision made, she squared her shoulders, picked a corridor at random and strode off, turned a corner, and came to a blank wall.

She regarded it with disapproval, turned about and marched off, stopping after she had taken two steps. She turned back.

"That's *stupid*. Why put in a corridor that leads up to a dead end? There must be *something* here..."

As she glared at the wall, one of the rivets surrounding the edge caught her eye. It looked... different. Experimentally, she pushed it, and was rewarded with a dull *CHONK* noise, and the wall swung open with a faint *squeeee*.

Agatha grinned, stepped through, and found herself at the lip of a vast pit. Her arms windmilling, she barely keept her balance upon the small ledge that surrounded it.

The room itself was lit by the lights of some odd-looking machinery that lined the far wall. Agatha noted that there was a much larger floor, as well as another door, on the other side, so she was preparing to inch her way around the pit when a deep booming voice addressed her from the darkness.

"Ah! You must be the Villain's Beautiful But Misguided Daughter!" She almost lost her balance again.

When she had stabilized herself, she looked up. Agatha saw a large burly man suspended over the pit by an excessive number of chains. A vast complex of devices were attached to various points on his head, and an obvious bomb had been attached to his feet. He smiled at Agatha engagingly. "You're just in time!"

SIX

"Jägermonsters are hard to kill, because the devil don't want them in Hell."

—PEASANT SAYING

"I'm the *what*?"

"You're the Baron's beautiful daughter, surely."

"I am *not* the Baron's daughter."

The hanging man looked nonplussed for a moment. His brow furrowed around the visor that hid his eyes. "Are you sure? I'm usually very good at spotting the offspring of evil geniuses…" Then his face cleared. "Ah! Then you must be the plucky lab assistant here to set me free!"

Agatha began to feel like she was on stage and didn't know her lines. "I'm sorry, who *are* you?"

The man grinned and, astonishingly, managed to make himself look imposing, even restrained as he was. "Ah, allow me to introduce myself. I am Othar Tryggvassen—Gentleman Adventurer!" He smiled modestly. "Perhaps you've heard of me. I'm told the stories are getting around."

Agatha felt her feeling of unreality increase. "Othar. *The* Othar. The man who defeated the wooden warriors of Dr. Krause."

"That would be me, yes."

"The hero who saved the hamlet of Lunkhauser from the ever-widening moat."

"The very same."

"The savior of the town of Mount Horeb from the rain of mustard."

Othar's grin slid off his face. He chewed his lip. "I... uh... I'm afraid you have me on that one."

Agatha nodded approvingly. "I made it up." She peered down the shaft below. Much to her surprise, the bottom was quite visible, as were the gigantic gears that would swiftly grind anything that fell into them into a fine lubricating paste. She looked back at the again-grinning Othar. "You don't seem too worried about..." She gestured downwards.

"About being a prisoner in a seemingly hopeless predicament? Well I'd be lying if I said it wasn't inconvenient, but I'll escape eventually. I *am* the hero, after all, and *you* are just what I need!"

"An audience?"

"Ye—*no*! You can be my spunky girl sidekick. I'm fresh out at the moment. Release me and we'll blow up the Baron's Dirigible of Doom, escape by the skin of our teeth, and then it's cocoa and schnapps all around!"

Agatha folded her arms. "'Spunky girl sidekick.'"

"Sure! It'll be *fun*!"

Agatha nodded and began to resume her edging around the pit towards the far door. "Look, no offense," she said, "but I've been around Sparks and their labs most of my life."

Othar's grin faltered. "Oh?"

"Uh-huh, and I'd rather *not* end up being the Easily Duped Minion Who Sets the Insanely Dangerous Experiment free. *Or* the Hostage Who Ensures the Smooth-Talking Villain's escape."

"Ah…"

"I don't have any *proof* that you really *are* Othar Tryggvassen, or even that you're really *human*."

"Er…"

Agatha reached the far side and dusted herself off. "This Girl Sidekick job doesn't call for a lot of *smarts*, does it?"

The hanging man had the grace to look embarrassed. "Um… Not as *such*, no, but no matter who or what I *am*, is it *right* to leave a fellow sentient strung up like this?"

Agatha considered this. "That depends on the nature of the experiment."

Othar frowned. "I *think* you spent a little *too* much time in those labs."

Agatha looked surprised. "Really? Why?"

The door behind her slammed open. "Vot is all dis yakkink—" A Jägermonster shambled through the door and stopped dead upon seeing Agatha. "GOTT'S LEEDLE FEESH IN TROUSERS!"

He rushed over to Agatha as another monster soldier entered and surveyed the prisoner. "Anodder shtupid easily duped *minion*!" He waved at Othar. "Don't you know dis iz an *insanely* dangerous guy?"

"I *knew* that!" Agatha responded defensively.

The other Jäger turned towards them. "He's shtill secure." He jerked a large thumb over to the other side of the pit, where the door that Agatha had used to enter still swung open. "She came in throo dot idiotic secret door. Dey *gots* to get rid of dot ting. Vell, let's just keel her." He turned towards Agatha. "Ve ain't suppozed to let anybody in here," he said apologetically.

"*Fiends!*" roared Othar. "Kill her and I'll tell the *Baron!*"

"Vell mebbe ve keel you too, schmot guy."

The other Jägermonster began to look troubled. "Gorb..."

"Vat?"

"Gorb, dis iz turnink into von of *dose* plenz... The kind vere ve keel efferbody dot notices dot ve's keelink pipple?"

Gorb deflated slightly. "It is?"

The other Jäger nodded and slung a friendly paw over Gorb's shoulders. "Uh-huh. Und how do dose *alvays* end?"

Gorb muttered, "The dirigible is in flames, everybody's dead, an' I've lost my hat."

His friend smiled. "Dot's *right!* Und any plan vere you lose your hat iz—?"

Gorb struggled for a second. "A bad plan?" he ventured.

That earned him a slap on the back. "Right *again!*"

"Look—" Agatha broke in impatiently, "How about *you* don't kill *me,* and *I* won't mention that *you* let me get in."

Gorb looked troubled. "But..."

His companion beamed. "Hoy! *Excellent!* Vut a schmot gurl!"

Gorb spoke up. "Stosh, you mean dis iz vun of dose plenz vere ve dun keel *hennybody?*"

Stosh nodded glumly. "Yop. 'Fraid so." He turned to Agatha and leered. "Zo, howzabout I ezcort hyu beck to you qvarters, Meez—?"

"Clay," she responded automatically. "Agatha Clay."

The Jägermonsters stared at each other in astonishment. Gorb looked sheepish. Stosh smacked him in the head. "See? *See?*" he roared. "*Dis* iz vhy dot 'keelink evverbody' plan iz no goot! Hyu never know, now *do* hyu?" Another smack on the head.

"Know *what*?" asked Agatha.

Stosh and Gorb spun to face her. "Ve has orders regadink a meez 'Agatha Clay.'"

There was something different about him. About them both. With a chill she realized what it was. Nothing she could actually point a finger to, but they weren't... *funny* anymore.

"O... orders? What orders?" she asked. A tiny analytical part of her brain wondered how much of their daily behavior was an act put on to put those around them at ease.

Stosh shattered the mood by whooping and sweeping Agatha up over his head. "I gots to take hyu to a *party*!" And with a loud "Wheeeee!" scurried off with her down the hall.

Othar and Gorb stared after them for a moment until Othar sighed and remarked conversationally, "No one ever takes *me* to parties."

Gorb looked at him and smiled. "Ve haff our own party. Hyu ken be da piñata!"

After being rushed along several halls, Agatha realized exactly *where* the Jägermonster was holding her and demanded loudly to be put down. He did so with a laugh and they proceeded onwards.

"Zo. Agatha Clay, hyu *iz* da gurl who helped Master Gilgamesh fly smek into General Khrizhan's qvarters?"

"Well... I..." she saw the look of amusement in the soldier's eyes and gave up any thought of pretense. "Yes."

"Heh heh. I bet he vas sooprized. So vat heppened?"

"Your Master Gilgamesh was doing the steering, and he..." she paused, and grudgingly amended her narrative, "*we* didn't look where we were going and plowed right into the Castle. We smashed through the wall into your general's room. He was sitting in a chair reading a book and we skidded right *into* him and he reached out with one hand and WHAP—" she clapped her hands, "we stopped *dead*. Can you *believe* that?"

Stosh's face was filled with wonder. "You *saw* him *do* dat?"

Agatha nodded. "Amazing, huh?"

The Jägermonster just shook his head. "Reading a *book*. Da tings hyu gots to do ven yous a general."

"HALT!" The order came from behind them. They turned to see a Lackya hurrying up to them.

Agatha turned to look at her companion and saw that he looked... stupider. It was something about the face...

"Vot hyu vant?" he asked the footman. The newcomer drew himself up and sniffed disapprovingly at the soldier.

"There was an intrusion in one of the Baron's labs. Equipment was damaged. I am to bring in all personnel that I find in this sector."

The Jägermonster slowly scratched his jaw while glancing at Agatha. She realized that she was acting nervous and forced herself to relax. "Vos de Baron hurt?"

"No one was hurt, but valuable equipment *was* damaged, and we were ordered to find the culprits." Unseen by the footman, the Jäger's mouth twitched upwards approvingly.

He slowly turned back. "Ho vell, den itz not impawtent.

Schtuff break all de time. Goot luck." He turned to Agatha. "Letz go."

The footman darted forward, reaching for Agatha. "You will both come with me *now*!"

Agatha did not see the Jäger move, but suddenly the footman's hand was grasped within the soldier's paw. The footman hissed, exposing fangs that caused Agatha to take a step back in surprise.

"I dun gotta answer to hyu," the Jäger said lazily, "and dis gurl iz vit me, so hyu dun gotta vorry about her needer."

The footman's arm suddenly *twisted* and his hand was free. The Jäger was surprised, but covered it instantly. The footman smirked. "All personnel in this sector *includes*—"

The Jäger interrupted him. "To be 'personnel,' hyu gots to be 'person.' I is *Jägerkin*, vitch is *better*. Vere as *hyu* is jumped-up lackey boy mit delusions of authority."

The footman began to vibrate and started hissing. His eyes swiveled towards Agatha. "You will come with me—"

Agatha took a step backwards, and felt her hand deftly tucked into the crook of the Jägermonster's arm. "De lady has chosen. Now ve gots to be goink."

The footman stood and stared at them until they turned the corner. Agatha looked at the Jäger beside her. He was obviously thinking hard. "You won't get in trouble, will you?"

Stosh looked at her in surprise and grinned. "Trouble?" His tongue shot out for a quick raspberry. "The Lackya are veak." He glanced back at Agatha. A troubled look crossed his features. "But dey *is* vindictive. Vatch out for dem. Ve do not know how dangerous dey is yet."

"You don't?"

"Mm. De Baron inherited dem ven ve smacked down de Gilded Duke last year. Dey is zuper-engineered sqvirrels or zumting. Dey gots to serve *somebody,* so de Baron has dem delivering messages and annoying pipple. He keeps dem busy."

Agatha nodded. "Ah, like he took in the Jägerkin after the Heterodynes disappeared."

Stosh grabbed her and swung her about until they were face-to-face. "Iz not like dot *at ALL!*" he roared.

He would obviously have said more, but a large door next to them opened, and the massive form of General Khrizhan filled the doorway. "Vot iz dis shoutink?" he rumbled.

Stosh snapped to attention. "Dis iz Mizz Agatha Clay, who smells verra nize, but tinks der Baron iz kippink uz like dose poncy useless Lackya." He thought for a moment. "Sir," he added.

The general stared at Agatha through narrowed eyes. "She sees dot, does she?" He stared for another moment and then closed his eyes and rubbed his forehead. "Thank you, Stosh, I vill talk to her. Beck to hyu post."

Stosh grinned triumphantly at Agatha. "Hah! Hyu *tell* her, sir!" With that he wheeled about and strode off.

Agatha and the general looked at each other for a moment, then the Jägergeneral pushed the door open further. "I tink dat der are tings ve should tell each odder, Meez Agatha Clay. Pliz to com inside."

It was a different room from the one that Agatha and Gil had crashed through earlier. It was smaller and cozier, with a large ceramic stove warming the room. An enormous brass samovar hissed upon a table. Agatha glanced at it and saw, to her shock, that it was decorated with naked female demons. Trying to find someplace else to set her eyes, she discovered that all of the walls were filled with paintings and drawings of a similar nature. She settled for staring at her shoes, realizing belatedly that she did not want to examine the pattern on the rug underneath them too closely.

General Khrizhan coughed, and Agatha thought he sounded embarrassed. "Hy must apologize for the decor. General Zog does not belief dot age, or de dignity of his office, should interfere vit a rich fantasy life."

"Dose are *memories*, Alexi, un don hyu *forget* it!"

Startled, Agatha's head snapped up and saw two other creatures entering the room. The one that had spoken was shorter than General Khrizhan, but was obviously older. The fur that covered his body was snow white, and his teeth were yellow and uneven in his mouth. His clothing looked like it belonged, not to a soldier, but some sort of barbarian warlord. Despite his evident age, however, he moved with a fluidity that Agatha found hard to follow. The effect was startling.

The last creature was the oddest of all. For one thing, he was gigantic, even next to General Khrizhan, towering a full four meters tall. His mouth was easily a meter wide and filled with what appeared to be hundreds of small sharp teeth. Thick brass goggles hid his eyes, and a small brass dome, scratched and battered by the passage of the years, appeared to be screwed directly onto his skull. His large hands ended in small, delicately clawed fingers. General Khrizhan gestured towards them.

"Dis iz General Zog—" The ancient Jägergeneral nodded his head while keeping his eyes locked on Agatha.

"And dis iz General Goomblast." The tall monster executed a perfect courtier's bow that he had evidently been practicing for the last three hundred years.

His voice was a surprisingly pleasant contralto. "And dis must be de Meez Agatha Clay dot made such an impression on our compatriot. Velcome."

General Zog spoke up. His voice rasped and buzzed like his voicebox was constructed from shoe leather and horn. "Vas hyu involved in dis trouble in der Baron's lab?" he asked.

Agatha looked at the three creatures. Would they know if she lied? Agatha didn't lie, as a rule. If for no other reason than she had discovered that she wasn't very good at it. "Well... it was an accident," she confessed. All three of the generals broke into huge grins.

"Ho!" Zog slapped her on the back, almost sending Agatha into a wall. "En *exident*!" He leaned in and spoke confidentially. "Vun ting de Jägerkin understand is dat krezy exidents *heppen*, right, boyz?"

"Hoo boy, yaz"

"*Dot's* de trooth."

Agatha could well imagine. "Yes, that's all very good, but why am I here?"

General Khrizhan opened a large cabinet and pulled out a small chest that Agatha recognized with a start as one from the Clays' home in Beetleburg. Opening it up she discovered—"My clothes! My stuff!"

General Goomblast nodded. "It vas collected ven you vas taken from Beetleburg. Somehow, it vas mizplaced, und ve just discovered it. Ve thought hyu vould vant it as soon as possible."

Agatha nodded happily, but as she repacked the outfits, her movement slowed and her brow furrowed. "Yes... but you *could* have just sent them to the dormitory."

General Khrizhan shrugged as he fiddled with the controls

on the samovar. "Oh. Yaz, I suppose hyu is right. Oh vell. Vould hyu like sum tea? To make op for de inconvenience?"

Agatha realized that she was hungry again. How could that be? "Oh, I..."

"Ve effen t'row in sopper."

"But I..." Agatha's stomach growled. "Supper?"

General Goomblast offered her a silver platter piled high with warm tea cakes. Agatha could see that some were stuffed with custard and jelly, sprinkled with nuts and topped with a thick sugary glaze. Some appeared to be covered in thick chocolate, and a few were evidently stuffed with fruit. A second plate appeared, covered with warm pastries that Agatha could smell were stuffed with savory meats and baked cheeses. "Iz goot! Ve not eat bugs. I svear!"

General Zog looked at his plate disappointedly. "No bugs?" General Khrizhan shushed him with a glare.

Agatha smiled nervously and graciously plucked a small meat pastry from the tray and gingerly nibbled at it. Onions and spices she was unfamiliar with suffused her mouth and she let out a muffled, happy squeak. It was delicious. Intensely so. In three bites it was gone.

General Goomblast was obviously pleased. He poured her a cup of tea and gestured towards the platter. "Hyu like? Take anodder."

Agatha looked longingly at the platter, but the manners that Lilith had drilled into her stayed her hand. "Oh, I couldn't—" she began, but was stopped by General Zog's reaching forward, tilting the platter, and dumping half of the cakes upon Agatha's plate.

"De gorl is starffing," he said conversationally, as he put

the tray back down. Turning to Agatha he said, "In enemy territory hyu neffer know ven you is gonna eat. Don't pass up an opportunity." With that he scooped up the remaining cakes in one hand and dumped them into his mouth.

General Khrizhan took a deep breath and smiled alarmingly at Agatha. "General Zog has been a varrior longer dan any uf us. He sees efferyting in terms of... practicality." He gestured at Agatha's plate. "Dis doz not mean dot he iz wrong. Please eat up."

General Goomblast had stared at the empty platter for a second, sighed in disappointment, and from a sideboard produced an enormous cake pan. Lifting the lid allowed the spicy odor of gingerbread to begin filling the room. A crock on the table was opened, revealing its contents to be thick yellow whipped cream. The large creature showed Agatha how to stir a spoonful into her tea, which, he informed her, came from a friend of the Baron's in China.

After some steady eating, Agatha felt herself starting to relax, a fact the three Jägers noted.

"Zo, my dear Meez Clay," Goomblast began while refilling her cup, "vere iz hyu family from?"

Agatha looked at him warily. "Beetleburg?"

"Iz dot so? Mine people still liff in Mechanicsburg."

"Ah. The Heterodynes' home. Of course. I've never been there, but I always wanted to go." Despite her reservations, the very inanity of the topic was reassuring, Agatha found herself relaxing and discussing the various merits of different towns. Off to one side, the other two generals quietly sipped their tea and observed.

General Khrizhan leaned closer to the older Jäger and

muttered behind his hand. "Vot you tink?"

General Zog glanced at him and snorted. "Hy don *gotta* tink. Hy knew ven hy smelt her clothing." He considered Agatha with a scowl. "Could be a forgotten second cousin, or a by-blow..."

"A by-blow? *Dem?*"

Zog smiled at his colleagues' astonishment. "Dey *vas* hooman."

Khrizhan nodded reluctantly. "De kestle vould know," he said quietly.

Zog shook his head. "De kestle iz mad. Dyink. *Useless.*"

Khrizhan's shoulders slumped. "Den it iz op to us." He leaned into the conversation, which had come to a lull. "Tell us about you parents."

Instantly a wall of suspicion slammed down behind Agatha's eyes. "My father's a blacksmith, and my mother gives piano lessons. I'm worried about them," she admitted.

"Yez. Dey haff disappeared und ve cannot find dem. Dey obviously do not *vant* to be found, but dey *vould* vant to know dot hyu vas safe, jah?" Khrizhan shook his massive head. "Iz qvite puzzling."

"They're probably hiding," Agatha admitted. "They don't... trust the Baron."

Goomblast waved a hand dismissively. "Who does? Ve's *used* to pipple hidink. Vat's strenge iz dot ve cannot *find* dem."

Agatha absorbed this information and deliberately reached for another tea cake. There were few left. "These are *very* good," she said, and smiled at Goomblast, who frowned at her in annoyance.

General Zog, who had been pacing around the room,

168

dropped into the chair next to Agatha. He smelled like ancient leather boiled in vinegar.

"Zo," he said brusquely, "hyu vent flyink mit der young master." He leaned closer. "Vot hyu tink of him?"

Agatha flushed. "Well…" she struggled for words. As she did so, the general's nostrils flared, and a smile crossed his features. General Khrizhan's hand smacked the back of his head, sending Zog's fez flying.

"Vot kind of schtupid qvestion is *dot*?" Khrizhan roared.

"Vell it vould make tings really *simple* if—"

"I *know* vat hyu is *tinking*! Bot hyu ain't *tinking* tinking!"

"Tinking iz *overrated*!" Zog roared, and tapped his nose. "*Dis* tells me—"

Khrizhan grabbed Zog's vest and shook him violently. "Be *qviet* you *idiot*!"

Agatha scrunched down in her seat as the generals roared about her. Two delicate furry hands effortlessly scooped her up and deposited her before the door. "I tink hyu better go," General Goomblast muttered.

Agatha picked up the box with her belongings. "Did I say something wrong?"

Goomblast smiled at her in what he thought was a reassuring manner. "No, no, madam waz qvite charmink. But ve gonna haf a leedle discussion now, and dey can get kind ov loud." He opened the door and called out, "Minsc!"

A tall Jägersoldier with a particularly toothy grin appeared and snapped to attention. "Yezzir?"

Goomblast pushed Agatha forward. "Dis iz Meez Clay. See dot she's get beck safely to—"

A scream of rage from within the room was all the warning

they got as the samovar caromed off of the back of the general's head. Spinning about, Goomblast's head appeared to split in half as his mouth opened wider than Agatha would have thought possible. A scream like tearing metal filled the hallway and the Jägergeneral leapt back into the room, slamming the door behind him. Minsc grabbed Agatha's arm and dragged her down the hall. "Ve go now," he advised.

The sound of breaking furniture followed them down the hall, until there was a sudden final shattering of glass and then silence. Minsc turned to Agatha and grinned. "Zo. Vere to, dollink?"

"Um... the student dormitories?"

Minsc brightened. "Ho! Excellent!" He licked his hand with a purple tongue and slicked back his hair. "Mebbe I see my sveetie."

Agatha stopped dead. "Your—*who*?"

"De gorgeous Von Pinn."

"Your sweetheart is *Von Pinn*? *The* Von Pinn is your sweetheart." No matter how many times she said it, it still sounded wrong.

Minsc shrugged slightly. "Vell, if youz gonna get *technical* about it, not *yet*. But I am confident dot she *vill* pick me!"

"Pick you out of *what*?"

"All of der Jägermonstern iz desirous of her," he confided. "She iz zo sharp... zo *dangerous,* like a pudding bag full uf *knives*!" He growled at the thought.

Agatha swallowed. "Ah. And that's *good* is it?"

Minsc's eyes went misty and a beatific smile played across his face. He sighed. "Tvice I haff felt de touch uf her hand as it caressed my face." He pointed proudly. "See der scars? Vunce her elbow lingered as it vas buried in mine kidney. And vunce, ven her teeth seek mine throat, I gaze into her eyes und—"

"You're *crazy*!" Agatha screamed, "She was trying to *kill* you!"

Minsc stared at her and then his face slid into a sly, knowing grin. "Ho, ho, ho. Hyu iz still a leedle gurl in der vays of luff." He patted her shoulder. "Hyu vill learn."

Agatha swallowed. "I sure hope not." She looked up. To her surprise, they had already arrived at the dormitory door. "Thanks. I guess—"

"Miss Clay! Don't move!"

Agatha and Minsc whirled and saw Von Pinn racing towards them, her hands outstretched, a look of fury on her face.

Agatha squeaked in alarm and froze. Minsc grinned and stepped forward while pushing Agatha through the doorway. "Hyu moof along now, kiddo."

"But she's after me."

"Hee heh," Minsc smirked as he straightened his hat. "I guarantee dot a kees from me vill make her forgets all about *hyu*!"

Von Pinn was almost on them and Minsc stepped forward into the crazed construct's outstretched arms. "Hey beautiful, it's *me*, you *Minsc*!"

"MOVE OR DIE!"

"Whoo! Already mit der sveet tok!"

At this point the massive door closed behind Agatha and all she heard was a sound that reminded her of a fight she'd witnessed in the biological oddities lab when a soon-to-be-deceased lab assistant had neglected to lock a number of cage doors. A large object slammed into the door, shaking Agatha out of her shock. She raced into the main room and saw a plump young man sporting a yarmulke coming out of the kitchen clutching a large number of bottles. She ran up to him. "Von Pinn is *killing* one of the Jägermonsters!"

The young man raised an eyebrow. "Oh. So?"

"So we've got to *help*!"

He considered this for a second, then shook his head. "I think Von Pinn can handle them by herself."

Agatha thought she was going mad. "No," she explained through clenched teeth, "we've got to help *him*."

The light dawned. "Oh!" He then turned back to the stairway. "No, I don't think so."

Agatha raced around him and pointed at the door, where the noise had grown even more frenzied. "Can't you *hear* that?"

The young man looked at her patiently. "That's what I mean," he explained. "It's taking much too long. If she *really* wanted to kill him, it would be over very quickly. She's just warning him off." A pained squeal rose through the air and was cut off with a sharp wet sound. "Ah, Minsc. I should've guessed."

Agatha stared at him. "Oh." She leaned wearily against the wall. "This is a very strange place," she observed.

The young man considered this. "You think so? I don't get out much." He awkwardly shifted his load of bottles so that he could stick out a hand. "I'm Hezekiah Donewitz." Agatha gingerly shook his hand. "You must be Agatha," he continued. "You should come to Theo's room. Gil is here! He's telling us about Paris."

Agatha scowled. "I wouldn't—"

Hezekiah interrupted her. "Aw, come on!" He jiggled the

load of bottles. "We're going to reinvent the corkscrew. You can help! I hear you're brilliant at systems analysis."

Agatha blinked. "What?"

"Sure. Gilgamesh said you really improved his flying machine."

"He *did*?"

"Yeah. He says you're really smart." He leaned forward: "I think he really likes you."

Agatha looked closely at Hezekiah's face, but could detect no trace of irony. Her head felt funny and she desperately wanted to sit down, and the last thing she wanted to do was face Gilgamesh Wulfenbach. "I'm afraid I'm so tired that I don't think I could stay awake if he was telling you about his trip to… to America by way of the moon. I'm sure I'll hear all about it tomorrow."

Hezekiah shrugged with a clink. "Fair enough, from what I'd heard, you've had a busy day. Good night."

Agatha realized that it *had* been a busy day, and as she climbed the short stairway to her room, she felt weariness drop onto her like a blanket.

On the wall next to each of the bedroom doors, Agatha had noticed a set of thin metal pockets mounted to the wall, labeled with the occupant's name. As she approached her door, she saw that the second pocket had been labeled with her name, and that there was an envelope within. She unfolded it and found a notification that in the morning, she was to report to Minor Mechanical Workshop Number 311. There was a map showing the way from the dormitory. She studied it a moment and then realized that she was swaying slightly.

She pushed open the door and was startled to see a large white cat eating off of a tray of food that had been left on the desk of the room's other occupant. In a flurry of white, the cat leapt down and vanished under the other bed.

Agatha got down on her hands and knees and peered under the bed. Two large glowing green eyes stared back. "Hiya, cat," she said. The cat scrunched itself further back into the corner.

Agatha sat back on her knees. "How many cats do they have running around here anyway? Well, you don't want to come out? Suit yourself."

The door opened and a tall, aristocratic-looking young lady walked in. She had a long, thin face, pale skin, and an elegant mass of long auburn curls. Her outfit was a standard Wulfenbach overall, but it had been tailored to fit, and shiny brass buttons replaced the regular issue. From the state of her outfit, it was apparent that she had been engaged in heavy labor. Upon seeing Agatha, she stopped dead. In an eyeblink her tiredness had vanished and was replaced by an air of graciousness. "Ah, you are awake. You may rise."

Agatha realized that she was still on her knees and hastily scrambled to her feet.

"I am Her Highness, Zulenna Luzhakna, a princess of Hofnung-Borzoi. We are to be roommates, it appears." She extended a hand. "And you are?"

"Agatha Clay."

A faint frown flitted across Zulenna's face and the hand was smoothly withdrawn. "Clay," she mused. "Not a… noble house. Which member of your family possesses the Spark?"

"Ah, none of them. My father's a blacksmith," she offered hopefully.

"A blacksmith. How utilitarian." Zulenna sat down on her bed and surveyed Agatha. "So, why *are* you here?"

"Baron Wulfenbach captured my... my boyfriend. He's a Spark."

"A captured..." Zulenna's eyes narrowed. "Do you mean Moloch von Zinzer?"

"You've heard of him?"

"I keep tabs on all of the Sparks aboard Castle Wulfenbach. So *you* are Herr von Zinzer's bedwarmer." She jumped up, obviously greatly annoyed, and leaned into Agatha. "I have heard about you, and I trust there will be no nonsense within this room."

Agatha found that she was so tired that her outrage barely flickered. "Look," she said evenly, "there seems to be a mistaken impression that I'm some sort of—"

"How *dare* you!" Zulenna interrupted furiously. Startled, Agatha saw that she was holding the tray she'd seen the cat eating from. "This was *my* dinner. I work the late shift. The kitchen is closed! It was on *my* desk! How *dare* you touch it! And how dare you make such a mess!" Indeed, food was scattered across the desktop.

"Oh, now wait a minute!" Agatha objected hotly, "I didn't *touch* your stuff. The cat was up on the desk eating it when I came in!"

Zulenna cocked an eyebrow. "What cat?"

"I thought it was yours. It's a big white cat. It's under your bed."

Zulenna looked at Agatha for a moment, a look of uncertainty passed over her face, and she gracefully dropped to her knees and raised the coverlet to peer under the bed. When her head came back up, she was glaring furiously. "You can't even *lie* competently."

"What?" Agatha looked under the bed. No cat. Hurriedly she looked under her bed. No cat. A quick look around the small room showed that there was certainly no place a cat could hide, and she knew it hadn't left when Zulenna opened the door...

"But it *was* there!" Agatha looked under Zulenna's bed again. A small, flat underbed chest, which would have to be removed to be opened, and a ventilation grate were all that were to be seen.

"There's a ventilation grate here, maybe it—"

Zulenna's hand snapped down and whipped the coverlet out of Agatha's hand. Her voice was icy with disdain. "That vent cover is held in place with two snaps. I doubt that any cat, even one as fabulous as the one you saw, could open them. Therefore I must conclude that in addition to being a person of low moral character, you are a liar as well as a thief. I expect nothing less from the lower classes, but I'll be damned if I will sleep in the same room with you. I imagine your parents expected you to sleep in the foundry; I suggest—"

The smack to her face caught Zulenna by surprise. The force of it spun her around causing her to slam into the wall. Before she could recover, she found herself hoisted up off the floor by an Agatha who was radiating rage.

Agatha felt the fury roaring through her body like a lightning storm. A part of her realized that she had never been *allowed* to be this angry before. Whenever she got mad, a headache seemed to come along to snuff out the rage. But not this time. For the first time in her life, Agatha could vent all the fury that she was capable of feeling, and a part of her reveled in it. She screamed as years of pent-up emotions found voice.

Zulenna had been about to deliver a solid kick to Agatha's stomach, but an older part of her brain looked into Agatha's face, overrode her conscious mind, and she stopped struggling and went limp.

"One thing my parents taught me," Agatha said in a voice that set off fresh alarms, "was that nobody gets to badmouth my family. I will tell you this one last time. I didn't eat your dinner. There was a cat. I have had a very long day. And I am *not*—" this was emphasized with another slam into the wall— "von Zinzer's... like that." The embarrassment she felt over this last admission seemed to sap her strength. Zulenna felt her feet touch the ground. She eyed Agatha warily.

Agatha was fading fast now. She felt a great weariness roaring over her, and merely stood there, her hands still grasping Zulenna's clothes.

Zulenna gingerly reached up, and found that she could remove Agatha's hands without effort. She stepped sideways. Agatha didn't move.

Zulenna considered slamming Agatha face first into the wall, but at that moment, Agatha's face turned towards her, and the thought fled. She stepped back and tried to project self-assurance. She jerked her clothes straight.

"Never touch me again." She braced herself for another attack, but Agatha ignored her and simply shuffled past her to drop onto her bed. "And I want you out of my room."

Agatha looked at her, and then closed her eyes. As... exhilarating as the rage had been while she was experiencing it, now that it was gone, she felt sick, exhausted and ashamed. "Nothing would please me more," she whispered, "but tonight I'm sleeping here."

Zulenna glared at her and stepped forward, then hesitated. With a disdainful sniff, she turned, disrobed and got into her own bed. She reached out to extinguish the light and stopped. Agatha was already asleep. Zulenna began to ease out of her bed, then reached up and touched the tender spot on her face. Agatha made an odd humming noise in her sleep, then began to breathe deeply. Zulenna crept out of bed, selected one of the fencing foils that was on the rack, and carefully climbed back into bed with it placed between her and Agatha. She left the light on. It was quite a while before she slept.

In Agatha's dreams, the great celestial machine warped itself slightly. The teeth of the gears grew longer and sharper, and began to fly off and chase Von Pinn, and Zulenna, and Gilgamesh Wulfenbach, and as they ran squealing in terror, Agatha found herself enjoying the show until she realized that the largest and sharpest gear was bearing down upon herself.

She came awake with a jerk, dropping a jeweler's wrench upon a benchtop which was littered with parts. She looked around in surprise. She was in an empty machine shop. But it wasn't Adam's. Where was she? A voice behind her—

"Miss Clay? Good heavens."

Swinging about, Agatha saw the Baron's secretary Boris, and Moloch, both looking rather dumbfounded.

Years of training as Dr. Beetle's assistant kicked in and she leapt to her feet, smoothed back her hair and stood at attention. "Good morning, sir. I... I was asleep, but I am ready to begin."

This only seemed to make Boris even more uncomfortable. He glared at Moloch. "I dare say she is."

Moloch tried to control a grin. "Um... Didn't you *forget* something—er—darling?"

Agatha looked at them blankly. "What do you—" belatedly she noticed the direction of Moloch's gaze. Looking downward she saw that she was dressed in naught but her camisole and pantalets. With a shriek she barreled between the two men and dashed from the room.

Once she had vanished around the corner, Boris rounded on Moloch and shook several fingers at him reprovingly. "You are expected to get *work* done, Herr von Zinzer. Perhaps a *different* assistant..."

"No!" The last thing Moloch wanted was someone who could tell he knew nothing. "Um... she's... it's just—the science stuff, it... um... it really gets her... excited."

Boris rolled his eyes. "Ah. One of *those*." He shrugged. "Well, as long as you're discreet and it does not interfere with your work. But—" he warned. "Tell Miss Clay not to flaunt herself in front of the Baron or his son. They have no tolerance for such things." Satisfied that he had cleared up the matter, he steered Moloch deeper into the lab. "Now the one example we saw of your work was rather crude, but the Baron found aspects of the design quite remarkable. *He* believes that with access to *proper* materials, your work might be well worth his full attention."

Moloch smiled weakly. "Great."

Boris nodded. "If this is so, you will subsequently report to the Baron directly. For now, however, he is interested in seeing what you can produce independently."

"I'll bet."

There followed a quick tour of the lab, ending with Boris indicating a small electric bell. "And finally, whatever you need, be it supplies, assistants or food, simply ring this and it will be provided. We look forward to seeing what you will do." As he left, he passed a fully dressed Agatha coming the other way. Tactfully, neither said anything.

Agatha entered the lab to find a despondent Moloch rummaging about in the chemical locker. With a grunt of satisfaction, he pulled out a large carboy of clear liquid and filled a beaker. He swigged fully a third of it down before he sat on the nearest stool.

Agatha examined the label. "That's supposed to be used for cleaning machine tools," she pointed out.

"So I'll die clean." Moloch saluted her with his glass and polished off another third. "Now what the heck were you doing? Do you *always* work in your underclothes?"

"No!" Agatha began to pace back and forth in agitation. "I don't *know*! I *never* used to walk in my sleep!"

"Well you sure made a mess of the workbench." The two of them examined the bench, which did show all the signs of heavy use. "But I don't see what you were working *on*." It was true. Tools and parts littered the area, but there was no device anywhere in sight.

Agatha slumped against the bench. "Probably nothing," she admitted. She straightened up and turned away. "Well, at least I don't have another *failure* staring at me."

From an upper shelf, a small device paused in its labors. A small lens focused on her, ascertained that she did not require its assistance, and resumed its task.

Moloch finished off his drink just as the beaker began to dissolve. He tossed it into the trash. "So now what?"

Agatha grinned. "Take a look at this!" She turned away and reached into her shirt and hauled out the airship manual and handed it to him.

Moloch looked surprised. "Where'd you get this?"

Agatha shrugged. "Just found it."

Moloch paged through it, then handed it back. "This has possibilities. There's a lot of traffic, there's supply balloons coming and going all day long. Unfortunately, stuff like this will be guarded all the time. But look over here—" He took Agatha's arm and brought her over to a rack of packages mounted on the wall near the main exit to the lab. A small sign explained how to prepare the devices for use. "This might be easier. These are personal balloon gliders for if they have to abandon the dirigible. You can use these to just glide down to earth, and they're located throughout the Castle. The problem with these, is that people would see you jumping off the Castle. At night the damn things glow."

Agatha nodded. "Hmm. Modifying one of them might be our best bet. It glows? We could paint it with tar or something."

Moloch looked surprised. "That's a good idea."

"I want to get out of here too." She thought for a minute. "I'll bet they notice if we start messing about with one of these things, in fact, I wouldn't be surprised—" She stepped over to the rack and examined it closely. She gave a grunt of satisfaction and motioned Moloch over. "Look. See this? There's a wire running through these rings. Probably some sort of tripwire, I'll bet. When one of these things is pulled off the rack, it sounds an alarm somewhere. Makes sense, really, even if it's a genuine emergency." She studied the wire closely. "This is going to be tricky." She looked at Moloch. "We can't afford to do it wrong the first time."

Moloch sat down heavily. "I wouldn't even have looked for something like that," he admitted. He brightened up. "On the other hand, I got to be pretty good at disarming booby traps."

"How good?"

"I'm still here, ain't I?"

"Fair enough. I think I might be able to build some stuff that could help."

Moloch looked at her askance. "You said you couldn't build anything."

Agatha paused. "Yes, but I... I think I know what I did wrong. I have some ideas..." She shook herself. "But whatever we do, it's going to take some time, and we've got to make it look like you're doing *something*." She looked around. "An inventory."

Moloch looked up. "That's always a good one. Place like this, we could kill a day or two at least before they expect us to produce anything."

"It'll work better if you can fake it a bit." She snatched up a tool from the nearest bench. "Now this, is a wrench."

Moloch glared at her. "I *know* it's a wrench."

"Ah, but what *kind* of wrench?

"A 3/17 Occipital Left-Leaning Heterodyne wrench."

Agatha whipped the wrench up to her face and stared at it. It was. She glared at Moloch. "How did you know *that*?" she demanded.

Moloch smiled bitterly at her from his chair. "*These* days, machines are more important than soldiers. If you know how to *fix* machines, it makes you more valuable." He stared off into the distance. "My brothers and I, there were nine of us, we crewed this walking gunboat for the Duke D'Omas. Mad as a bag of clams, of course, but it was a good berth. Snappy uniforms, fresh food, and plenty of it, and he paid in gold." Moloch sighed. "Then it all turned to dung. Wulfenbach blew up the Duke's mountain and we had to start raiding the countryside to keep the gunship repaired."

"But why would you do that?"

"Ah, well, you see, the peasants didn't like the Duke. Which meant they didn't like *us*. After the Baron took him down, the gun was the only thing keeping us alive. We figured our best bet was to get out of there, so we headed for Paris. We had to go through Wulfenbach land, sure, but if you keep to the Wastelands and the dead towns, you can travel for days without seeing a soul, which was the plan. But just our luck, we ran into one of the Baron's patrols, led by this... this *crazy* woman! We'd have *surrendered* if she'd *asked*." Moloch's eyes showed that he was far away. "I think Bruno and the kid made it, but I don't know about anyone else. Nobody but Omar and me. And now it's just me."

Agatha placed her hand on his shoulder. "That's... that's really rough. I didn't know."

Moloch jerked his shoulder away. "Of *course* you didn't know. You're just a spoiled townie. The big towns are important. They get cleaned up, repaired, disinfected. Not like the rest of the world." He stalked over to the carboy of cleaning solution and hunted about for another beaker.

Agatha stood behind him. "Oh, *that* will help."

Moloch furiously turned upon her. "Get out!"

"But... but the inventory—"

"Screw it. I want to be alone." He pulled out a beaker and discarded it for being too small. "I'm expected to act like a brooding unstable psychopath? Great. Here's a chance for me to rack up some extra credit."

Agatha turned to go, took two steps and then wheeled about. "Now you're just being stupid."

Moloch didn't even look up from his pouring. She continued: "A brooding, unstable psychopath? Fine. But you've got to convince the Baron that you're a brooding unstable psychopath who's having way too much fun to ever *want* to leave. They've got to see you eager to get to work in this beautiful lab they've given you!"

Moloch looked at her and frowned. He harrumphed. "That *does* make sense," he admitted. With a sigh, he poured his drink back into the carboy and tossed the beaker into the trash. "Okay. Inventory it is, then."

They turned and looked at the room. It was a large space, twenty meters square. The main central area was clear, surrounded by benches and work tables. Overhead were lights and a set of winches on motorized tracks. Lining the walls were cabinets and bins filled with various parts, chemicals, tools. The shelves were easily four meters tall. They looked around, but failed to find a ladder.

"Guess we use this a little sooner than I'd thought," said Moloch as he pressed the bell button.

Less then a minute later, the door opened and an immense man entered. He was over two meters tall and everything about him was proportioned to fit. He wore a gray overall covered in pockets. His head was the thing you looked at, however. His face was open and friendly, but above it was a bald pate that showed the obvious signs of multiple, extensive surgery.

"Hello!" he said in a booming, cheerful voice. "I..." He suddenly appeared to be having trouble remembering something. "I am Dr. Dimitri."

Moloch and Agatha were surprised. "Doctor?" Moloch exclaimed.

Dimitri nodded enthusiastically. "Yes! I am a doctor! Yes I am!"

Moloch smiled apologetically. "I'm sorry we disturbed you, Herr Doctor, I thought we were ringing for an assistant."

Dimitri beamed and slapped his chest. "Yes! Yes! I am assistant! Yes!"

Moloch and Agatha glanced at each other. Right.

Moloch spoke slowly. "We need a ladder."

Dimitri brightened. "I will get a ladder! Yes! I could *make* you a ladder! A *giant* ladder that will go up to the sky!"

Moloch blinked. "No thanks. Just a regular ladder."

"Yes! Yes! A ladder that will carry you up and down by itself! I could make that! I could! Up and down and up and down and up and—"

"No, just a regular ladder."

"Ah! Yes! Yes! I understand! You want it to *look* like a regular ladder, and when you are at the tippy top, the *blades* come out and—"

"Enough!" Moloch shouted. Dimitri looked hurt. Moloch turned to Agatha. "Miss Clay, you'd better go with him." He thought for a moment. "Get us something without blades."

"I'll try." At this Dimitri began to look worried. Agatha looked at him. He reminded her of some of the faculty back at the University. She gently took him by the arm and pulled him out into the corridor. "Okay, Herr Doctor, where do we keep the ladders?"

"But *I* go! Yes, me!"

"Well I'll just go *with* you." Dimitri looked very worried now, but he reluctantly began to move down the hall. "I don't understand what the problem is," said Agatha. "All we want is a ladder."

Dimitri looked slightly reassured. "Yes, ladder. We just go to get ladder."

They quickly came to a large door labeled "LABORATORY SUPPLIES." Dimitri spun the locking wheel and the door eased open, revealing a large dimly-lit store-room, neatly crammed with crates and barrels, cans, jars and tools. Agatha quickly spotted a rack of ladders and moved toward it.

"This looks like what we need—" She paused. Hidden behind the ladders, she saw a small, neat cot.

She turned back to Dimitri. "Oh, do you sleep here?" She stopped because the giant's face was now set in a rictus of fear. She looked back at the bed. There was nothing there, except...

A closer examination revealed a number of small objects. Agatha picked one up... "Why they're *bears*!" she exclaimed in delight. "Made from rags! They're adorable! Did you make these?" So saying she turned back to Dimitri, only to find him huddled upon the floor at her feet, his tear-stained face raised in supplication.

"Please," he whispered, "please don't give them to the Baron."

Agatha looked at the rag doll in her hand. "What, these?"

Dimitri nodded frantically. "Yes, *please*..."

Agatha gently placed the bear into Dimitri's trembling hands. "Why would I give them to the Baron? They're yours."

The large man clasped the toy to his chest. "Yes! Mine! *I* made them! *Me!*"

"But... if the Baron really *wanted* them, he'd just *take* them... wouldn't he?"

At this, Dimitri's face underwent a startling change. A look of pure determination crept into it, although it obviously took a great deal of effort. "He doesn't *know*!" His voice, too, was different. It was a voice that was used to wielding power, but it was obvious that it was power long gone. He jerkily turned towards Agatha. The look he gave her was of someone who was unaccustomed to asking for help, but who had no choice, and had known it for a long, long time. "It's my last secret. He's taken all the others, but not them! I've kept them *safe*!"

Awkwardly, Agatha patted his massive shoulder. "Well... *I* won't tell anyone."

Sudden hope flared within the kneeling man's eyes. "You... help keep my bears... *secret*? Keep them safe from the Baron?"

Agatha nodded. "Of course. I won't even tell that man I'm working with, von Zinzer."

Softly, silently, the large man began to cry. "Thank you! *Thank* you!" he blubbered. "I've been so *worried* about them."

An embarrassed Agatha looked about and grabbed a large rag, which she handed to Dimitri, who gratefully used it to scrub away at his face. "They'll be okay, I promise. Now let's get that ladder."

Once again beaming widely, Dimitri climbed to his feet. He wheeled about and addressed the row of bears lined up on the shelf. "Did you hear? She has promised to help take care of you. You will be safe!"

The watcher nodded. He'd heard.

* * *

Several hours later, after von Zinzer had dismissed her for the day, Agatha found herself swept up by Sleipnir and several other girls and dragged off to their fencing practice. Agatha had never held a sword, but she had always admired the way actors had flailed about with them onstage. Much to her surprise, the people she watched didn't seem to do any flailing at all. Indeed, the object appeared to be to hit your opponent while moving as little as possible. The analytical part of her mind found this intriguing, though she did miss the singing.

The girls warmed up by fencing with each other in various combinations, but after a while, Sleipnir went off and returned pushing a large cart which was topped by a vaguely humanoid figure possessed of a single arm, holding a fencing foil. Once activated, it turned out to be a fencing clank, and the girls took turns battling it while the others rested.

It took little encouragement to get Agatha to suit up in a padded outfit, and the girls looked on with interest while Sleipnir began to teach her the basics. A stream of humorous comments at her expense were made, but to Agatha's surprise, instead of feeling hurt, she found herself laughing along with them.

Relinquishing the sword, she sat and tried to ignore how the other girls now attacked each other while singing. It had seemed like an interesting idea at the time.

One of the girls, Sun Ming, handed her a cup of water, and asked her about her first day at the lab. Eventually, the conversation got around to Dr. Dimitri, though Agatha omitted any mention of his stuffed bears. "We call him Dr. Dim." Sun

Ming admitted. "I believe him to be some sort of construct that didn't work out."

"He's been here for years," Sleipnir chimed in. "He seems to be harmless."

The door to the changing rooms swung open and Zulenna strode towards them. She carried a gold foil over her shoulder. She nodded to several of the other girls, but a frown creased her face at the sight of Agatha. "Miss Clay. I didn't know you fenced."

Agatha experienced another wave of embarrassment at her actions last night. She resolved to try and be civil. "I don't, but Sleipnir said I should try it."

Sleipnir nodded. "Agatha has pretty good reflexes. I think that with some training…"

Zulenna interrupted, waving dismissively. "Really, Sleipnir. Taking a plow horse to the races?" Whereas Agatha had felt distress at last night's incident, Zulenna had been replaying it over and over again and getting more and more annoyed. She wanted a rematch. With a sword. And witnesses. Sleipnir blinked. Zulenna continued, "I would like to see these fabulous reflexes." She turned to Agatha. "If you're not afraid to face me when I'm armed."

Sleipnir looked back and forth between Agatha and Zulenna and tried to avert certain calamity. "No, I don't think that would be a good idea. Why don't we—"

Agatha interrupted. "Sleipnir, would fencing give me a chance to hit her with this sword in a civilized manner?"

"Well…" Sleipnir hesitated, "*theoretically*, but—"

"Let's do it."

Sleipnir closed her mouth and shrugged. Some things just had to be worked out.

Zulenna chuckled as Agatha's outfit was checked by Sleipnir. "Oh, this will be amusing."

Sleipnir muttered to Agatha as she finished up. "She's *very* good."

"Indeed I am," Zulenna confirmed brightly. "So just try to hit me."

Agatha and Zulenna moved into position. Tentatively Agatha reached forward with her sword, and, languidly, Zulenna flicked it aside.

Agatha frowned and whipped her sword around from the other direction, and again, Zulenna deflected it with ease. She had watched the other girls and the fencing clank, but even her untrained eye could tell that Zulenna was superior to them all. Fascinated, Agatha executed a series of attacks from any direction she could think of. The smirking girl easily batted them all away while moving nothing but her arm.

Agatha stepped back and wiped a trickle of perspiration from her brow. This was developing into a very interesting problem, and Agatha's anger at Zulenna began to fade as she considered it.

This detachment disappeared when Zulenna reached out with her sword and smacked the side of Agatha's head. Agatha whipped her foil upwards, but hit nothing. There followed a series of strikes by Zulenna, which Agatha found herself helpless to prevent. The few times she actually managed to hit Zulenna's sword, it simply slid off and connected with Agatha anyway. Her anger building, she decided to ignore the attacks and concentrate on striking back. There followed a series of attacks and feints delivered at blinding speed, which had absolutely no effect. Zulenna raised an eyebrow, and with an enormous grin, continued to strike Agatha at will while she deftly parried Agatha's furious attacks.

"As you can see, Miss Clay," she said with a smirk, "fencing is the sport of the highborn. There is far more to it than hacking and slashing." This was punctuated with a sharp poke to Agatha's stomach. "And while I'm sure you'd do very well with a sledge hammer, which is probably all you need for tavern brawling, fencing is all about finesse, the art of exploiting your opponents' *weaknesses*." A move too fast to see and Zulenna's sword cracked against Agatha's hand, causing her to drop her sword. Zulenna smiled and turned away. "This *was* entertaining." She glanced back over her shoulder. "Those *are* good reflexes, by the way."

A panting Agatha reached down and picked up her sword. Blowing a lock of hair from her face, she turned to a watching Sleipnir. "Hey…" she said between breaths, "I just figured out the difference between Dr. Dim and *royalty*. Dr. *Dim* is still doing something *useful*."

Zulenna froze, and then spun about, sword upraised to strike. "How *dare* you—*Oof!*"

This last sound was caused by Zulenna slamming herself directly onto the point of Agatha's foil, which had been aimed at her solar plexus. Zulenna dropped to her knees and tried to gasp in a lungful of air. Agatha leaned over her. "*Your* reflexes, on the other hand, could get you into trouble, your highness."

Zulenna shot Agatha a look of pure hate as two of the other girls helped Zulenna to her feet. When she could stand, she shook them off, wheeled about and stalked off. Sleipnir looked after her and shook her head. "You fight nasty."

Agatha slid the foil back into the rack. She didn't feel good about her win. "Back in Beetleburg, we didn't care much about royalty as such, what was important was if you had the Spark or not."

Sleipnir nodded. "Yes, we've been seeing that trend spreading out from the larger towns for some time. It's been giving Zulenna's family some real problems, apparently."

"Aren't most of you from noble families?"

Ming grinned. "Some of us, but the important thing here is your position vis-à-vis those who possess the Spark. Baron Wulfenbach needs to control those who can disrupt things, and the few royal families that still rule are desperately eager for things to remain calm. Zulenna's family is a case in point. They rule a small nation in the Germanies. Useful because it controls a pass that at least three major trade routes use. Their defenses were built by the Heterodynes, and thus they'd stood off a number of attacks by madboys until they were annexed by the Baron."

Agatha frowned. "I would think that would make her a little more willing to get along, not less."

Sleipnir sighed. "Yes, you would, wouldn't you? But Zulenna is determined to keep her position."

"What position?"

The other girls looked embarrassed. A dark-haired girl named Yvette explained. "Most of us came here as children, non? So there was established a pecking order."

"Sleipnir explained a bit about that," Agatha said.

A quiet blonde named Gunnlöd spoke up. "When she first got here, Zulenna ranked pretty high, if only because she was used to bossing people around. But as we all got older, things changed. Zulenna's family is just royalty. She's not here as a hostage, but because they're genuinely loyal to the Baron."

Sleipnir nodded. "Her being royalty is all that Zulenna has, so she tries to make the most of it." She looked Agatha in the eye. "Be careful. She'll not forgive you for this."

Agatha frowned. "Oh, come on. Surely, over time some of you have made similar comments, or worse. You grew up together."

"True enough," Sleipnir admitted, "but there is this pecking order thing…"

"Meaning?"

Ming gently patted her shoulder. "Welcome to the bottom of the heap."

The next few days were quiet ones.

Von Pinn gave Agatha a wide berth.

Agatha returned to her room one evening to discover that Zulenna had moved out.

The biggest change was in Agatha's sensations. Every day brought new smells, tastes and nuances of sounds that occasionally threatened to overwhelm her. Foods that she had grown up with revealed startling new flavors. For a few days, Agatha felt like she was starving. At meal times she ate until she felt ready to burst, but within the space of two hours, she would be prowling the kitchens looking for more. She worried about her clothes, but over the course of several days, they seemed to get looser, despite everything she was eating. Sleipnir actually got annoyed over this, until she confirmed Agatha's claims with a tape measure.

A noisy room became a rich aural tapestry of underlying rhythms. The most distracting was her sense of touch. She was aware of the textures of the clothing she wore, the surfaces of the tools in the lab. A prolonged shower left her gasping on her knees.

It was a difficult few days. Sleipnir was concerned. Agatha saw a medic, who examined her and found nothing wrong, and suggested that she was simply over-stimulated by being in a new, exciting situation. Agatha certainly had to admit that was a plausible possibility.

And, most glorious of all, Agatha's headaches, the Damoclean sword that had always checked her emotions, had stopped.

She noticed it the second day. By the third, she had actually tried to induce one and failed. That night, Sleipnir had found her in her room weeping. She'd never been able to have a good, solid cry, and by the time she was done, she felt wrung out like a rag and slept for twelve hours. After that, while her sensations and emotions remained much sharper than before, everything began to become much more manageable. Thankfully, Agatha found her appetite beginning to diminish.

The crisis had passed.

Moloch proved to be adept at finding his way around a lab. The inventory was completed. Agatha tried to create something that would interest the Baron, but these attempts always ended in failure. The biggest problem was caused by Agatha herself, who continued to sleepwalk each night, ending up in the lab, sprawled over one of the workbenches.

On this particular morning, she was awakened by Moloch tossing his coat on top of her. "I wish you'd build something we could *use* instead of just messing up the place."

Startled, Agatha thrashed around a bit, scattering tools and machine parts to the floor as she pulled the coat on. She glanced at a clock. "You're late. Did you oversleep?"

Moloch shook his head. "I wish. I got summoned before the Baron. He's getting *impatient*. He wants to *see* something."

"But what about those plans we've been working on the last couple of days?"

"He took one look at them and told me to stop cribbing D'Omas' designs. It's like I *told* you, every madboy has a *style* like... like a painter—and the Baron can recognize them."

Agatha drummed her fingers on the bench. "Well... I do have some ideas of my own..."

Moloch waved his hand in dismissal. "Those tiddly little clockwork things that don't work? Forget it. I'm supposed to be a Spark, not an idiot toymaker. I hand him plans for something like that and I'll be shipped off to Castle Heterodyne within the hour. We need something *Big*. Impressive."

"Well... Maybe stylistic similarities run in families. We could say that you're D'Omas' natural son."

Moloch grinned ruefully. "Not a bad idea, but D'Omas' taste in women was... well... let's just say it was lucky for him he could build his own. A lot of people knew it too. There were reasons why the public didn't like him. No, there'll be no D'Omas heirs showing up, except preserved in glass jars."

"Yech. Any ideas on escaping?"

"Only if I want to throw myself out a window, which I'm not ruling out, by the way. But for the moment, the plan is to get out alive."

Moloch paced back and forth several times and then whirled to face Agatha again. "You were *there* when that clank in

Beetleburg was built. That's what we need. You must remember *something*!"

Agatha shrugged apologetically. This was an old subject. "No. I woke up after it was gone. I don't know *anything*. I could do some research—"

Moloch slammed his fist down onto the bench hard enough to send several tools flying. "Stuff that!" he screamed. "You didn't see the Baron's face this morning! I need something *now*!" He loomed menacingly over Agatha. "I don't think you're really trying."

Apprehensive, Agatha tried to back up, and found herself bumping into another bench. "You said yourself that I'm no Spark! What do you expect me to—"

Moloch gripped her shoulders. "*Think*, you stupid cow! *You* have as much to lose as I do!"

Agatha shook herself free and glared at Moloch. "Wrong! *My* parents are long gone and in hiding. Even the Jägermonsters can't find them. You no longer have a hold on me, so if you want my co-operation, I suggest you change your attitude, or... or..."

A change had come over Moloch's face. His eyes looked dead. He reached out and, grabbing the lapels of the coat Agatha was wearing, hauled her forward. "Or what? You'll kill me too? Wrong. You're gonna help me out one more time. A lab accident, I think. That should buy me some more time..."

Horrified, Agatha watched as he raised his fist, and suddenly Moloch's eyes widened and he screamed and dropped her. A quick glance down revealed the white cat biting and clawing at the inside of one of Moloch's legs. As he danced away, trying to dislodge it, Agatha regained her balance, reached behind her and felt her fingers close around the handle of a large mallet.

* * *

Gilgamesh Wulfenbach strolled down the corridor, his brow furrowed in thought. Eventually he nodded. "Oh very well, I'll concede the point, it does appear alarming, but you shouldn't be afraid of it, I'm rather sure it's just a goldfish."

Beside him Zoing frantically waved his claws and discoursed at length in high-pitched squeals.

CRASH! A lab door slammed open beside them and the inert form of Moloch von Zinzer was booted out into the corridor. A second later his labcoat was flung over him. Gil and Zoing turned to see a furious Agatha standing in the doorway, clutching a broken mallet. "You pathetic *thug*! Don't you *dare* threaten me again! Come near me and I'll put *you* in a glass jar!" It was now that she noticed Gil and his companion for the first time.

"Lover's spat?" Gil inquired.

"I *quit*!" Agatha snarled. "I don't care if you put his brain into a *jellyfish*!"

Gil frowned. "But you made such a cute couple—" Without visible effort he dodged the mallet handle that sailed past his head.

"You know perfectly well he is not my lover! Now send me *home*! I have to find my parents!"

Gil looked serious. "Yes, your parents. I can certainly understand your concern. We still haven't been able to find them. The Jägermonsters haven't been able to find them. None of your neighbors has seen them. According to the University records you don't have any other family in Beetleburg. Do you have any other family *anywhere*?"

"I have an uncle, but he… he disappeared over ten years ago."

"Not much help then. Did they have any enemies?"

"Enemies?" Agatha looked shocked. "No!" Then certain things she had seen and heard over the years assumed a possible new significance. "At least, I don't know of any. Why?"

Gil sighed. "It is not uncommon, when my father takes over new territory, that during the confusion, some people take the opportunity to… settle old grudges."

"That's… that's terrible."

"Foolish, certainly. My father prides himself on maintaining law and order within the Empire, it's kind of the whole point really, and we come down very hard on things like this. Up until now, we've been assuming that your parents were hiding from us, but now we also have to consider the possibility that something has happened to them."

"Why? What's changed?"

"One of the things I did was place public notices throughout Beetleburg advising the Clays that we had you in our possession and providing an address where they could anonymously send you a message to at least let you know that they were safe. So far there's been nothing."

"I… I have to go back! I—"

Gil interrupted. "And do *what*? My worry now is that if someone is responsible for your parents' disappearance, they might be after you as well. Until we find your parents, I'm afraid my father will insist on you being kept here under protective custody."

"That's outrageous! He can't—" Agatha suddenly stopped as she realized who she was talking about.

Gil nodded grimly. "He most certainly *can*. Now I can

understand you not wanting to work with Herr von Zinzer—"
Gil nudged the prone mechanic with the toe of his boot—"But
I'm afraid everyone aboard the Castle is expected to justify their
weight—" Agatha opened her mouth—"Would you consider
working with me?"

Agatha's mouth hung open for a second, then closed with a
snap. Her eyes narrowed. "...Why?" she finally asked.

Gil ticked off points on his fingers. "I found your daily
reports to be concise and well-written, you very efficiently
re-organized the parts warehouse, and, most important, your
suggestions regarding my flyer's engine increased its efficiency
by seventeen percent."

Agatha looked pleased. "Seventeen percent? Really?"

Gil nodded. "Really. And I believe that by working together,
we could do even better. Interested?"

"Yes! Yes I am!"

Gil smiled. "Good." He casually reached down and with
one hand hauled Moloch up by the collar. "I shall deal with
Herr von Zinzer here. Be at my lab this afternoon."

Agatha drew herself up and performed the traditional bow.
"Yes, Herr..." she paused.

"Doctor," Gil supplied.

"Herr Doctor Wulfenbach."

Gil coughed discreetly. "Ah, there *is* one thing, Miss Clay...
If you're going to be working with *me,* I'd appreciate it if you
wore more clothes."

For the first time Agatha became aware of her appearance
and with a strangled "Eep!" vanished inside the lab.

Gil puffed out his breath and grinned. A slight movement at
the end of his arm caused him to set his face in sterner lines,

and he briskly slapped Moloch's face several times until the man began to thrash feebly. "All right you, let's go."

Moloch's eyes opened, rotated in different directions, focused upon Gil and then snapped open in terror. His feet began to move, but as they weren't touching the ground, nothing happened. When he became aware of this, he seemed to give up, and with a sigh, went limp. Gil cocked an eyebrow. "You're not a very good soldier, are you?"

Moloch shrugged. "That's why I became a mechanic, sir."

Gil nodded. "Now I believe this little charade has played itself out, hm? *You* are not a Spark."

Again Moloch spasmed within Gil's grasp. "No! Sir! I... I can *explain*!"

"Sh—sh—shhh! *Relax*." With an alarming smile, Gil gently lowered Moloch to the floor, and reached around to drape a friendly arm over Moloch's shoulders. Another smile and Gil had gently propelled him down the hallway. "I want to *help* you." Zoing gathered up Moloch's coat and scuttled along behind.

Inside the lab, Agatha leaned against the door, her head swimming. She looked over and saw the large white cat, which had bitten Moloch, sitting on the nearest bench glowering at her. "He listened to my suggestions! He actually tried out my ideas—and they *worked*! Nobody has *ever* listened to me!"

She hugged herself and did a quick jig over to the bench. The cat continued to stare. "And he asked me to *work* with him! Do you understand what that *means*, you beautiful leg-biting cat? Everybody knows that the labs on Castle Wulfenbach do the real, cutting-edge science! The stuff the universities only *dream* about doing! And I'll be working with the Baron's son! Doing *real* science, in a *real* lab, with someone who actually *listens* to me!" Overcome with emotion she scooped the surprised animal up and swung him around. "What do you think of *that*?"

The cat frowned and leaned into her and pointed at her with an oddly shaped paw. "*I* think," he said clearly, "that you'd better be very, very careful."

SEVEN

"With an anxiety that almost amounted to agony, I collected the instruments of life around me, that I might infuse a spark of being into the lifeless thing that lay at my feet. But wait, I thought, why not give it the ability to spit acid? Or a few extra claws? Or, yes! A total disregard for the sanctity of human life! That will show them!"

—A TYPICAL LAST ENTRY FROM
THE JOURNAL OF AN EMERGENT SPARK

Agatha stared at the cat. "Oh," she said carefully, "I'm dreaming again. How disappointing."

The cat rolled its eyes. "You work with mad scientists and you're surprised at a talking *cat*? *I'm* the one who's disappointed."

Agatha gently placed the cat back onto the lab bench. Instead of dropping to all fours, it remained on its hind legs, which

Agatha now saw didn't look like normal cat legs at all.

She took a deep breath. "Okay, I'm sorry. You really talk. You just startled me."

The cat nodded briskly. "Right. Now that we've got that settled, I'm here to help you."

Agatha nodded back. "Help me. Okay." She paused. "Do I need to get you some boots?"

The cat glowered at her and his tail lashed back and forth in annoyance. "I don't do the boot thing, so knock it off. I'm serious. We can't talk now." His ears flicked towards the door. "Someone will be here soon."

Agatha opened her mouth—the cat raised his paw peremptorily.

"Tonight. Your room. Bring something to eat." He leaned forward. Agatha found herself doing the same. "And be careful around young Wulfenbach. He's up to something. He knows that you're a Spark and—"

"*WHAT?*" The cat looked surprised at Agatha's outburst. "I am not a Spark," she said.

The cat frowned. "What? Of *course* you are!"

Years of worrying about the state of her mental health found voice and Agatha slammed her hand down on the bench, hissing: "Don't you make fun of me, cat. I—"

The cat swiftly but gently smacked her nose with his paw. Agatha's mouth snapped shut in surprise. "Shhh," the cat said, and gestured her closer. Gingerly Agatha leaned in and the cat put its muzzle up to her ear. "You talk in your sleep," he whispered. Agatha reared back.

Suddenly there was a *clack* and the door to the corridor swung open. With a fluid motion, the cat flowed off the bench and under a stack of gears, leaving Agatha alone. She whirled to face the door and saw Ardsley Wooster, his head discreetly averted, holding forth his large coat. "Good morning, Miss Clay. Master Gilgamesh informed me that you would require a cover-up as well as an escort back to your quarters. This afternoon I am to show you the way to the location of your new duties."

Klaus Wulfenbach was in a genial mood. He strode down the center of the corridor, marginally aware of the crowd that carefully broke before him and stood aside as he passed. Coming up to a large, reinforced door, he nodded to the Jägermonsters that were lounging before it. The nearest picked up a small book and leafed through it at random, then looked up. "Vat is de sqvare root uf 78,675?"

Klaus nodded in approval, thought for a moment, and then replied: "345."

The Jäger carefully checked the book before him and then grinned. "Dot is correctly incorrect. In hyu go." The other Jäger moved and spun the locking wheel on the door until it opened with a *chunk*.

Klaus stepped inside and waited until the door was shut behind him. He unlocked another door and then entered a small laboratory lit only with red lights. Humming a tune, he removed his greatcoat and began donning protective equipment. A small sound caused him to look over his shoulder and smile genially. "Ah, good afternoon."

In the center of the room, strapped down to a massive examination table, lay Othar Tryggvassen. His muscles strained against the bonds holding him. When this proved to be useless, his head thumped back against the neckrest and he settled for glaring at the Baron.

Klaus scanned a report in his hands. "Didn't sleep well? Quite understandable. Today is going to be a *very* exciting day."

"You'll excuse me if I don't share your enthusiasm, you twisted fiend!"

Klaus shrugged genially. "Quite all right. I'm used to it." Silence descended, broken only by Klaus quietly humming a waltz as he began to check a row of surgical instruments.

"No matter how you torture me," Othar declared, "I won't talk."

"If only that were true," Klaus muttered.

Othar stared at his back for several minutes. "So. What is it you want to know?"

Klaus turned, holding a small bone saw. "Why you're a Spark. What it is that makes you *different* from other people."

Othar chewed on his lower lip. "But I... I don't actually know that."

Klaus smiled and patted him on the shoulder. "Of *course* you don't. Neither do I. But I intend to find out."

Despite himself, Othar looked interested. "How?"

Klaus began holding up a series of drill bits against Othar's skull. Othar couldn't help but notice that they were getting progressively larger. "I will destroy selected parts of your brain," Klaus explained, "until you no longer *are* a Spark."

"You ah—" Othar tried to maintain an even tone to his voice. "You can *do* that?"

Klaus nodded. "Oh yes. Eventually."

Othar considered this for a moment. "And afterwards?"

Klaus sighed. "Ah. That whole 'quality of life' question." He ran a hand through his mop of hair. "I'm working very *hard* on that." He smiled ruefully. "And I'm getting *much* better."

Othar strained against his bonds. "But my *work*!" he shouted. "My *mission*!"

Klaus activated a device attached to a swing arm that descended from the ceiling. With a whine, a number of blades began spinning. "Yes, a bonus, that."

"You villain!"

"Yes, yes." Klaus muttered as he began to position the device above Othar's head. "Normally, there would be a lot more tests. You'd have a long, productive career working for me while I studied your habits and patterns."

"But?"

"But I'm afraid that *you* are far too dangerous." The device's whine took on a higher pitch. "Now look up…"

With a *clack*, the lighting changed from red to white. With a sigh, Klaus moved the device back up and turned it off. He turned towards the door with a frown. "Yes, Boris?"

The Baron's secretary nodded apologetically. "I'm sorry to disturb you, Herr Baron, but you *did* tell me to tell you the *moment* Herr von Zinzer said he had something."

"Indeed I did." He looked down at the smaller man who had been cowering behind Boris, his eyes taking in the scene before him. When he realized that the Baron was staring at him, he jerkily brought forth a sheet of paper and extended it before him.

"It's… um… it's all here!" The Baron made no move to take the paper, but continued to look at Moloch. The shaking of his hand increased so much that the paper itself rattled. "I… I know what I want to do, but I don't know where to get some

206

of these materials." He extended the paper upwards. "It's all here," he repeated.

The Baron plucked the paper from Moloch's hand and studied it. A frown crossed his features and he studied it again. After several seconds he pursed his lips and his massive eyebrows rose and all but disappeared beneath his hair. "Interesting," he said, like a man bestowing a great compliment. "Very interesting *indeed*. Yes, some of this will be *quite* tricky." He looked down at Moloch with new eyes. "This will take some time to assemble, but I look forward to the results."

Moloch blinked. "Really?"

Klaus nodded. "Yes. Boris? See that these items are secured, and make sure that I am informed when Herr von Zinzer is ready for the initial test run. I wish to attend."

Boris looked surprised. "Yes, Herr Baron."

Klaus handed the paper back to Moloch. "I must say that I was beginning to have my doubts about you, but this... this justifies my original estimates and *then* some. What was holding you back?"

Moloch started and then shrugged. "Oh, er... it... it was that assistant of mine. I... fired her this morning. She was very distracting."

Klaus nodded. "I see." He turned away dismissively. "And now I must—"

Boris cleared his throat apologetically. The Baron's shoulders slumped slightly. "Yes, Boris?"

"I'm sorry, Herr Baron, but as long as I have your attention... The city council of Hufftberg is still unhappy about the glassworks. They're really just feeling slighted because Tarschloss got the new university."

Klaus drummed his fingers on a nearby bench. "Tell them that I will cover the cost of a Corbettite rail terminal if they will supply the labor."

"But didn't the Corbettites petition us to place a terminal there already?" Klaus merely looked at him, and the secretary looked embarrassed. "Ah. Yes, I understand. No doubt they'll see it as very generous. But if they continue to be difficult?"

Klaus whirled. "Then tell them I'll have the Jägermonsters there in two days and the city council will *be* the labor!"

Boris smiled. "Yes, *that* should do it. Good day, Herr Baron."

As the Baron's secretary and a relieved von Zinzer left, Klaus leaned against a bank of controls and sighed. To Othar he remarked, "I swear, it is like running a kindergarten."

"What is that, Tyrant?" Othar asked snidely, "Does your precious Empire give you no pleasure?"

Klaus frowned, and he straightened up. "No," he admitted, "it gives me no pleasure. Politics always annoyed me, and now I have to play it every day. I *despise* the whole business. I haven't seen my *wife* in years—"

Othar started violently. "Your *who*?"

Klaus ignored him. "I haven't traveled or explored—"

"Who exactly *is* this wife you mentioned?"

"At least with the Heterodynes we had the adventures. The occasional fight. We expected people to at least be able to *govern* themselves after we cleaned the monsters out for them. Well, I won't make *that* mistake again. Now I just send in the armies, then the bureaucrats with mops. Same old formula, over and over again." He stared darkly at something only he could see, then shook himself free of his reverie and turned back to Othar. "Well, we do what we must. But I will confess that one of my few pleasures is in these rare moments of research." He patted Othar on the head as he started up the drills again. "So hold still, and rest assured that I am going to enjoy this *very* much."

Othar braced himself as the device began to descend, when a fussy voice from the doorway broke in. "Your pardon, Herr Baron?"

Klaus froze. Then he slowly and deliberately stopped the drills, removed his goggles and then turned towards the door. "Yes?" he asked politely.

At the door stood one of the Lackya in a state of high indignation. Standing beside him was a sullen Theopholus DuMedd.

"Sorry to disturb you, Herr Baron," the servant said in a voice that clearly didn't realize how annoying it was, "but young DuMedd here refused to report for grease trap duty this morning. He had hidden himself in one of the smaller machine shops."

"I wasn't *hiding*," DuMedd said testily, "I was *working*."

Klaus looked interested. "Working? On what?"

"On an automatic grease-trap cleaner, Herr Baron."

A large hand came up to try and hide a small smile that vanished instantly from the Baron's face. "Ah—hmm. Potentially useful, certainly, Herr DuMedd, but I must insist that such things be pursued in your free time. Think of this duty as inspiration."

DuMedd rolled his eyes. "I have a surfeit of inspiration, sir."

Klaus turned away. "Well, if that is all—"

Suddenly Othar shouted out, "Don't be *too* clever, lad, or you'll be on this slab next!"

"*Silence!*" Klaus roared. He swung back to Theo and fixed him with a piercing glare. "Master DuMedd is aware that he is under my *protection*."

DuMedd nodded vigorously. "Of course, Herr Baron." He said cheerfully, "Very much aware!" With a large grin on his face, he moved towards the door. "I apologize for causing you any annoyance, Herr Baron. I'll just be getting back to those grease traps. In fact, I'll put in a little overtime! Yes sir!" And then he was gone, the sound of his running boots echoing down the corridor cut off by the closing of the inner door.

The Lackya did not see Klaus move, but suddenly found the lapels of his greatcoat clasped within an immense fist, and a furious Klaus inches from his face.

"Idiot!" He said through clenched teeth, "You were told to never bring any of the students into this lab!"

"But, Herr Baron, the guards outside said—"

"You like to listen to them? Done! You are now a Jäger orderly until further notice!"

The Lackya went white. "No, Herr Baron! Please, I—"

"I could have you shipped to *Castle Heterodyne*?"

The terrified construct visibly considered this option, then sagged in the Baron's grasp. "Yes, Herr Baron."

Klaus flung him away. "Get out." The Lackya spun about and silently vanished.

"Confound that idiot!" Klaus muttered, "To jeopardize all my work with DuMedd—"

"That boy is not stupid," Othar said. "A web of lies can unravel at the lightest touch of the truth!"

Klaus whirled, smacked aside the massive drill, snatched up a scalpel, and grasped Othar's face in his other hand. He grinned fiercely. "This will hurt *slightly* less if you don't move."

A voice sang out from the doorway. "Ta-daaa! I am here!"

"GIVE ME STRENGTH!" Klaus screamed as he drove

the scalpel into the table scant centimeters from Othar's face. Composing himself, he turned about. "Bangladesh DuPree," he acknowledged.

"That's right! It's *me*!" A tall, shapely young woman sashayed into the room. Her dark, East Indian complexion was complemented by the crisp, white airship captain's uniform she wore. Her long black hair cascaded down her back until it was gathered in a series of small tufts. Ornamenting her forehead, a small skull-shaped bindi glittered.

Bangladesh was one of Klaus' freelance agents. She patrolled the wilder parts of the Wastelands, and was occasionally dispatched when circumstances warranted the use of a barely controlled homicidal maniac.

Bangladesh's mother had been a pirate queen, ruling one of the small remote islands of the North Sea. The princess Bangladesh had been away when the island populace had revolted and her mother was slain. Determined to avenge her, Bangladesh had taken up the family business and ruthlessly built up her own organization of air pirates, which had quickly earned a fearsome reputation throughout Scandinavia and northwest Europa. Preparations for the assault to reclaim the family island were almost complete when she returned from an expedition to find her fortress a burnt-out hulk, her fleet in ruins, and her crew dead or vanished. There was no clue as to who had destroyed them.

Then and there, she took a bloody oath upon her family's malevolent god to avenge them, but until she could discover who was responsible, she needed a job.

To her surprise, she was recruited by Klaus Wulfenbach. Klaus had followed her career from a distance, and realized that having Bangladesh working for him would be preferable to eventually having to fight her.

Bangladesh had accepted his offer on the condition that the Baron's intelligence gatherers seek out those who had destroyed her base. Klaus had agreed. However there were no other similar incidents, and in the subsequent three years, Klaus had successfully found useful avenues in which to channel DuPree's murderous tendencies for his own ends. When correctly applied, she was terrifyingly efficient.

There was also, he had to admit, something fascinating about her. DuPree was disarmingly open about her thirst for blood and destruction, and Klaus found that he enjoyed the challenge of keeping her in check. She was also one of the very few people who displayed absolutely no fear of the Baron whatsoever. She treated him like an equal in all things, which made for a refreshing change in some respects, though her familiarity sometimes caused him great annoyance.

She was also one of the nastiest fighters Klaus had ever seen. With some trepidation, he had asked that she instruct his son in combat techniques while he was in Paris. To her surprise, Gilgamesh had survived her instruction, and proved an apt pupil, though he had acquired several scars, some of which were physical.

Klaus was positive that he could take DuPree in a fair fight, but was equally positive that he'd never have a chance to prove it.

"I heard that you wanted to see me, and I *knew* you wouldn't want to wait." She got about halfway into the room when she saw Othar. A look of concern crossed her face. "Say, what are you up to here?" She looked at Klaus suspiciously. "Klaus, are you *torturing* this man?"

Klaus looked embarrassed. "No—"

"YES!" Othar shouted. "Help!"

Bangladesh blinked in surprise. "He asked me to help!" She grinned and a blackened stiletto materialized in her hand. "A wise choice! *Nobody* knows more about torture than *me*!"

"I *believe*," Klaus murmured, "he expected you to *rescue* him."

Bangladesh pouted and the knife vanished. "What—Is he stupid?"

"A bit." Klaus opened a slim leather volume that had been crudely adorned with hand-drawn skulls, scenes of decapitation, flogging and other acts of violence that Klaus carefully did not look at too closely. "I noticed something interesting in your latest log book..." He looked up. "A pity about that walking gunboat, by the way."

"Yeah, that was over way too quick."

Klaus opened his mouth, and then just sighed and shook his head. "What caught my eye was this note in your Phenomena Log."

"The rain of marzipan?"

"No—though that *is* intriguing. I meant the apparitions."

Bangladesh grew serious. "Yeah, those *were* weird." She thought back. All trace of frivolousness was gone now. "The first time was when I was watching that gunboat burn. There was this... crackling in the air, a kind of hole in the sky opened up, and there were these people... it was like they were right *next* to me. One of them looked like Gilgamesh, but—" She thought. "But older than he is now. Not a lot older, but—" She patted Klaus' great shoulders. "Bigger. Tougher. He'd been working out. And you could tell from his face that *this* guy didn't go around moaning about how miserable his life was; he made life miserable for other people," she said approvingly. "He looked right *at* me, like he could *see* me. And then he said 'maniac.' You know, I think maybe it *was* Gil, because he's always saying pointless stuff like that." Klaus forced himself to nod sympathetically.

"The second person was a girl. Light hair, fair complexion, a little shorter than Gil, big hips, but in good shape, not fat. Big glasses. She was running some sort of mechanism. When they appear she's in mid-sentence and she says, '—A little earlier. How's this?'

"A third guy, he's shorter, darker, trim beard and moustache, kind of rumpled. Looks like a minion. He's looking at the burning gunboat and he starts jumping up and down and shouting, 'Yes! There they go! They made it!'

"At this point a Geister enters from the right. The others don't even blink. She seems to be addressing the girl, and she says, 'Mistress—you are needed.'

"The short guy says 'Thanks.' and the girl smiles and does something to the controls and the hole in the sky kind of collapses in on itself." Bangladesh paused. "I just remembered. Gil was dressed like one of the Geisterdamen. It didn't really suit him. Does any of that make sense to you?"

Klaus shook his head.

Bangladesh shrugged and continued. "Then, two weeks later, I'm investigating this burnt-out town, Furstenburg, which I did not do, when—ZAP! There's another hole in the air. Same group of people, same situation. The girl says, 'Okay, there's Bang.' Like she knows me, you know? Then she says, 'You see your friends?'

"The little guy looks around and says, 'Um... no, this isn't the right place.'

"Gil notices that I've pulled my shooter and he says, 'Hey mistress—'"

"Mistress?" Klaus asked sharply.

"That's what he said. For what it's worth, he looked kind of annoyed, and he's saying it like he's saying something stupid. So he says, 'Hey mistress, she's getting ready to shoot you.'

"The girl looks at me and says, 'Don't worry. I'm going to try—' And then it was gone. Say, are you okay?"

This question was asked because Klaus was staring grimly at nothing, and his hands had crushed a metal canister without his knowledge. When he spoke, it was obvious that he was trying to project a calm demeanor. "This is very important news, DuPree. Thank you."

To her astonishment, Bangladesh found that she was upset at Klaus' obvious inner turmoil. She realized that she relied on Klaus' imperturbability as a sign that all was well. Awkwardly, she reached out and patted him on the shoulder. "Hey. Don't worry. What do I know? It couldn't really have been Gil. You've had him caged up here for the last couple of months, haven't you?"

Klaus went still, and the air of worry vanished. He turned to Bangladesh and nodded. "You are correct, of course. Thank you, DuPree."

Bangladesh relaxed. "Always am. So. Any news about my problem?"

Klaus shook his head. "No. I told you I'd let you know."

"It's *been* three years."

"And I've heard nothing."

Bangladesh sighed, then shrugged. "Well, a group that tough can't hide forever. I'll be in dock for the next three days if you need me to burn down Sevastopol or something."

Klaus waved his hand in dismissal. His brow furrowed in thought as DuPree strode out. "This is very bad," he said conversationally. He turned towards Othar. "Surely even *you* realize—"

The examination table was empty. The restraints cut cleanly, as if by a scalpel. From behind, Klaus heard Othar's triumphant voice, "Ha, villain! Realize that your reign of evil is at an end!"

Klaus sighed.

Agatha and Wooster stepped through a giant set of metal doors, and Agatha stopped in confusion. This was a different lab, still filled with a bewildering array of machines and benches, but the ceiling was easily thirty meters high. Almost one entire wall was covered in glass, revealing a magnificent cloudscape, as well as several dozen of the Wulfenbach support fleet. On an outside ledge, several gargoyle clanks squatted motionless. The center space was dominated, and almost filled, by pieces of a gigantic clank. With a shock, Agatha recognized a section of the exterior carapace, which was hanging from a set of enormous chains.

"It... that's Mr. Tock!"

High above, Gilgamesh's head and shoulders popped out from inside a cavernous hole in the massive chest plate. Agatha saw a large clock mechanism hanging beside it, waiting to be placed within. "Ah, Miss Clay! Wooster, do show her in!"

Tossing aside a large wrench, Gil clambered out onto a

precariously balanced ladder, which began to fall backward. Agatha gasped, then blinked as Gil calmly stood on the falling ladder until it passed a hanging chain, which he snagged with one hand, as he kicked at the ladder with one foot. The ladder swung back into place with a *thunk,* just as Gil touched the ground next to Agatha and Wooster. "Today, I'll just show you around the lab and let you settle in."

"Shall I fetch some tea, sir?"

Gil looked around and, not finding what he was looking for, shrugged and nodded. "That would be excellent, Wooster, thank you." With a short bow, Wooster glided away. Agatha looked up at the immense clank.

"What are you doing with Mr. Tock?"

Gil blinked. "I'm fixing him, of course." He patted a gigantic toe affectionately. "He's too much a part of Transylvania Polygnostic's history and tradition." He then turned serious. "Dr. Beetle may be dead, but the University his family built will continue as he wanted it to."

Agatha smiled. "That's good." They stood looking at each other awkwardly for a minute. Agatha looked around. "So how many labs do you have?"

Gil smiled. "Four. You've seen the flight lab, and you—" he coughed discreetly—"saw the entrance to the chemical lab. This is the large mechanical lab, and my private lab and library are through those doors."

"You really need four different labs?"

Gil snorted. "My father has forty-three onboard the airship, plus two ground-based complexes. As far as I'm concerned, I'm a model of efficiency."

Agatha felt a light tug on her skirt and, looking down, saw

a single eye staring at her from under an oversized hat. "Hello again." Agatha smiled.

"Ah. You haven't been properly introduced." Gil reached down, lifted the small creature up and deposited him on a nearby bench. Try as she might, Agatha could only see the tips of large blue claws peeking out of fleece-lined cuffs and two long-jointed antennae. Everything else that might have given a clue as to the little creature's nature was hidden beneath layers of clothing.

"This is Zoing." The little creature clicked its heels and bowed slightly. Gil continued, "Zoing, this is Miss Agatha Clay. She will be helping *us* now."

Zoing studied Agatha for a moment and then turned back to Gil. "Schmeka teee?"

Gil shook his head. "No, that's still your job." He paused, then looked guilty. "Although, I couldn't find you a moment ago, and I believe Mr. Wooster is fixing us some now."

Zoing squealed like a penny whistle and, faster than Agatha would have believed, leapt off the bench and scuttled away, furiously waving its claws.

Gil rubbed the back of his neck. "I'll hear about that," he sighed. A crash of crockery from the next room seemed to verify this.

"What *is* it?" Agatha asked.

"My *friend*," Gil replied tersely as Wooster gave a yelp of pain. "I'm sorry, I meant—"

An entire china cabinet collapsed now. Gil held up a hand and, closing his eyes, took a deep breath. He opened his eyes. What sounded like a fire alarm went off, and then was silenced, if the noises were any indication, by being pummeled with a live animal. Gil resolutely ignored it. "It's understandable. He's a construct. I made him when I was younger."

"He was *eight*," Wooster informed Agatha. Unruffled and impeccable, he set a laden tea tray down upon a bench. From the next room could be heard a frantic hammering, as if from inside an overturned cauldron.

"Eight?"

Gil shrugged. "Even my father was surprised."

Wooster handed Agatha a sturdy triangular mug. She tasted it and realized that the mixture was exactly as she preferred it. Wooster hadn't bothered to check her response, but was pouring another mug.

"As well he should have been. Eight is *very* young. Most of the gifted break through in their *teens*—or even later. Master Gilgamesh is a very strong Spark indeed."

Gil accepted his mug with a shrug. "This is Ardsley Wooster. He does my bragging for me."

Wooster smiled. "I had the pleasure of meeting Master Gilgamesh while we were both students in Paris. After graduation, he kindly arranged for me to be his assistant here. This was before I knew who he was, of course." Wooster looked down in surprise. A third mug of tea had apparently materialized in his hand. He shot Gil an exasperated look.

Gil smirked and raised his mug. "You should have seen his face!"

Wooster raised his mug in return, and took a sip. "Very sneaky, sir. Most amusing."

Gilgamesh took Agatha's elbow and steered her towards a series of work stations. "To start with, you'll be giving me general assistance when I require it. When it *isn't* required…"

They stopped before a small bench that was littered with old tools and scraps from other projects. "You have permission to work on your own projects here, as long as they don't interfere with your other duties."

Agatha looked at Gil, the hand holding her tea mug frozen midway to her mouth. "My own... I can work on my own projects?"

"Certainly."

"This is my space?"

"Yours and yours alone, as long as it doesn't interfere with your other work. Later today you can clear it off and set it up for your requirements."

Agatha turned towards the bench and slowly ran her hand along it. She put her tea down, quickly picked it back up, found a large gear and used it as a coaster. She turned back to Gil. "Thank you.I've never had... I mean, at the University I couldn't... they..."

Gil awkwardly patted her on the arm. Their eyes met and locked. Gil felt his breath stop as he realized that Agatha's eyes were the largest and deepest he'd ever seen.

Agatha saw eyes that regarded her as someone with thoughts and ideas that were worthwhile. Eyes that saw her as she had hardly dared to see herself. The moment seemed to last forever until a small gasp of pain broke the spell. Whirling about, the two saw Wooster trying to maintain a semblance of dignity, while attempting to dislodge one of Zoing's claws from his foot. Gil opened his mouth to say something, looked at Agatha, and instead, gently pulled her away from the gyrating figures, over to a large series of bookshelves. "You will also be in charge of my library."

Scores of books filled the racks, books of every type. Large leather tomes framed and braced with metal clasps, scrolls in intricately decorated bamboo cases, roughly bound manuscripts and notebooks were mixed in with scores of the cheaply printed textbooks that were used by university students. Agatha noted that while the sciences predominated, books on an astonishing range of subjects were present, many showing signs of use, such as cracked spines or thickets of bookmarks sticking up from the pages. One rack in particular caught Agatha's eye. These books, cheap though they were, obviously were part of a set, and a familiar set at that. "You collect the Heterodyne Boys books?"

Gil looked embarrassed. Agatha pulled down *The Heterodyne Boys and Their Pneumatic Oyster*. "These are so much fun!" A thought struck her. "Oh, of course! Your *father* is in these, isn't he?"

Gil mumbled, "I... uh... I don't really remember..."

"Of course he is! Here we go...

'Hey Klaus, what are you doing in that vat?'

'You put it under the hatch you great idiot! Help me out!'

Punch scratched at his massive head. "Wull, iffen you hadn't been running away..."'

Agatha stopped. "Oh. Oh *dear*."

Gil gently took the book from her and tucked it back onto the shelf. "Yes, well... I'd appreciate it if you didn't mention these."

"Of course." Another set of books caught Agatha's eye. They were gaudily bound in red, white and blue, and looked quite new. "What are these?" She read a title: *Trelawney Thorpe, Spark of the Realm*?

Gil's face lit up. "Ah, these are terrific! Total British propaganda, of course, but really good!"

This last comment was clearly heard by Wooster, who paused while carrying a large, thrashing sack over his shoulder. He frowned. "Oh, I *say* sir—as I have *told* you *before,* Miss Thorpe is a real person."

"Yes, yes, and I'm *sure* that these stories are *just* as accurate as the Heterodyne series."

Wooster wagged his finger. "Ah, but *these* publishers are British."

Gil gave up. "Of course." He turned back to Agatha, who was sliding several of the volumes around on the shelf. "Feel free to borrow any you like,"

Agatha pulled a book out from behind the others. "This one must've slipped back—" The title caught her eye: "—*In the Seraglio of the Iron Sheik*?"

Wooster waggled his eyebrows. "A favorite, I believe."

Agatha did not actually *see* Gil move, but suddenly there was a different book in her hand. "I'd recommend that you start with *this* one."

"*The Glass Dirigible*? Sounds interesting."

Gil glared at his servant. "Wooster, take Zoing and help him clean the flight lab." A blue claw punched through the sacking and missed closing on Wooster's ear by several millimeters. Wooster sighed. "Very good, sir."

Agatha looked up. "But about that seraglio one—"

Quickly Gil reached up and pulled a large lever. "Oh, hey! What do you think of *this*?"

With a hiss part of the wall folded back to reveal a series of figures. They were animals, dressed in formal evening wear, arranged as an orchestra, equipped with instruments. From the center, a small figure, which looked disturbingly like the Baron, rose from a hidden cavity with a pneumatic hiss, and raised a slim baton. After a brief pause, the tip of the baton glowed, and the orchestra began to play a light waltz. Small statues that Agatha had thought were merely there to hold lighting fixtures began to sing a melodic counterpoint. Agatha began to notice the little details: how the rabbit playing the piccolo, managed to twitch aside its ears every time the trombone slide approached from behind; the small mice with penny whistles that occasionally popped out of the bells of various horns. She was entranced until she felt a light tap upon her shoulder. Gil bowed. "Would milady care to dance?"

Agatha shyly curtsied. "I would." She felt Gil's strong hands grasp her hand and shoulder, but resisted slightly. He looked at her enquiringly. "But later, I want to see how it works."

Gil smiled. "I expected nothing less," and with that she allowed him to swirl her around in time to the music. Never had Agatha felt so grateful to Lilith as she did then, for the endless dance lessons that she had endured, acting as a prop for Lilith's male students. Seeing that she was no novice, Gil nodded in appreciation, and increased the complexity of the steps. With a gleam in her eye, Agatha returned the favor, catching Gil off guard, but with a delighted laugh, he carried through on the change, and, locked together, they swirled around the floor in a graceful arabesque that, when the music ended, deposited them exactly where they had started. But now they were closer to each other, their eyes again locked, their hands grasping the other's, and their breathing slightly faster than even the exertions they had completed would account for.

With a hiss, the orchestra bowed in unison and went still. After a moment, they both, reluctantly, released each other's hands. "That..." Agatha ventured, "that was wonderful dance music. Who wrote that?"

Gil smiled modestly. "I did. When I was a student in Paris."

"If that's any indication, you really liked Paris."

Gil nodded. "I loved it. It's beautiful. You can be anything you want there." He glanced at Agatha and visibly pulled himself back from the past. A calculating look flashed across his face. He crossed over to a large wall cabinet and, reaching inside, pulled out a large globe of blue glass which was mounted upon a small brass figure of a man holding it, Atlas fashion, upon his shoulders. Several nozzles and connectors were placed upon the exterior, and a small brass trilobite was mounted upon a band that ran down the center. "This is a genuine Heterodyne artifact I found at a curiosity shop. Unfortunately, I haven't been able to figure out what it is yet. What do you think?"

Agatha looked at the device for a moment and then looked at Gil over her glasses. "It looks like a lamp."

Gil frowned and pulled it back. "It is *not* a lamp. I've been fiddling with it a bit. But nothing I run through it seems to do much. Unless it just takes an enormous amount of power, I must be doing something wrong." He displayed several sides of the object to Agatha. "I'd like to open it up, but as you can see, there are no visible screws, hinges or access plates. I'd hate to take a chance on breaking it just to find out what it does."

Agatha nodded. "Your father knew the Heterodynes. Maybe he would know what it is."

"I'm sure he would, but where's the fun in that? I'll get it eventually."

As Gil was placing the globe back in the cabinet, Agatha's eye was caught by a large ceramic tube festooned with cables that seemed to be surrounded by charred equipment. "What's this?"

Gil's eyes lit up. "Lightning generator. Watch." So saying, he activated a small control unit and instantly a bolt of electricity crackled through the air and a copper globe vaporized into molten fragments.

Agatha whistled in admiration, but Gil was shaking his head in annoyance. He held up his hand with the control unit and clicked it a few times, but nothing happened. "It still needs work. At the moment it takes way too long to recharge."

Agatha took the control unit and peered up at the glowing tip of the generator while flicking the switch a few times herself.

Over the next half hour, Gil showed Agatha the layout of the labs and explained the procedures she'd need to know. Eventually they came to a large room that looked to Agatha like a gymnasium, complete with several racks of fencing swords. There, the battered, spider-like clank that dominated the middle of the room looked even more out of place than it ordinarily might have. It had a large humanoid torso, with a single left arm, which clutched a dueling saber. Its lower half consisted of four triple-jointed legs, which were crouched down, bringing the torso almost to the floor. The only ornamentation that Agatha could see was a small, cherry-red heart, which was located in the center of the clank's chest.

"That looks nasty," She remarked.

Gil nodded. "It is. I wanted a more… realistic fencing clank to practice with. The ones the students use are kind of tame, don't you think?"

Agatha frowned. "I don't fence, actually."

Gil looked at her speculatively. "You should. It comes in useful." He picked up a foil and tossed it to Agatha, and nodded in satisfaction at the way she snagged it out of the air. "Plus, it's fun. You should ask Zulenna to teach you. She's really good."

"Zulenna doesn't like me."

Gil grimaced. "Ah. That stupid ranking game of hers. That girl needs a good smack upside the head."

"I tried that. It didn't work."

Gil stared at her. Agatha's face reddened, and she concentrated on swinging her sword about. "I'm not proud of it, but she was asking for it. She was insulting my parents."

Gil nodded. "That sounds like Zulenna, all right. Well, she's going to do some occasional work for me here, so I'll expect you to be civil to her, and I'll expect the same of her. Is that clear?"

Agatha nodded. "Yes, Master Wulfenbach."

Gil rolled his eyes. "Please, call me Gilgamesh."

"Yes, Master Gilgamesh."

"Miss Clay—"

At that moment, Agatha's sword tip smacked into the small red heart of the fencing clank. With a burst of steam, the device reared up on its multijointed legs. Three slots irised open, and an additional three arms sprang forth. One was equipped with a Japanese *sai*, one carried a small but lethal-looking hand axe, and the last terminated in a circular sawblade, which began to spin faster and faster until the gleaming teeth faded into invisibility.

Agatha stared entranced until Gil pulled her aside as the axe swept through where she had been standing. "Amusing," she commented. "How do you shut it off?"

Meanwhile Gil had grabbed a sword and was blocking the clank as it lashed out again with its own weapons. "You hit the heart again!"

"Oh. Well that seems pretty straight forward."

Gil moved to block the clank's sawblade and found his sword trapped within the *sai*. With a quick twist, the blade was snapped. He dropped the weapon and found Agatha ready with another. He swept it up and deflected the other three arms in a flurry of motion. "Straight forward, yes, but it's a really *good* fencing clank."

A small oilcan flew through the air and smacked onto the heart. The clank froze, and with a hiss, began to relax. Gil turned in surprise and looked at Agatha. "I don't fence," she explained. "So how is this thing more realistic?"

"Ever traveled the Wastelands?"

"No, but I've heard... oh."

"Uh-huh. But there are still some problems..."

With a roar, the fencing clank snapped back into action. Gil pushed Agatha back as the sawblade swung through the air in front of them. "There's a forty-three percent chance of spontaneous restart within thirty seconds," Gil shouted.

"Okay," Agatha acknowledged. "That's a problem." She scooped up a small wrench and fired it at the heart. Casually, the clank brought up its axe and deflected the missile before it could hit.

"That's not the problem," corrected Gil, "that's a design feature. The *problem* is that it learns from its previous encounters."

Agatha looked impressed. "But that's great."

Gil pushed her aside and a sword blade ripped through his sleeve. "Thanks. But I'm afraid that with all the test fighting I've been doing, I've been reaching the limits of my ability." He leaped back as a pointed leg slammed into the ground where he'd been standing. Agatha studied the fight for a moment and then stepped forward.

"Miss Clay? What are you *doing*?" Gil lunged towards her, but was beaten back by a flurry of steel. Meanwhile Agatha calmly walked up towards the clank, and gently tapped the device's heart. Again it froze and began to power down.

Agatha blew out her breath in relief and turned towards Gil. "No attack, no response," she explained.

Her grin faltered when she saw the look of fury upon Gil's face. "You could have been *killed*!"

"I... It was an experiment—"

"I will not tolerate lax procedures in this lab!"

Agatha flushed. "You're just mad because I beat it twice."

"I AM NOT!" Gil froze, and took a deep breath. He held up a hand to forestall any further conversation and looked up at a large clock. Agatha joined him in watching the ticking progression of the second hand. After thirty seconds had passed without any movement from the clank, they both relaxed.

It was then that Othar Tryggvassen crashed backwards through one of the doors in a shower of fragments. Looming within the doorway was Klaus Wulfenbach. His shirt and vest were in tatters, and it was obvious that Othar had managed to get in a few good punches of his own. What struck Agatha was the expression of enjoyment on the Baron's face. He turned to Gilgamesh and shrugged. "Sorry, son. I got a bit carried away."

Othar slammed into the floor and bounced back up. He looked remarkably unharmed. Taking in his surroundings, he snarled, "Gilgamesh! So—ALL the vipers are now in residence!"

Gil's shoulder's slumped. "Get *wound*, Tryggvassen. I can't believe you still talk like that." He turned to Klaus, who was leaning nonchalantly against the doorway. "Father, why is he here?"

Klaus shrugged. "I don't think we can do any more damage to *my* labs."

"No, I mean why is he still on his feet? I know you could—" He stopped and a look of fury crossed his face. "You've been sizing him up as a fighter." He glanced at Othar. "There isn't a real mark on him. This is another stupid *test*! I'll bet you let him loose on purpose!"

Klaus examined his fingernails.

"Nonsense!" Othar boomed. "I escaped using naught but my wits!"

"And a knife or a key or coat hanger my father left within your reach, right?"

"Um…" A brief moue of uncertainty crossed Othar's face.

Gil nodded. "That's what I thought. Well, I can't have you running around." So saying he jumped and spun in midair, lashing out with his foot so that the heel solidly caught Othar's jaw. The big man dropped to the ground.

He pushed himself up and found himself looking up at Agatha. "Why, 'tis the fair maiden! Have no fear! I shall rescue you from this den of evil and—"

Gil stepped up and brutally smacked the back of Othar's head with a large wrench, sending him face forward to the floor. "In your dreams," he muttered as he tossed the wrench aside.

Klaus clicked the stem of his stopwatch and looked pleased. "Well done, son."

Gil visibly kept himself under control as he spoke. "Father, this was very irresponsible. He should be kept locked up. You *know* what he could do!"

Klaus prodded Othar's inert form with a booted toe. "And he isn't even damaged."

"Believe me, if I had my way, but I don't want a repeat of that business with Beetle." As he said this, he seemed to remember Agatha. And glanced towards her. Agatha was in shock. Her face was white at the casual brutality with which Gil had taken Othar down. She had seen numerous fights in Heterodyne Boys shows, and read about them in novels. This had been nothing like that at all.

Klaus nodded at Gil's words and his face went somber. "Yes, that was a pity."

Gill appealed to the heavens. "Not that anybody cares, but he *did* throw a bomb at me."

"Hold on." Agatha stepped forward. "Is this really *the* Othar Tryggvassen?"

Gil nodded. "I'm afraid so."

"But isn't he a *hero*? You know... one of the good guys? How could you—"

Gil stepped up to her and cut her off. "Miss Clay, a *good* assistant is one who *trusts* her employer. A *healthy* assistant is one who doesn't meddle in things she doesn't understand. Now please go fetch the maintenance staff."

Agatha looked at him for a moment, and then wordlessly whirled about and dashed off. Gil turned back towards Klaus, but the old man peremptorily held up a hand until the lab door closed behind Agatha. Then he scowled at his son. "Assistant?"

Gil scowled. "She's a *good* assistant, Father!"

"Even Glassvitch's assessment said otherwise, and he *liked* her."

"Her work with von Zinzer—" Klaus cut him off.

"Von Zinzer *fired* her! And she was his—" Klaus stopped. He blinked a few times, and looked at Gil in a peculiar way that made the young man nervous. "Ah." Klaus nodded. "Of course. I see."

Gil looked blank. "You do?"

Klaus looked over towards the door. Conflicting emotions flickered behind his eyes. A grudging resignation won. He sighed. "You're young, and she *is* quite comely..."

Gil's face went scarlet. "Father!" he gasped.

Klaus awkwardly tousled his son's hair. An act so rare that it shut Gil up as his father continued. "These things must run their course." He caught Gil's eye. "*Discreetly,* I trust." Gil sucked in an outraged lungful of air—

"Obviously," Klaus mused, "it is time we found you a suitable bride."

"A *what*?" Gil squeaked.

"Someone from one of the Great Houses preferably, though we *are* having some problems with the Southern border states..."

"But... but..."

"Yes. I shall see to it." He turned towards Gil and spoke seriously. "These sort of negotiations take some time, so I expect you'll be able to keep her through the summer, which—" a flicker of memory softened Klaus' features for a moment— "is the best season for that sort of thing." His usual sternness returned. "But I want her set aside come mid-September at the *latest*. We can get her a job in a library or some such in one of the northern towns easily enough, and a harsh winter will help persuade her to find someone else to keep her warm, I expect." Klaus nodded in satisfaction and strode out of the room. Gil realized that his mouth was hanging open and shut it with a snap. He felt a slight tug on his pant leg, and looked down to see Zoing staring at him with concern.

"Ugettagurl?" Zoing inquired.

"You heard that! He thinks I hired Miss Clay because I'm... because she..." Words failed him and he flailed his arms wildly until another memory surfaced. "AND he's talking about marrying me off! Most of those stupid princesses have trouble remembering their own *name*!" He slumped in place. "This *couldn't* get any worse."

A brawny arm snaked around Gil's neck and jerked him back. "Nonsense!" Othar chuckled. "The Baron could find out about your *actual* taste in women. Now if I were to suggest a side trip to the Island of the Monkey Girls—"

Effortlessly, Gil reached back and Othar found himself being slammed to the floor. Gil stood over him and said conversationally, "I really hate you." With that he aimed a vicious kick that drove Othar's head into the floor hard enough to cause the giant man to go limp. A gasp from the doorway caused Gil to spin about. Agatha, flanked by a couple of the Lackya and Mr. Rovainen, stared back at him.

She nervously licked her lips. "They... they're here for Othar," she whispered.

Gil felt his rage dissipate. He glanced down at the unconscious man at his feet, noted the bruise which was already coloring the side of his face, and a feeling of embarrassment swept over him. He stepped forward. "Miss Clay, I should—"

Agatha's expression was wooden, but she flinched slightly as his hand approached. Gil froze. His face darkened and he turned away, gesturing dismissively at Othar. "Clean this up."

"Yes, 'Master.'" Agatha intoned.

Again Gil froze, but it was only momentary. Without looking back, he strode from the room and pulled the great metal door closed behind him.

The others released a gust of breath. Wordlessly, the Lackya bent down and seemingly without effort, hoisted the unconscious Othar up and began to haul him away. Agatha stood and stared at the door through which Gil had departed. Mr. Rovainen, having directed the Lackya where to take their charge, turned to the troubled girl.

"He just *struck* him. Kicked him when he was down," she whispered. Mr. Rovainen nodded approvingly, but Agatha failed to notice. "I was just starting to *like* him. But he... he can be so horrible."

Mr. Rovainen's voice rasped from beneath the bandages on his face, "Will you... leave his employ?"

"Yes!" Confusion crossed Agatha's face. "I mean—No. I... I don't..." A bizarre sound that Agatha realized was Mr. Rovainen's attempt at a chuckle, filled the air.

The smaller man shook his head. "It is part of the power of the gifted. Those around them wish to aid them. To... *serve* them. Even when we know them to be monsters." Within his enormous coat, he suddenly shivered, stopping himself with a jerk.

Agatha nodded slowly. "Must he be a... monster?"

Mr. Rovainen shrugged. "With that one, it is too soon to tell. The best thing we can do is advise them. Try to influence them." He glanced down and casually patted Agatha's rump. "You, at least, have methods of persuasion at your disposal that I do not." Again he chuckled, but it was cut off sharply by Agatha grabbing a fistful of his shirt and hauling him forward.

"You *disgusting* little man," she snarled. "Don't you have something you should be doing? Somewhere *else*?"

The harmonics in Agatha's voice caused Mr. Rovainen to flinch, and he gasped out a feeble, "Yes."

With that, Agatha flung him against the nearest wall and said through clenched teeth, "Then go *do* it!"

For a moment, Rovainen resisted, then caught Agatha's eye, and with a whimper, he spun and loped off with a muttered, "Yes, Mistress."

Agatha stood until he was out of sight, and then stalked back to the dorm to take a shower.

Later, around the dinner table, Agatha regaled the others with the events of the day.

After she was finished, Sleipnir added a few castle-grown strawberries to her dish of rommegrot, and frowned. "Othar Tryggvassen. Are you sure you got the name right?"

Agatha nodded. "I heard both the Baron and Gil say it."

Sleipnir looked pensive. "I can't believe it's the same person. Othar Tryggvassen is a hero. We've all heard of him. Theo even has some of the new books about him. He hides them under his bed."

Theo choked on a cup of tea. "How did you—?"

"I found them when I was looking for my shoes." Theo blushed. The others looked interested.

The mood was altered by Zulenna standing and declaring, "If the Baron has confined him, he must have just cause, books or no. You shouldn't believe everything you read. Anyone can *say* they're a 'hero.'"

Nicodeamus raised an eyebrow. "I'd say it has to do with how a person acts, wouldn't you?"

Zulenna shrugged dismissively. "I suppose *some* people would allow themselves to be rescued by just *anybody*." Nicodeamus rolled his eyes. Agatha also stood up.

"Where are you off to?" Sleipnir asked.

"I have some letters to write. There are people in Beetleburg who might have news of my parents."

Sleipnir noticed the dish that Agatha was loading up. Agatha shrugged. "Writing letters. Hard work."

"For some of us," Zulenna said to no one in particular. Without a word, Agatha straightened up and walked back to her room and very carefully closed the door. She then leaned back against it, closed her eyes, and took a deep, slow breath. "Cat?" she whispered.

"My name is Krosp," said a voice from atop an armoire. Gracefully, the cat leapt to the floor where Agatha had placed the dish. "What's for dinner?"

"Fish."

Krosp sat on his haunches and gave her a thumbs up. He then reached out for the linen napkin, and tied it around his neck. Satisfied it was in place, he buried his nose in the food and began devouring it. Agatha watched this all with fascination.

"So, what *are* you?" she inquired when Krosp came up for air.

"I'm a construct. A cat with human intelligence. No milk?"

Agatha shook her head. "I didn't think of it. Sorry."

Krosp shrugged and again attacked his plate. Within minutes it was clean. He sighed, sat back, and daintily dabbed at his mouth with the napkin. "Anyway, I was declared a failure and was 'scheduled to be terminated,' but I escaped."

"A failure? But you sound pretty intelligent to me."

"I hid that. Which, in retrospect, might have been a mistake. But the intelligence wasn't the point."

Agatha looked confused. "Then what—?"

Krosp held up a paw. "I'm the Emperor of all cats. Think about it. Cats can go anywhere. They're invisible. Nobody looks at them twice. Imagine if you could order them around. If you could use them as spies, messengers, saboteurs. Well, you tell me what to have them do, and I can give them their orders."

Agatha nodded, impressed, then she saw Krosp's slumped shoulders. "It didn't work," she guessed.

"Oh, it worked *perfectly*. I'm the highest-ranking cat there is. They all listen to me."

"Then why—?"

Krosp whirled, his fur a-bristle, "Because they're *cats*! They're *animals*! They can't grasp complex concepts! Their attention span can be measured in *microseconds*! Even if I can get them to understand what I want, they're only under my command until they fall asleep, or see something move, or blink! It was a *moronic* idea!" He collapsed into a small, dejected shape on the bed. "Sometimes I think I was supposed to be killed because I was too embarrassing to live."

Agatha sat down next to him. "I understand. I feel like that a lot."

Krosp looked up. "You do?"

Agatha nodded. "I... I want to *make* things. I *see* them in my head—but they never work! I got headaches! I can't concentrate! I feel so useless sometimes. Why am I like this? I must be good for something, but I feel like my head is full of *junk*! I can't do anything useful!"

Krosp blinked. "You get me something to eat."

Agatha looked at him for a moment and then slumped over onto her side. "Oh, of course. I see. My destiny is to serve the King of the cats."

The effect of these words upon Krosp were electric. Thoughts raced through his head, and then a grim resolution filled his face and he nodded once. With great gravitas, he stood and placed his right paw upon Agatha's forehead. "I accept your fealty," he said. "Next time, don't forget the milk." He straightened and looked at her seriously. "Now we have to figure out how to escape."

Agatha sat up. "Escape? From what?"

"From the Baron. I can live here, but you can't. Not safely."

"What are you talking about?"

Krosp looked at her. "You placed yourself in my service. You're my responsibility now. I can't guarantee your safety here, so we have to leave."

"Why would the Baron care about me?"

"The Baron studies the Spark. One of the ways he studies it is by destroying it. He 'studied' my creator, Dr. Vapnoople." Krosp looked away. "I couldn't save him, but I have vowed to help save his work, and..." Krosp sighed, "and what's left of him." He gave Agatha a look she couldn't interpret. "And now I must try to save you."

"But I don't have the Spark. I seem to have the opposite. Nothing I build even works."

Krosp sighed in exasperation. "What do you think you DO at night?"

Agatha looked wary. "I don't know. I'm asleep. What *do* I do at night?"

"You build things."

"But there's never anything there when I wake up."

Krosp folded his arms. "They always run away."

Girl and cat stared at each other for a minute. Finally, Agatha said carefully, "Why?" Krosp shifted uncomfortably and looked away. Agatha folded her hands and continued to look at him.

Krosp hunched his shoulders. "I chase them," he whispered. He looked up at Agatha with lowered ears. "I can't help it." Now he looked annoyed. "And I can't *catch* them."

Agatha took a deep breath and a new thought struck her. "Othar Tryggvassen, he's a Spark. Would the Baron really hurt him?"

Krosp considered this. "He'll destroy his mind, certainly. It might kill him eventually, but I don't think he'll go out of his way to *hurt* him—"

"But Othar, he's supposed to be a good person. He's helped people. Why would the Baron do that?"

"The Baron sees a bigger picture." With that, Krosp leapt with surprising grace back on top of the armoire. "I've got to go." With a deft motion, he hooked the ventilator grill with a claw and popped it from the wall. Agatha snapped her fingers.

"There's another one of those under the bed."

Krosp nodded. "Think about what you want to take, if anything, and keep it with you. Opportunity will dictate our schedule."

"Wait. If you're going to rescue someone, rescue Othar. I'll be fine."

Krosp's head looked out at her from the depths of the

airshaft. "Othar isn't my responsibility." With a muffled *click,* he pulled the cover back into place, and was gone.

Agatha stared at the vent for a moment and then nodded to herself. "Well. Then I guess he's mine."

EIGHT

"It is a terrible thing, to see your loved ones moving, and yet know they are dead."

—SURVIVOR'S REPORT, AFTER THE DESTRUCTION OF THE TOWN OF BERNE

Mr. Rovainen froze halfway through the door. In a dim pool of light, a familiar figure was hunched over a series of microscopes. "Dr. Vg," he said. "Why are you still here? It is very late."

Vg nodded without turning to face him. "I couldn't sleep." He delicately placed a pipette on a dish, and sat back with a sigh. "I think I have found a way to determine the age of the Hive Engine."

Rovainen scuttled forward. "Really?"

Vg removed his pince-nez and buffed them on his sleeve, always a sign that he was pleased with himself. "Yes. It will

240

involve disassembling part of the control unit, but once we have, we can compare the crystallization rates of the brines."

Rovainen peered up at the massive Hive Engine that dominated the room. He nodded. "That would work." He hesitated, then awkwardly placed a hand on Vg's shoulder. "I have... always admired your brilliance, Doctor." Vg was so surprised by this statement, that the shock of the blade passing through his chest was almost an afterthought. "I am so sorry," Mr. Rovainen whispered as he gently lowered the stricken Vg to the floor.

Vg felt the life draining from him. "You... you have killed me!"

Mr. Rovainen stood over him and deftly reinserted the long steel blade into the spring device in his coat sleeve. "No, old friend. I have spared you." He stepped up to the Hive Engine, and with three sure motions, activated it. "Spared you from that which is to come."

Vg struggled, but only felt himself grow weaker. "You've activated it! Are you insane?"

Rovainen looked at him askance. "Alas, that comfort is denied me."

Vg's brain made one final leap of logic. "You're a servant of the Other. You're a revenant!"

"Yes."

"Fight it! Don't do this! The Other is dead! Gone!" The effort caused a gout of blood to cover his lips and he fell back.

Mr. Rovainen turned back to the now-glowing Engine. "Oh no. The Other lives—and I have seen her."

* * *

Agatha floated in the middle of the universe and saw that it was an engine, endlessly ticking. She saw how it was put together. She reached out and grasped a tiny part which was, as she saw, connected to everything else, and *twisted*—"Yes. Now I see. Wrench."

A small silver wrench was delicately placed into her outstretched hand. A final twist and she stepped back from the large cylinder before her. A movement to her side caught her eye and she realized that the wrench had been handed to her by a small brass clank that was the size and shape of a large pocket watch. It had diminutive arms and legs, and the single great eye set in the center of its face watched her intently. Agatha gave a small gasp of delight and leaned forward to study it. "What are *you*?" she breathed.

"You should know," a voice remarked from behind her. Agatha whirled in surprise. There, perched upon a lab stool looking tired but exultant, was Gilgamesh Wulfenbach. He waved a hand. "You built them."

It was only then that Agatha realized that the lab they were in, Gilgamesh's she realized, was literally crawling with hundreds of small clanks, no two of them alike and all of them small enough to fit in her hand. Half of them seemed to be disassembling parts of the lab and its equipment, while the other half were reassembling said parts into new, unfamiliar shapes.

Agatha shook her head. "No, I couldn't have built all these. There are too many of them."

Gil shrugged. "I think you started a few nights ago—in your sleep."

"But still—all of these..."

"That's the best part. They're self-replicating." He snagged a small, domed clank that was moving across the floor by fits and starts. "I watched as this one was built by three others tonight." Agatha peered at it and noticed that the rivets were misaligned along half of the little clank's carapace. Its single eye rolled towards her slowly. "It doesn't seem to be as well made as the others," Gil remarked.

Agatha stared at him. "But they work. I built something that works."

Gil shrugged. "You'll have to get used to that—being a Spark and all."

Agatha felt like she was watching the conversation happen to someone else far away. "I built something that works," the far-away girl said. She turned and looked Gil in the eye, to see if he was making fun of her. "A Spark," she said.

Gil grinned. "I certainly *hope* so." He gently took hold of her shoulder and swung her around. "Because if you're *not*, then I'm *never* going to figure out what *this* is about."

"This" was a tall, barrel-shaped clank standing motionless upon a pair of powerful, jacked legs. Attached to its back was a tapering, green metal pod that looked vaguely insectoid. The whole thing was startlingly familiar, and it suddenly dawned on Agatha where she'd seen it. "Is… is that your *fencing clank*?"

Gil nodded. "The fencing clank, part of the wrecked flying machine, bits of the furnace *and* the mechanical orchestra, my *good* lathe—" he looked at her quizzically "—and a pneumatic nutcracker."

Agatha looked embarrassed. "I really like nuts."

Gil nodded. For a Spark, this was solid stuff. Any number of devices had been built because "The cats on the moon *told* me to."

Agatha frowned. "Wait. You don't know what this is? But if you saw me put it together—"

Gil shrugged. "Oh, I know most of *how* you did it—You had me playing assistant half the night. But that's a lot different from actually firing it up and seeing what it *does*. Maybe I'll get Wooster to do it."

"*What?*"

"Just kidding." Gil grinned. A part of Agatha noted with a touch of embarrassment how much she enjoyed seeing his smile. He pulled a bizarre pocket watch out of his waistcoat and clasping her wrist, began to check her pulse. His hand was warm and comfortably strong. "Hmm. Accelerated pulse. So, how are you feeling?"

Agatha thought about it. "Good," she realized, with a touch of surprise. "A little tired. Hungry."

Gil snapped the watch lid shut and gestured towards a long table along the wall. "Hardly surprising, you've been working all night. I had the kitchens bring up some food. Help yourself."

A large covered basket revealed a stack of warm crusty loaves of French-style bread. A block of sweet Irish butter was surrounded by several different types of cheese, including a sharp orange cheddar webbed with fiery spices, a buttery gouda baked into a flaky crust and a pungent bleu which contained small salt crystals that crunched between your teeth. Platters of cold meats, an astonishing selection of various puddings and sausages and smoked fish from all over the Empire. Several small crocks contained pickled vegetables.

Hungry as she was, Agatha swiftly constructed a massive sandwich and was in the process of topping it off with a potent garlic mustard that was a Beetleburg favorite, when she realized that the young man was observing her closely. He nodded when he saw that she had noticed. "You seem very…" He considered his words carefully. "Together."

Agatha quickly checked her attire and then hefted the finished sandwich self-consciously. "Yes—I'm all dressed and everything."

Gil waved that aside. "No, no. When a Spark breaks through, it's usually very *traumatic*. A fair number go mad. Since they're made during these periods of great emotional pain and confusion, breakthrough devices usually cause a lot of destruction. It's how a lot of Sparks get killed. But *you*—even your first clank in Beetleburg was fairly benign. You haven't *broken* through so much as *eased* through. My father will find this very interesting."

Agatha swallowed. "You're telling your father?"

Gil nodded. "Oh yes! He was totally wrong about you! He still thinks *von Zinzer* is the Spark! Hee!" It was obvious that catching his father in a mistake was the best thing to happen to Gil in quite some time.

"But I don't *want* to be 'studied,'" Agatha objected. "What if I end up like… like Dr. Vapnoople?"

Gilgamesh was instantly serious. "What makes you think you'll end up like Dr. Vapnoople?"

Agatha blinked. "Oh. Ah…"

Gil's eyes narrowed. "How do you even know who he *is*?"

"I don't really, but his cat warned me." The sentence actually formed in Agatha's head, but common sense kept it from being spoken. Luckily, she was spared further interrogation by a blast of sound that came from a set of whistles set into the wall. Both Agatha and Gilgamesh clapped their hands to their ears. "What is that?" Agatha shouted.

Gil leaned close to her and shouted back. "Evacuation alarm! There isn't a drill scheduled, so let's move!" With that he grabbed her hand and took off for the exit. Pipes were whistling all through the section, and Agatha saw people emerging from various doorways, some of them frantically clutching armloads of papers or equipment.

"Evacuation?" she yelled over the din, "You mean off the Castle?"

Gil shrugged. He seemed remarkably unconcerned. "Probably not," he shouted back. "Just out of the labs. If it's *really* bad, we'll head to one of the support dirigibles."

Agatha stopped suddenly, almost jerking Gil off his feet. "Wait! My little clanks!"

Gil frowned. "You don't have time to collect them!"

Ignoring him, Agatha cupped her hands and roared down the hallway, *"FOLLOW ME!"*

From the doorway of the lab, a glittering carpet of tiny devices poured out into the hall. Suddenly the flood paused, and the giant mystery clank smashed through the doorframe. It moved quickly, but with a delicate mincing step that managed to avoid crushing any of the smaller machines that swarmed around its feet.

"But what are they even *good* for?" Gil yelled.

"If I leave them behind, we'll never know!"

With that the two again headed towards the exit. Agatha noticed that the hall was now empty, except for them. Gil explained, "We're experimenting with dangerous stuff here. Once the alarm goes off, we have two minutes to get out of the labs before they're sealed off."

"Does this happen a lot?"

Gil shrugged. "Every couple of weeks. You'll get used to it." They turned the corner and saw the exit doorway. Beyond it an anxious crowd was gathered, arms loaded with items. At the sight of Gil and Agatha, they raised a cheer and called encouragement. On the doorframe itself, lights were blinking, and a digital display across the top was counting down the seconds. As Agatha watched, it clicked to 21. With a gasp, they crossed the threshold. Agatha felt embarrassed at how out of shape she was, and with a guilty start, realized that she was leaning on Gil's arm. She jerked herself off just as Gil's hand was about to delicately ease itself onto her shoulder. With only a slight hesitation, said hand smoothly fished out his watch instead. He nodded.

"That's cutting it a bit fine. But now we should find my father and help—"

"WAIT!" Agatha had screeched to a halt. "The prisoner!"

Gil looked at her blankly, then he frowned. "*Othar?* What about him?"

"He's still locked up in your father's lab. If it's something dangerous, he'll be helpless!"

"Your point being... ?" Agatha frowned. Gil lowered his eyes. "Look, you've got to understand. I've known Othar a long time. He's completely insane. He's probably the *cause* of this alarm. He's very dangerous, especially to you—because—"

A collective gasp from the crowd caused him to look up in time to see Agatha darting back down the corridor just as the counter clicked to "0," and the great metal doors clanged shut. Instantly, a shrill metallic keening arose from the floor. Everyone looked down and saw the swarm of little clanks frantically scrabbling at the closed door. The crowd shrieked and scuttled away, anxiously checking skirt hems and pant cuffs. Gil sighed and rolled his eyes, then squatted down and addressed them. "If you want me to go in after her, you'll have to help me *open that door*!" The array of little machines stared back at him. He sat back upon his heels and felt slightly foolish. *Why had he allowed himself to succumb to the impulse to talk to them like they could do could actually do anything—*

With the sound of a thousand tiny relays flipping to a new setting, the little clanks pulled out, re-arranged themselves into, or simply grabbed a neighbor who was thus revealed to be part of, a vast set of miniature tools, with which they instantly attacked the great metal doorway that stood between them and their mistress.

On the other side of said door, Agatha was having second thoughts as she raced back down the corridor. Turning the bend, she almost plowed into the large mystery clank, which was jogging towards her. She swerved to the left, caromed off the corridor wall and kept on going. The clank jabbed a leg forward, pivoted around it with a screech until it was facing the way it had come, and then clanked off after her.

"What am I doing?" she muttered. "The Baron's labs are probably even bigger than Gilgamesh's. How can I find Othar *quickly*?"

"A-*ha*!" a voice rang out from an open doorway. "The reticent damsel answers the call of *adventure*!"

Agatha skidded to a halt and looked in. For a fellow who was chained upside down surrounded by an array of spring-loaded weapons all aimed at him, Othar looked remarkably cheerful, not to mention a bit smug. Agatha took a deep breath and went up to him. Behind her, the great metal clank tried, with qualified success, to ease itself through the doorway without causing too much damage.

"You okay?" she asked.

"Ha! Othar Tryggvassen *laughs* at such a question!"

"Probably because all the blood's in your head."

"That's certainly part of it," Othar cheerfully conceded.

Suddenly the great clank stepped forward. With a *hisss,* the four great fencing arms, topped with their various weapons, unfolded. "Subject Othar—" Its voice was an astonishingly melodious three-part chorus "—I am here to rescue you!"

With a scream, the great circular sawblade on its lower right arm roared into life and, with a flourish, cut through the chains holding Othar aloft, centimeters away from his fingers. Instantly, the spring-loaded weapons released, and were deftly deflected by the remaining arms quickly enough that the machine was able to grab Othar by the leg before he had time to crash onto the floor. Triumphant music erupted from the device and it waved Othar about like a baton as it lumbered back through the doorway, all consideration for the doorframe's integrity forgotten.

Agatha raced after it, opened her mouth, and ran straight into a billowing expanse of ribbed fabric. Backing up, she saw that the pod upon the clank's back had opened, and a vast set of green, bat-like wings, supported by an intricate cluster of rods and levers, was unfolding and snapping into position. "Fear not!" The clank sang joyously, "Soon you will be safe!"

"Wait!" Agatha screamed. "We're inside! You can't fly in here!"

For a split-second, the device paused, and then spun about and lumbered forward, gaining speed as it headed for a vast bank of windows. Seeing this, Othar frantically doubled his efforts to escape the device's clutches, but to no avail, as without hesitation, the clank, and its unwilling passenger, smashed through the tempered glass and plunged into the empty sky. Agatha dashed to the gaping hole, and clutched the edge, fighting against the great winds that tore at her long enough to hear a final triumphant "Be free!" along with Othar's fading scream as they dropped out of sight.

"Well," she said distantly to no one in particular, "at least now I know what it was for."

A sudden silence caused her to look around. "The alarm is off. Now what was *that* for?"

At the far end of the gallery, a door creaked open. A large insectoid head poked through, along with several long multi-jointed arms. Agatha froze. Everyone was trained to know what a Slaver wasp looked like.

Klaus' quarters were large and opulent, in a restrained and tasteful way. Many of the quarters aboard the Castle were snug at best. Here, there was space, despite the great canopied bed and the large solid items of furniture that occupied the area. At the moment, it was filled with people, many of whom were in the process of coming or going, while a core group collected reports and sent messengers out anew. In the center of it all was the master of Castle Wulfenbach, who was finishing off a goblet of warm wine while his valet finished buckling on a great bandoleer fully loaded with immense shells. The gun that used these shells was strapped into a large holster on his hip. The other hip was taken up with a scabbard holding a villainous-looking greatsword almost two meters long.

The main doorway was filled by the large, bulky form of Jägergeneral Goomblast. "Herr Baron—der outfliers report Slaver warriors all over your main labs."

Boris nodded. "Yes, the Hive Engine has been activated. Do you have any *new* information for us?" Goomblast shook his head.

"A revenant onboard," Klaus muttered. "How many were in the labs?"

Mr. Rovainen hunched his shoulders. "We're not sure. A few technicians cleaning, Dr. Kirstein's team was running their lizard-candy experiment... oh, and the prisoner, of course."

Klaus rolled his eyes. "Of course. Where is Dr. Vg?"

Mr. Rovainen polished his left lens with a bandage-wrapped finger. "Ah. No one has seen Dr. Vg since last night," he admitted.

Goomblast broke in. "Dere iz some goot news—All der bogs dey haff seen so far iz *varriors*!"

Klaus perked up. "So there's a chance that the actual swarm is still gestating? That *is* good news! How soon before we're ready to go in?"

"Hyu giff der order und ve go. Ve haff a mixed team of Jägerkin, Lackya, clenks und crew at each entry."

"Excellent. I am pleased at the lack of rivalry."

Goomblast drew himself up. "Sir—dere iz a time to twit nancy-boy feetsmen and a time to crush bogs." The head Lackya bristled while Boris rolled his eyes. Klaus blinked.

He was saved from any comment by the arrival of Von Pinn, who entered through the door with a creak of leather and an expressive leer from the Jäger at the door. "The children's ship is away," she rasped. "The older ones were not happy."

A pair of booted feet sticking out from a shadowed chair uncrossed themselves and Bangladesh DuPree leaned forward. "Well of course. They're kids. They want to fight! It's fun!"

Von Pinn swiveled and glared at the seated woman. "I teach restraint."

DuPree eyed the leather-clad form and grinned. "So your dressmaker's an 'A' student then?"

Von Pinn hissed and DuPree slowly began to rise from her chair, her grin even wider. "You're losing air, sweetheart," she crooned.

The two jerked upright as Klaus' voice snapped out. "Enough!" Crisply, Klaus gave orders and assigned positions. With a rush, the soldiers left to implement his orders. Klaus turned to an airman who had been patiently waiting off to the side.

"Present Captain Patel with my compliments and tell him to continue the evacuation. If he does not hear from myself or my son in two hours, or if the wheelhouse is about to fall, he is to scuttle the Castle." The airman looked nervous, but his voice was steady as he repeated back the orders, saluted and left.

Klaus turned back. His group consisted of General Goomblast, Bangladesh, Boris, and a squad equally composed of Jägers, Lackya and Castle Wulfenbach's own marines. He patted his greatsword and for the first time, grinned. "Let us take some exercise."

Agatha was running flat out down the hallway. She was glancing behind her when she took a corner and smacked into Gilgamesh Wulfenbach. "Miss Clay! Are you all right? Ow."

Gil was the first one to move, but it was Agatha who hauled

252

him to his feet. "No! Slaver wasps! Coming fast!"

A look of loathing crossed Gil's face. "That cursed Hive Engine! What was Beetle *thinking*?"

Unsteadily, they broke into a trot towards the exit. "What were *you* thinking?" snapped Agatha. "How did you get in here?"

They turned the corner and skidded to a stop. Before them a tide of small machines ran to meet them, swarming around Agatha's feet, producing a noise that sounded suspiciously like small, tinny cheers. "Your little clanks," Gil explained. "They opened the door. They're amazing."

Agatha felt a surge of hope. "That's great! Then we can leave!"

She turned to run, but Gil grabbed her arm and hauled her in a different direction. "No," he explained, "I had them seal the door behind us. I didn't know what was in here."

"Then... then we're trapped!" She glanced back and slowed at what she saw. "Wait—my little clanks can't keep up."

Again Gil jerked her forward. "They'll catch up, and they're in no danger. It's us the wasps want. Now hurry! My main lab is just ahead. If I can seal it off, we can wait for my father."

They turned another corner, but outside the lab doors, they saw several of the insect creatures freeze briefly, and then scuttle rapidly towards them.

With an oath, Gilgamesh steered them into the first room they found and slammed the door behind them. They looked around, panting. The room was bare of furniture, but was lined with shelves, cabinets and bins filled with racks of various devices.

"This is your electrical parts storage locker," Agatha noted.

Gil finished securing the door to a sturdy rack of shelves with a coil of heavy-duty cable. As he stepped back, the door shuddered as something slammed into it from the other side.

"That might do," he muttered. "But we've no time to waste."

"But we should be okay now, right?" Agatha looked around with interest. "Once we equip ourselves from your arsenal, those things shouldn't stand a chance."

Gil looked blank. "My what?"

"Your weapons. The stuff you've built." Agatha rubbed her hands together in gleeful anticipation. "I wondered where they were. So any chance of a good Death Ray? That'd be perfect!"

Gil looked appalled. "I don't have a Death Ray!"

Agatha blinked. "What, it's an early prototype or something?"

"I don't have a Death Ray."

A sudden realization filled Agatha. She blushed in sympathy and with a gentle smile she placed a hand on his arm. "I'm sure that next time you'll build a much bigger one, but trust me, right now any Death Ray, will do, no matter how—"

"I. DO. NOT. HAVE. A. DEATH. RAY!" Gil shouted.

Agatha stared at him in disbelief, and with an exasperated puff blew a lock of hair out of her face. "Don't be ridiculous. Dr. Beetle had stuff like that all over the place. You must have something." She scratched her nose. "Sonic Cannon?"

"No."

"Disintegration Beam?"

"No."

"You must have some sort of Doomsday Device. We can modify it. Come on, it'll be fun."

"I don't have *anything* like that!"

They stared at each other.

"Fine. So what you're telling me is that you—Gilgamesh Wulfenbach—the person next in line to be the despotic, iron-fisted ruler of the Wulfenbach Empire—have no deadly, powerful weapons lying around whatsoever! That's just great! What kind of an Evil Overlord are you going to be, anyway?"

"Apparently, a better one than I'd thought," Gil said, suddenly thoughtful.

At that, with a series of sharp thuds, a swordlike arm punched its way through the door. It was joined by several others, and using the opening, rapidly expanded it.

A canister of old fencing swords was next to a cupboard. Gil grabbed two and faced off against the wasps struggling to get at them. "Build something!" he ordered Agatha.

"What?"

"I'll hold them off, you build your own damn Death Ray!"

"But I don't know how! You should—"

"You can't fight—but you're a Spark!"

"But—"

"Or we'll die—or worse!" With that he turned away from her and sliced away at a wasp that had managed to cram itself through the door.

Agatha backed into a corner. "Got to think." She gasped as a razor-edged claw sliced through Gil's boot. Deliberately she turned away. "Got to think!" The noise was becoming overwhelming. It sounded like dozens of creatures hammering and tearing away at the metal door. Sounds became magnified. The sound of sword striking chitin, the smashing of equipment, the slow rending of the metal door, even the slow steady breathing of Gil as he wove a curtain of death before him.

"Too much noise," Agatha whispered. "I have to think." And softly at first, then quickly gaining strength, a complicated atonal humming filled the room. Agatha stood stock still for several seconds, and then her head snapped forward, her eyes filled with a furious purpose.

Meanwhile Gil found himself being slowly pushed back by the sheer weight of numbers. It didn't help that the wasps seemed capable of taking an extraordinary amount of damage before their brain admitted that they were dead, and even in death, they tended to lash out, as the numerous tears ands gashes covering his arms and legs attested to. "I'd better be right about you," he muttered. One of the swords bent as it hit an internal structure. He was only barely able to wrench it out in time to parry a darting bladelike arm. A wrenching groan was his only warning, but he was able to leap backwards as a section of the ceiling collapsed, raining a fresh wave of Slaver wasps across the floor. Another step backwards and he found himself surrounded by empty canisters, which were just tall enough to hamper his movement. Suddenly his swords were occupied and another bug flashed towards him, its saberlike arms upraised.

A pair of copper rods drove into the wasp's eye. And a cascade of sparks erupted. The creature jerked frantically and then collapsed. The other wasps froze in surprise. Gil looked behind him.

There stood Agatha, a fierce grin on her face. In one hand she had the mysterious Heterodyne sphere. Connected to it was a supple cable, which ended at a bizarre-looking swordlike object, which crackled and continually threw off great arcing Jacobs ladders. "HA!" she cried. "It works!"

Gilgamesh scrambled to his feet. "You did it!"

"Sure did." Agatha tossed him a large rubberized gauntlet, identical to the one she was wearing on her right hand. He quickly slid it on as she tossed him another sword, which was also attached to the glowing blue orb. "Here. You're the fencer."

Together they returned their attention to the again advancing bugs. Whenever they touched the wasps, the insects jerked and died instantly. "You used part of my lightning generator," Gil observed.

"Yes, the Heterodyne device can recharge it instantly."

"Good job. I never thought to test it as a power source, but I'd really thought there was more to it." As he said this, both he and Agatha smacked the same bug at the same time. It jerked once, crackling, and when they swung their swords away, it clattered to the ground like a collection of scrap iron.

They pushed out into the hallway, effortlessly scything down wasps. Gil nodded approvingly as Agatha swept her sword in an arc that took out three wasps at one swipe. "I thought you didn't fence," he remarked.

"This isn't fencing!" she retorted. "This is swinging wildly!" A frantic series of such swings on both of their parts brought them almost face to face, slightly tangled in the cords. Gil's face was glistening with sweat and a small cut oozed on his cheek. Agatha was breathing heavily and grimly determined. Their eyes locked. They froze and swayed fractionally closer—and then whirled away as an attacking arm slashed through the place they'd been.

"Couldn't you have used a longer cable?" Gil groused.

"It's what was there," Agatha snarled.

Gil shrugged. "Okay. So now what do we do?"

Agatha looked at him askance as she fried an unwary wasp. "Um… we should try to get out of here?"

"We could head for the exit," Gil conceded, "but that won't solve the problem."

"You're saying we have to stop them at the source. We've got to destroy the Hive Engine."

"As long as we're here."

Agatha drove her sword up into a wasp's mouth causing its head to explode. "Then we'd better get going."

Around Castle Wulfenbach, the ever-present cloud of attendant airships began to shift. Ships carrying emergency crew and marines began to head towards loading docks, while shuttle and passenger ships removed non-essential personnel.

One such ship was carrying away the students and other children. On one of the observation decks, Theo had commandeered the largest of the great brass telescopes and was training it upon the laboratory decks. "Well," he reported to the others, "there's wasps all over the place. But I still don't see any resistance."

"Let me look," said Sleipnir. Theo yielded the telescope.

"At least I couldn't see any outside the lab area," he said, "so I guess the doors—"

"Omigosh!" Sleipnir yelled. "It's Gil and Agatha! They're in the labs! They're fighting wasps!"

"Let me see!"

Sleipnir defended her position with a deft kick to Theo's knee. "They're using swords and—wait. They just vanished!"

"What?"

"No—There they are. I must've—no, they're gone—they're back—" Sleipnir furiously knuckled her eyes. "What the heck is wrong with my eyes?"

Sun Ming pushed her aside and peered through the eyepiece.

"No, I see it too. They're vanishing," she announced. "I wonder how they're doing that?"

Theo scribbled a quick note and handed it to Von Tock, the boy with the clock in his head. "Have the message light send this to the Baron right away. He's got to know." The boy nodded and dashed off. "I hope the Baron can get to them in time."

Sleipnir grinned. "Why wait?"

Theo's eyebrows perked upwards. "Go rescue them ourselves? Intriguing…" His eyes slid over towards Zulenna. "But the life gliders will be guarded."

Zulenna tossed her head. "Probably by a man." With that she gave her torso a supple little twitch that caused Theo to blink and swallow. "And there's no male guard on this ship that can resist a beautiful and oh-so-lonely princess."

Theo nodded as he picked up a large spanner and cheerfully smacked it into his palm. "That's the truth."

Behind them, Sleipnir rolled her eyes. "I cannot believe that works every time."

Hezekiah shrugged. "It always works on me."

Leaving the younger children in the care of the governesses, the students slipped out into the main hallway. Moving through the ship proved to be almost disappointingly easy, as things were so confused that their passage went unnoticed. The bay they had chosen for their departure was indeed guarded by a lone soldier. He was young and good looking, and was lounging against the entrance, quietly eating an apple while gazing at the panorama of ships spread out before him.

Zulenna looked him over, gave Theo a silent thumbs up, and then wandered into the bay.

Instantly the apple disappeared and the soldier snapped to attention. "This area is off limits, Miss."

Zulenna appeared startled. "Oh, I'm sorry, I was just..." She shuddered. "It's all so horrible. I was just looking for something... someone to take my mind off what's happening." She looked up at him with large luminous eyes, which blinked in surprise as she saw the guard's weapon pointing at her chest.

"It *is* very horrible, Miss. I remember when wasps wiped out my village. It started with people acting all odd."

Zulenna faltered, then gamely rallied with a shy smile. "Really?"

The guard's weapon didn't move a millimeter. "Oh yes. For instance, if a snooty little princess who had, just last week, upbraided a hard-working member of the ship's guard because he'd neglected to do up a collar button even though he was off duty, suddenly came slinking in like a Parisian streetwalker, just waiting for the proper moment to burst into soppy crocodile tears—why that'd be suspicious enough that any experienced soldier'd haul her off to the brig." He prodded the now scarlet-faced Zulenna in the stomach with the end of his rifle. "Now let's move along, eh?"

Mechanically, Zulenna wheeled about and strode off, causing her captor to hurry after her, which helped explain why he didn't see Theo step out from behind a duct and smack him smartly across the back of the head. He collapsed forward onto the deck.

Zulenna saw Sleipnir valiantly trying to keep from laughing. "Very well, I will concede that there's one who *can* resist."

Sleipnir shrugged. "Personally, I'm rather glad the Baron's troops are so well trained. I feel so much safer, don't you?"

Zulenna did not deign to reply, but carefully placed the soldier comfortably against a bulkhead, and then delicately arranged his arms so that one thumb was in his mouth while the forefinger of the other hand was lodged deeply within his nose.

"Now you're just being petty," Sleipnir observed.

Zulenna rose and dusted her hands together before smiling beatifically. "Quite."

Meanwhile the others had found the personal flyers. These were small dirigible shaped balloons attached to harnesses fitted with large bat-like wings, which the user could control with long rods. For emergency use only, the flyers were capable of slowing a person's fall enough that they would have an excellent chance of surviving should they have to abandon one of the great airships in mid-flight. The students had long ago discovered that the flyers could also be used to glide from ship to ship, provided that the ship you started from was sufficiently higher than your destination. This was, of course, strictly forbidden, and it had been weeks since they'd done it last.

Zulenna and Sleipnir entered just as Theo finished circumventing the tripwire alarm. Nicodeamus was using the gas tanks to inflate a pair of flyers for the girls. "You know, this is really stupid," he cheerfully informed them.

Sleipnir buckled herself into her rig while Zulenna checked her connections. "Oh. You just noticed?"

Zulenna patted his shoulder, then began to pull her own flyer on. "You can stay here."

Nicodeamus waved. "Nah. Just making conversation." He snuck a quick look at Zulenna, who pretended not to notice, but once Sleipnir had patted her shoulder and turned away, Zulenna leaned in and placed a quick kiss on his cheek.

They joined the others lined up at the opening. Before them was the vast bulk that was Castle Wulfenbach, stretching away in all directions. Scale was provided by the support ships that were moving to and fro between them. Theo pointed out the nearest windsock, and then to a landing deck several hundred feet below them on the Castle. "We'll aim for Docking Bay 451. That's closest to an armory." Nicodeamus tossed out a scrap of paper. With an aeronaut's experienced eye, they all watched it flutter away in the wind and plotted their trajectories accordingly.

Theo moved up to the lip and grinned. "Okay, you brats, let's go!" Without pause, he launched himself over the edge, and with a whoop, the others followed.

A troop of Jägers sloped down the hallway, looking like a parade sergeant's personal vision of Hell. Sloping was a combination of loping and slouching developed by the Jägerkin. To the untrained eye, it looked like they were ambling along in a disorganized fashion. A closer look and you saw that they were traveling at a respectable clip, and prolonged observation revealed that they could do it for a very long time over a wide variety of terrain. As with many Jäger practices, it had been developed to annoy other people. Particularly Boris.

Despite the haste, great care was taken to keep their uniforms straight, and several were brushing their hats and buffing their braid even as they moved forward. There was a palpable excitement amongst them, and many boasts and declarations regarding the number of wasps that were about to be killed, stomped, and (possibly) eaten.

The other Castle personnel hastily hugged the side of the corridor as they approached, and only dared to breathe again when they had passed. With each yard they covered, they became more and more excited, until they poured around a corner into a large intersection and stopped dead, the ones in the back flowing forward until the entire corridor was a solid sea of Jägerkin.

Before them, in the center of the intersection, stood Von Pinn. Still as a statue. As soon as they stopped moving, she slowly moved with a leathery creak. Wordlessly, she approached them and glided from one end of the crowd to the other. As her gaze swept them, each Jägermonster felt themselves snapping to attention, some of them for the first time in years. Without a word she spun away and headed off down the hallway ahead of them. Three meters away, she stopped, twisting about, gave them a toothy come-hither look over her shoulder, and whispered, "Well? What are you waiting for? Let's go squash some bugs."

With a roar that was heard throughout half of the Castle, the Jägers leapt forward and headed for battle.

The Baron's squad moved into position. It moved slowly because of the constant stream of unicycle messengers that darted in and out with reports from other parts of the vast dirigible.

Boris scanned the latest missive. "The main troop of Jägermonsters have engaged the bugs in Docking Bay 422." He waved the note. "They seem especially enthusiastic."

Klaus nodded. "It's been a while since they really fought."

From the corridor behind, a young voice rang out. "Personal message for the Baron! Clear the way! Stand aside!" Noiselessly, a tall brass unicycle wove through the crowd and the rider slid from the seat in front of the Baron. From a large pouch on the front of her uniform, she pulled out a note, which the bright yellow paper identified as being from the Heliography Corps. Klaus unfolded it, scanned it quickly, and went pale.

Concerned, Boris leaned in. "Are you all right, Herr Baron?"

"Gilgamesh has been spotted within the laboratory section. He is fighting wasps." Klaus' voice was rock steady, but Boris noticed that the note had been crushed. Klaus took a deep breath, and continued. "He is my son. He will survive." He looked around at the retainers gathered around him. "But he still needs a talking to. Let's go get him, shall we?" With a shout of affirmation, the group broke into a trot and headed off down the hallway.

Agatha gasped and dropped to her knees. By a supreme effort of will she kept the point of her sword up, but nothing impacted upon it. She looked up. Gil stood over her, a light sweat covering his face. His left sleeve was in tatters from where an extremely agile wasp had managed to get a bit too close. Blood oozed from several lacerations, but he breathed easily, his head and sword gliding easily back and forth keeping the wasps that surrounded them at bay.

They had entered a larger room, Agatha noticed. It was filled with crates and large barrels. The wasps, while certainly visible, had pulled back, and were circling them warily. "But they've stopped attacking."

Gil nodded. "Yes, of course. We're already heading towards the Slaver Engine."

"But I thought they were defending it."

"To a degree, but once they've established a perimeter, they'll begin to herd everyone inside it towards the Engine at the center. Once the actual Slavers hatch, then we'll be taken over and it will be our job to defend the Engine."

Agatha looked ill. Everyone knew what happened to people who were taken over by Slaver wasps. She looked up at Gil. "Kill me first," she whispered.

Gil nodded slowly. "I will." That said, he offered her his hand and helped her to her feet. As they moved deeper into the room, the wasps began to scuttle backwards, losing themselves within the dimly lit stacks. By the time they came to the next hallway, the bugs had all vanished.

The hallway was dark and low ceilinged. The few lighting fixtures they could see had been smashed. They turned a bend and the next room came into view. It was one of the experimental bays in the Baron's section of the lab. The ceiling faded into the distance, and the metal walls were dimly lit by a collection of glowing machinery. Suddenly a massive form in the center shifted and Agatha realized that it was the activated Hive Engine.

The great sphere had split, and the creature within had uncoiled itself. A messy collection of things that might have been tentacles, or simply entwined pipes and cables, had spilled out around it. A pool of thick liquid collected around the base. Rising upward was a horrible amalgamation of flesh and machinery. Two glowing red eyes blinked myopically while it snorted and gasped like a broken steam radiator. It shook itself and rose higher, not stopping until it was almost four meters tall.

Gil looked sick. "How do we kill that?" he mumbled.

Agatha dug her fingers into his arm. "Quickly," she whispered back.

Suddenly, on the various bits of machinery adorning the creature's head, a series of lights flicked on. Its eyes rolled up into its head, its great lantern-fish jaw dropped open and a long low note boomed out. Gil stiffened.

"What was that?" Agatha asked.

"Bad news," Gil replied. "The Slaver swarm is about to hatch. If we're going to attack it, we have to do it now!"

Just as Agatha nodded and tensed, the walls around them unfolded to reveal dozens of Slaver wasps, which had been hiding in the darkness. Moving almost too fast to see, they reached out and grabbed Agatha and Gil and held them steady. The swords were knocked from their grasp and clattered to the floor, sparking uselessly.

Above them, the Slaver Queen shuddered, opened its maw even wider, and a single insect-like creature darted out. It zipped upward and then paused.

Agatha felt her arms pulled tight and her head tipped backwards, forcing her mouth open. From the corner of her eye, she saw Gil suffer through the same procedure.

Then the tiny Slaver wasp twitched its body, folded its wings and dove straight towards her open mouth.

NINE

Little Mary has bugs inside her head—
Inside her head, inside her head.
Now The Baron's gonna come and make her dead—
Make her dead, make her dead.
But Mary puts bugs in little Karl instead—
In Karl instead, in Karl instead.
So little Karl has bugs inside his head—
Inside his head, inside his head.
Now The Baron's gonna come and make him dead—
Make him dead, make him dead...

—CHILDREN'S NAMING GAME

Agatha struggled, but it was hopeless. Every limb was secured by several of the Slaver warriors. Before her, Gilgamesh thrashed wildly, but to no avail. Two of the creatures delicately inserted their barbed spear-like

267

forearms into his mouth and slowly forced it open. Gil's eyes rolled frantically, but his head was held tight. Agatha realized that despite the fact that they were being clasped tightly by a multitude of the sharp-edged creatures, they were not being harmed. "They want us healthy enough to defend the Queen," she realized with a sick feeling.

Above their heads, the first of the mind-controlling drones swooped downwards towards Gil's open gullet. With a final futile shudder, Agatha felt herself begin to panic. "Let us GO!" she screamed.

Several things happened at once.

The assembled slavers froze and Agatha felt the pressure upon her arms and legs begin to relax, when a glittering orb darted through the air and, with a small electrical burst, fried the small flying Slaver just as it was about to dive into Gil's mouth. The orb hovered, revealing itself as one of Agatha's small clanks, held aloft by a furiously spinning propeller. Suddenly a carpet of the diminutive clanks poured into the room and began attacking the remaining Slaver wasps, who seemed nonplussed by the nature of this new enemy, and began to skitter away in confusion, releasing their captives.

Gil scooped up his sword and began laying about with it, dropping every insect within reach. He noticed Agatha standing with a perplexed look on her face. "Come on," he yelled as he plucked up her sword and put it into her hand. "We're lucky those little clanks of yours showed up to distract them. This must be an old engine. That's a bit of luck! The Slaver swarm should have been huge—and fast! We've got to try to destroy the Queen before she can generate any more of them!"

With that, he swung away and fried another dozen warriors,

who having a more traditional enemy in front of them, were once more beginning to attack, but, Agatha noticed, in a hesitant, half-hearted manner.

"They let us go... when I told them to," she whispered. The idea was patently absurd, but...

"You!" Agatha directly addressed a group of wasps that were drawn up before the massive Queen. "Stand aside."

Gil had his back to her, and was engaged by several foes, so he merely obeyed her and stepped aside. Thus, he didn't see the group that Agatha addressed dipping their heads and reluctantly drawing back, until they had opened an empty corridor between Agatha and the Queen.

Agatha stared blankly for a second, shook herself, grabbed Gil by the upper arm and yelled, "It's clear!"

Gil spun about and, although he was clearly taken aback by the sight before him, he responded to Agatha's tug on his arm. The two of them leapt forward, reached the base of the Queen, and as she swung her massive head towards them, sank both of their swords deep within the pulsating flesh.

As they pulled their hands back, the flesh quivered and smoked and the entire creature began to squeal and jerk spasmodically, ripping cables loose and smashing bits of imbedded machinery until, with a final snap, it crashed to the floor, flattening a phalanx of soldier wasps and buckling the deck beneath it.

Agatha and Gil stared at the dead behemoth. It began to slowly deflate. The warrior insects were frozen in place, not even defending themselves against the continued attacks of the small clanks.

Agatha felt an upwelling of emotion unlike any she'd ever

felt. A great wave of exultation flooded through her and it felt like every part of her body was electrified. She realized that Gil still had his arm around her shoulders, and with a growl she pulled him towards her and fiercely kissed him. Gil's initial astonishment caused him to hesitate, but the urgency of her lips upon his quickly caused him to wrap his arms around her in a crushing embrace and return the kiss with interest. Agatha felt as if a ball of fire was expanding outwards from her chest. The sensations coming from her lips, chest and head almost caused her to pass out from excitement. They broke, panting and wild-eyed, still clutching each other. They looked questioningly at one another for several seconds, then Agatha closed her eyes and pulled him back towards her—

A liquid noise caused them to freeze, lips scant millimeters apart. They swiveled their heads in time to see a section of the Queen's corpse beginning to swell alarmingly. With a sound like bubbling oatmeal, the large swelling burst, releasing a swarm of angrily buzzing Slaver wasps.

"Run!" They yelled in unison and pelted off down the hallway.

"What do we do now?" Agatha asked.

"What DO we do now?" Gil panted, "What was my father thinking? What would he—" He grabbed Agatha and dragged her off in another direction. "Of course!"

"Of course...?" she prompted. They entered another short corridor off the main room. It was lined with small, identical metal panels. Gil handed Agatha his sword.

"My father would have a fail-safe here. It'll be disguised but..." He began counting off squares. Several wasps buzzed around the corner and accelerated when they saw the two

Sparks. Behind them Agatha could hear the clattering rustle of the warrior wasps approaching. By frantically waving her sword back and forth, Agatha caught the two wasps in midair, and they exploded and dropped, smoking, to the deck.

As they hit, Gil finished his calculations, and snapped off a metal panel that appeared no different from its neighbors. Beneath it was a control panel with several levers and the legend "VESPIARY CONTROL."

Hitting the first switch caused a steel door to roll down into place. Unfortunately, two of the warriors scuttled under the descending door and approached, saberlike arms at the ready.

Gil assessed them coolly. "The entirety of the lab should be sealed," he told Agatha as he reached for the second switch. "And this one will flood it with gas." Just as he was about to hit the switch, Agatha's hand stopped him. "Wait! Somebody activated that Engine on purpose." She tossed Gil the swords. "Let me look at this first."

Gil made a moue of annoyance, but quickly turned to dispose of the warrior bugs. As the swords connected, Agatha was astonished to see Gil apparently blink out of existence. She was only slightly less astonished when it happened again.

She was about to speak when something caught her eye in the machinery before her. By the time Gil appeared at her side, she was halfway into the opening.

"Anything?" he ventured.

"Oh yes," Agatha's voice came from within the depths of the wall. "This gas line has been rerouted, to what I think must be the main ventilator for this area." With a delighted wiggle she extricated herself, and held up a small valve in a grimy hand. "Everything on this level *except* the hive's lab would have got

271

the poison." She dropped the valve into Gil's hand. "It should be okay now."

Gil nodded and threw the second switch. Within the walls, pipes boomed and a great roaring was heard.

"He didn't even check my work," Agatha thought to herself, and a warm feeling filled her that was almost entirely unconnected to the sight of white gas gushing from vents in the room outside, and the subsequent death throes of the assembled bugs.

Gil moved up behind Agatha. She felt the heat that rolled off him, and smelled his sweat. She was very much aware of his hand gingerly hovering above her shoulder. She knew that all she had to do was lean into it, and he'd never remove it. She shivered in anticipation, swayed gently—and they both jumped as a warrior slammed into the window before crashing to the deck.

Agatha looked at Gil, but the moment was gone. "Looks like it worked," she said lamely.

Gil cleared his throat and nodded. "Yes…" A puzzled look eased its way onto his face. "You know, from everything I've learned about Slaver wasps—I would have thought defeating them would have been more difficult."

Agatha considered this. "Maybe because it was an old engine."

Gil frowned and then reluctantly nodded. "Makes sense." His face brightened. "At least my father will have an easy time mopping up."

The hanger bay was a charnel house. The Wulfenbach forces laid about with a desperate ferocity, but the wasps were quicker and more ferocious than any they had ever encountered. Klaus stepped back from a smoking wasp to assess the situation as he levered a fresh round of radium bullets into the chambers of his ancient pistol.

To his right, Boris kept any wasps from approaching, his four swords weaving an impassable wall of glittering death. To his left General Zog was using the mangled form of a warrior wasp as a flail to beat back others, while roaring orders to the horde of Jägermonsters that fought before them. Those with weapons used them with a deadly precision that, to someone who had only seen the monster soldiers clowning around, would have been terrifying. Those without weapons used their teeth and claws so effectively that one questioned why they bothered to use weapons at all. Beside them fought the Lackya, still adorned in their long, elegant coats, but they moved like lightning, and dealt death with an elegant precision. Standing like pillars amidst the swarms of insects were a row of the great mechanical soldiers, wielding giant claymores almost three meters long that swept back and forth, destroying dozens of wasps with each swipe. Striding amongst the bugs were an eclectic sampling of the Spark-spawned creations that Klaus had collected and sworn into the service of the House of Wulfenbach over the years. Rumbletoys spun and smashed bugs wherever they moved, Radioheads crushed and pounded wherever their diminutive masters directed them, and deep within the enemies midst moved the Dreen, two unearthly, terrifying creatures garbed in dark, wide-brimmed conical hats and long, obscuring veils. They killed with but a touch, and they alone seemed to scare the Slaver wasps. Everywhere they drifted, a circle of emptiness opened around them as wasps desperately tried to escape.

The destruction the Wulfenbach forces were dealing was horrific, but to Klaus' eye the story of the battle was inescapable.

He glanced at General Zog with a look of inquiry. The general bared his teeth in a fierce grimace and growled. "Dis iz not goink vell."

"FALL BACK!" Klaus roared.

Gil touched a switch and the metal door rolled back into the ceiling. "I suppose my father will be sorry that he missed all the excitement," he sighed. A glint caught his eye, and he stepped behind Agatha. "Wait. You have something in your hair." His fingers ran through her tresses and he briefly marveled at its delicate smoothness before he encountered the object he sought. He dropped it into Agatha's hand.

It was a small circular piece of shiny silver metal. Agatha looked at it blankly, then her face cleared. "Ah. It's some sort of connector from the gas system. It's kind of pretty."

Gil nodded as he plucked it from her hand. "Yes. It's perfect." With that he gently but firmly took Agatha's left hand and slid the connector over her ring finger. "Here. A little souvenir."

Agatha felt herself flushing as she took her hand back. Self-consciously she re-examined her hand. The connector was stamped with a tiny little Wulfenbach House sigil. She felt a wave of joy beginning to fizz upwards through her body. She was so happy that she almost missed that Gil was talking.

"Now come on. As pitiful as they are, the rest of the wasps should keep my father busy for a while." He slipped her arm through his, and turned towards the exit. "We can grab one of the support gigs, sail down to the nearest town and be married before he even knows that we're gone."

Agatha stopped so suddenly that Gil, still hooked through

her arm, found himself spun around to face her. Agatha's face was blank. "Married?"

Gil patted her shoulder. "Don't worry. He won't be mad once he finds out that you're a Spark! He's talking about marrying me off anyway—it'll serve him right when I run off and do it on my own."

Agatha gazed upwards into Gil's excited face. Her lips parted and she burst out laughing. This was not the reaction Gil had expected and he looked surprised. "What?"

Agatha took a moment to wipe the tears off the inside of her glasses as she continued to giggle. Finally she took a deep breath, and smiled. "That's the worst marriage proposal I have ever heard."

Gil swallowed. "You... get a lot of them?"

Agatha crossed her arms. "You want to marry me to annoy your father?" She sighed dramatically and theatrically raised her hand to her brow. "How romantic."

These were unknown waters for Gil, but he was smart enough to realize that by flailing desperately enough, he might still come through.

"NO! No! No!" He waved his hands frantically. Agatha cocked an eyebrow. Still interested. Good.

"I... I know we haven't known each other long. But I really think we'd be very well suited... for each other."

Glance. Eyebrow down. Not good. Panic.

"Look—I've known a lot of girls and they were—" At this point Gil could feel heretofore unused parts of his brain screaming at him to shut up. He didn't even bother to look at her now. "No. Wait! That's unimportant!" What *is* important?

He looked at Agatha. She stood there, outlined in the early

morning light coming in through the window. Her hair was the most magnificent reddish gold he had ever seen. He took in the entirety of her and realized that he wanted to hold her in his arms and never ever let her go, and then he looked once again into those dazzling green eyes and knew that if he could spend the rest of his life watching them experience the things he could show them, then his life would be complete, and more importantly, that without her, his life would be forever empty and bereft of purpose. For the rest of Gilgamesh's life, whenever he thought of Agatha, the first and most enduring image, the one that was burned into his heart, was this one, where she stood and looked at him and listened to him babble and tried to decide whether he would live or die.

With this realization, a great clarity washed through him and he realized that if he wanted her, all he had to do was tell her why. His mouth finally got the message and snapped shut in mid-burble.

He straightened up and looked Agatha full in the face. Agatha blinked and uncrossed her arms. Gil stepped closer. "Agatha, I—"

"Ha-HA!" There was a swoosh, a blur of gold, and a "Gloof!" from Agatha. And she was gone.

Gil spun around and saw Agatha being carried off by Othar Tryggvassen, who was effortlessly swinging through the air on a long cable. "HEY!" he yelled.

Othar gracefully turned, and he and Agatha landed atop a ceiling girder. She twisted out of his grasp. "Do you *mind*?" She hissed, "I was *busy* here!"

From the floor Gil called up frantically. "Agatha! Get away from him!"

"What's the matter, Wulfenbach?" Othar called back jovially. "Didn't expect a hero to rescue the damsel from your unwelcome advances?"

Gil shook his fist. "They weren't unwelcome, you idiot!"

Agatha shoved forward. "Just a minute! I'm not done *yelling* at you yet!"

Othar gently pulled her back from the edge. "Well, yes you are." He reached into his side holster and pulled forth a bizarre little steam pistol. "We've got to go." He aimed the gun at Gil: "And he's got to die."

Just as he fired, Agatha grabbed his arm and yanked with all her might. This threw Othar off balance and he swayed precipitously on the edge of the girder. Below, the bullet smacked into the wall centimeters from Gil's head. With a grimace, Gilgamesh ducked down into the maze of machinery and was lost to sight.

Othar sighed. "Drat." He turned to Agatha. "He got away… for the moment."

Agatha stood braced for Othar's fury. "I won't let you—"

He wagged a gently admonishing finger in her face. "You should be more careful. You could have fallen. You're lucky I caught you."

The events of the last twenty seconds replayed in Agatha's mind. "But you *didn't*—"

"I hope you're not going to be one of those *clumsy* girl sidekicks who always need rescuing during my final showdown with the villain," Othar remarked.

"I AM NOT YOUR SIDEKICK!"

Othar laughed. "Of course you are! You came to rescue me!"

"If I'd known you were going to run around trying to

shoot people who were *proposing* to me—!"

"Oh, that was just the once." The sheer number of things that Agatha wanted to say to this temporarily overwhelmed her ability to speak. Othar, unfortunately, did not have this problem. "Now, your innocence does you credit, but you'll soon learn that Evil deserves no pity! And young Wulfenbach is certainly evil."

Agatha rolled her eyes. "*Clueless* I'll give you, but—"

Her words were left behind as Agatha herself was swept off the girder by Gilgamesh swinging through on his own cable. They lightly touched down on an adjoining girder. "If being like you is the alternative," Gil remarked to Othar, as he relinquished his grip on the cable, "then I'll gladly take being evil."

The released cable vanished into the dimness of the ceiling, followed by several squeaks and a faint *fwap*. This caused Othar to pause and peer upwards into the darkness, which may have been why he missed seeing the beam which swung down from the side, caught him square in the ribs and smashed him through the plate glass wall and into open space. As he arced downwards, they heard him admonish them with a final declaration of "Foul!" before he vanished into the cloudscape below.

Agatha rushed over to the window and stared down in shock. "You threw him out of the airship," she cried. "I went to all that trouble to *rescue* him and you've *killed* him!"

"But he was shooting—" Gil realized this was a futile line of argument and switched tactics. "He'll be fine. I've seen him survive worse." Agatha looked at him incredulously. "Trust me. When you get to know him better, you'll want to throw him out a window yourself."

As he spoke, Gil casually slipped off a shoe and with a

moment's calculation tossed it down into the machinery below. It hit a lever and a winch began to creak, lowering a hook on a large chain past their girder. Gil casually looped his arm around Agatha's waist and snagged the chain. They held each other tightly as they headed for the distant deck below.

"I occasionally want to throw any *number* of people out a window—" Agatha said looking significantly at Gil—"But I *control* myself."

But Gil wasn't listening. "Uh-huh. Forget eloping."

Agatha blinked. "Oh. But—"

"We're going straight to my father. I'll have him announce that you are, in effect, married to me already."

The thudding of their feet upon the deck broke Agatha's shocked silence. She ripped herself free of Gil's arm. "How dare you? What do you think—?"

"Any number of people are going to try to grab you. So the sooner the world sees that you are *mine*, the safer you'll be." Gil calmly retrieved his shoe and slipped it back on. He turned back to Agatha and froze. Agatha's fury poured off of her like a physical force, and it took all of his strength not to step back. Every instinct he possessed warned him that he was close to death and he frantically tried to figure out why.

"I am not your personal property, *or* Othar's!"

"I *know* that! But you're going to wind up *someone's* personal property unless we act now!"

"I thought the Baron outlawed slavery."

Gil rolled his eyes. "You've never been outside Beetleburg. You couldn't understand—"

"Don't assume I'm too *stupid* to understand—*explain* it to me!"

Gil reeled as if he'd been struck. His shoulders slumped. "You're right."

Agatha had been prepared for more arguing. She paused, and released the lungful of air she'd gathered. Encouraged by her silence. Gil continued: "The reason I... I like you is because you're smart. I should treat you that way. Explain why I think this is in your best interest, as well as my own." Agatha raised her eyebrows encouragingly.

A small explosion shuddered somewhere in the distance. Gil's eyes hardened. "But I'm afraid I simply don't have the time." Agatha's eyes widened in shock as Gil took her wrist in a grip like iron. "You'll come with me now, and I'll explain—"

A massive fist came down and connected with the top of Gil's head with a meaty *BONK,* and he collapsed to the deck.

"Was this boy *bothering* you, dear?"

"Lilith!" Agatha shouted. "Adam!" For it was indeed her step-parents standing before her. To her surprise she saw that they were garbed in coveralls, peppered with small pockets carrying tools and useful bits of gear. The outfits appeared to be rather old and well-used, though Agatha was sure that she'd never seen them before. She looked down at Gilgamesh sprawled out at her feet. "You *hit* him."

The burly construct allowed himself a self-satisfied smile. But Lilith noticed the concern in Agatha's voice. "He'll be fine, dear." A touch of concern appeared on her face. "Who is he?"

Agatha leaned down and shifted Gil slightly so that his head was at a less awkward angle. "Gilgamesh Wulfenbach," she informed them. "He... um... wants me to marry him." A look of shock passed between the two constructs. Agatha continued, "In fact, he kind of insists."

Seconds later, Agatha found herself tucked under Adam's massive arm while her step-parents were running down a corridor. "So, you don't think I should, then?"

"We're leaving," Lilith informed her. "*Right now!*"

Agatha looked out the window at the flotilla of airships that attended the Castle. "How?" She thought for a second. "And how did you *get* here?"

"We've been following the Castle from the ground. We were planning on hijacking one of the regular supply ships, but today there was a flurry of activity, with dozens of ships bringing people to the ground." They came to a massive bulkhead door which had been sealed. Lilith began spinning dials.

"There was an evacuation of the labs," Agatha explained. "There was an accident with a Slaver Engine."

Lilith froze on hearing this and then, without further ado, simply ripped the massive door out of its frame. "We commandeered a pinnace and we'll leave the same way."

They found themselves in an enormous, dimly lit chamber lined with pumps slowly thumping away on either side. "But this place is huge," Agatha observed. "How did you manage to find me?"

Lilith shrugged. "We *have* done this sort of thing before, dear. We just looked for the center of chaos and there you were." She shook her head. "We knew something like this would happen if your locket was removed."

Agatha's hand automatically went to the empty place near her throat. "My locket?"

Adam and Lilith looked at each other. Adam shrugged, and Lilith nodded. "You started to break through at a *very* early age—"

"You knew I was a Spark?"

Lilith nodded. "Your uncle made the locket specifically to keep you from breaking through completely."

"But I was so *stupid*! How could you let me *live* like that?"

"We were *hiding* you!" Lilith answered hotly. "Young Sparks never survive without powerful protection! If they don't blow themselves up or get killed by their creations, they're likely to go mad and kill everyone around them."

They turned a corner and Agatha began to note signs of the fighting. Smoke drifted through the air, and a single dead wasp warrior lay crushed beneath a gas cylinder that had obviously been taken from a stack of the same that lined the wall. Lilith grimaced, and continued: "Your uncle was gone. Beetle wasn't strong enough, and the Baron would have taken you instantly." She broke off and caught Agatha's eye. "And you don't ever want that."

Agatha opened her mouth to question, but Lilith plowed on. "In the country you would have been killed by the peasantry. Even burned as a Witch. Plus you're a girl. Girls with the Spark, they usually just disappear. Even the Baron's people have noticed that there's a disproportionately low number of them, but they don't know why. Every power in Europa is going to try to kill you or control you. You've already seen that with young Wulfenbach."

"But I don't understand," Agatha cried. "There are a *lot* of Sparks wandering about. Why would *I* be in so much danger?"

Lilith stopped dead in front of the door. Her head briefly slumped forward enough that it rested on the cool metal surface.

"I suppose there'll *never* be a good time..." she muttered. She looked at Agatha. "Your family. We never told you." She leaned on the door, which, surprisingly, was unlocked, and began to creak open. "You're the daughter of—"

The opening door revealed a large room lined with galleries extending several stories upwards. The room was filled with people, constructs and clanks. They all turned towards the opening door, revealing, at the center of the crowd, none other than the Baron himself.

Silence spread, until Klaus, his eyes wide in surprise at the figure in the doorway, stepped forward. "Judy?" he whispered.

TEN

Go to sleep, lay down your head,
The Heterodynes, they are not dead.
They will return to us someday,
And send the monsters far away.

—CHILD'S LULLABY

Lilith went white. "Klaus!"

Adam set Agatha down and moved forward. Klaus saw him and his brows lowered. "Punch?" Without taking his eyes off of the little group he snapped out orders. "Contain them, and find my son!" Several of the guards began to spread out, and a small squad raced off, no doubt to try to encircle the three. The others began to move forward, but the Baron checked them with an upraised hand. Agatha noticed that he was dirty, and that his clothes were torn; with surprise, she saw that his left hand was bandaged. Another part of her mind took note of the fact that she was shocked that he could be injured. The rest of the group had obviously been through a tough ordeal. Many were injured, and all looked weary.

"Something very odd is going on here," Klaus muttered.

Lilith swallowed. "Klaus, we—"

Suddenly a lone Jägermonster pushed its way forward until it was right behind the Baron. A distant memory was obviously fighting its way to the surface of its mind. "Vait! Meester *Ponch*?"

Without hesitation, Klaus backfisted the Jäger in the face and it dropped to the ground unconscious. "Damn! He'll be a problem." To the others he said, "Seal the area, and keep the Jägers out of here."

At this point Agatha didn't know what was happening, but thought to correct things before they got further out of hand. "Herr Baron," she piped up, "there's been some sort of a mistake. These are my parents: Adam and Lilith Clay."

Klaus nodded slowly. "Punch and Judy. So *you're* the unfindable Clays. This explains so much. But the girl—she's not your *real* daughter."

"She's just an orphan we took in," Lilith interjected.

"I'm sure she is. Lucrezia and Bill's, I imagine. Or is she a surprise from *Barry's* past?"

Agatha blinked. It almost sounded like the Baron knew her parents. He must be confused. They'd had many a laugh around the dinner table about the coincidence of the names—

A shriek caught them all by surprise. A wild-eyed Von Pinn pushed her way to the fore. Klaus put up a hand to check her progress, and she glared at him while she panted in short, excited bursts. "Yes!" She spoke in a strained voice. Gone now was the controlled fury that Agatha had seen before. "She is the daughter of Lucrezia Mongfish! When first she came, she gave to me an order, which I obeyed without thinking!" She whipped her head around and glared at Agatha with unreadable emotions distorting her face. "That will not work again, Girl Agatha. Now you are mine!" She clutched at Klaus' hand and, shockingly, pleaded with him. "She—Klaus, she is mine! Nothing have I ever asked, but now—!"

"Hold." Klaus did not speak loudly, but Von Pinn instantly went silent, and returned to staring, quivering, at Agatha. The Baron closed his eyes, and pinched the bridge of his nose.

"Yesss... so *she* was the Spark in Beetleburg. It's so obvious now." He sighed. "I must be getting old."

Lilith took a small step backward. "Klaus, we're going to leave now."

The Baron's eyes snapped open. "Oh no. Not this time. Not without an explanation. I was gone for less than four years, and I came back to a world in ruins! Death, destruction, chaos—the endless fighting—it was like the Heterodyne Boys had never *existed*. Things were worse than *ever*.

"So I stopped it. And I did it my way this time. No more negotiating, no more promises, no more second chances. Rule by conquest and peace by intimidation because that was all the geniuses I dealt with could understand. And I did it alone because I had to. All my friends and companions were gone, gone without a trace! I thought them all dead and gone and no one even knew what had happened to them—and now here you are, the Heterodyne Boys' steadfast companions. I had considered us mutual friends; I had always thought of you as people, decent people, and yet you've obviously been *hiding* from me for all these years.

"Well, I will find out why you were hiding from me. I will find out where the Heterodyne Boys went and I *will* find out what else you have been hiding from me, because I assure you, you *will* tell me."

Lilith glowered. "You always *could* play to the gallery, Klaus, but Barry came back."

Klaus sighed. "Wonderful. More puzzles. Apparently that's supposed to worry me?" He waved a hand dismissively. "Soon enough. Katz!" A Lackya stepped forward. "Have these people locked up—In separate quarters. I want them guarded by at least two guards each around the clock." Klaus frowned. "And not by the Jägers; in fact they're not to know of this until I've sorted this mess out."

Katz nodded. The door swung open. Everyone tensed, but the only one there was Bangladesh DuPree. She was obviously trying to keep herself from laughing about something. "Hey, Klaus," she announced, "we found your boy! Babbling a bit, but that's pretty normal. Get this—Says his fiancée knocked him out."

Few announcements could have broken Klaus' concentration, but this certainly appeared to be one of them. "His *what*?"

He spun about in time to see Agatha wearily rest her face in her hands. He went white. "Ah," he said a trifle unsteadily. "I see that history repeats itself. That will stop—"

Again DuPree interrupted. "Hey! That's her!"

Klaus tensed. "Explain."

Bangladesh waved towards Agatha. "That girl I told you about. The one in my Phenomena Log, the one with Gil and the Geisterdamen. That's *her*!"

"Worse and worse! All right, in addition to being confined, this girl is to be kept *sedated*—"

With a hollow sound, the head of the Lackya standing next to Klaus snapped back and the guard dropped to the deck.

In the next second, a small object tore through the Baron's leg. He roared with pain and dropped to one knee. Almost simultaneously, another object glanced off of Boris' skull and knocked the wind out of Bangladesh, sending them down.

A brief pause as Adam poured another handful of rivets into his immense hand. Lilith touched his arm. "I'll get Agatha out of here. Meet us at the dock." Adam absentmindedly blew her a small kiss as, in the space of half a second, six more rivets flew to their targets, taking out one of the giant battle clanks, a Radiohead, and three crewmen. The only surprise was Von Pinn, who coolly plucked the rivet out of the air and dropped it to her feet. Before it hit the deck, Adam had sent another dozen at her. She darted forward, her arms blurring into invisibility as she successfully deflected them all, but this did prevent her from being able to stop Adam himself, who, moving like a juggernaut, caught her with a roundhouse blow to the jaw that snapped her head to one side. But even as her ruby-red monocle flew back, her arms whipped upwards and grasped Adam's arm. Adam tried to recoil and he blinked as his arm remained where it was. With that, Von Pinn flashed him a toothy grin of triumph, and effortlessly tore his arm free from its socket.

Adam stared in shock as a gout of purplish fluid pulsed from his shoulder, then he gasped as Von Pinn tossed his arm aside and then swung back and punched her hand through his chest, crushing his spasming heart in her grasp before tossing it to the deck.

Adam blinked, then his eyes rolled up into his head and he pitched forward. Agatha found herself screaming until a hand grabbed her arm and brutally dragged her up to Lilith's terrifyingly calm face. "Go." Her voice was as calm as her face. "Get to *Castle Heterodyne*. It will *help* you."

Before Agatha could respond, she felt herself flung upwards. She caught a brief glimpse of Von Pinn centimeters away from Lilith, who was smiling calmly. "We love you!" She called out, "Now *run*!"

Agatha arced upwards and sailed over the railing of the balcony that circled the room. To her astonishment, she saw a huddled mass of wide-eyed figures, onto which she landed. Desperately she clawed her way back to the railing, in time to see Von Pinn finish ripping Lilith to bloody bits. Just as Agatha realized what she was seeing, Von Pinn's head snapped towards her with a glare that burned its way into her memory, where it resurfaced in nightmares for several years to come. Upon seeing Agatha, Von Pinn shrieked, "MINE!" and darted out of the room.

A hand dropped onto Agatha's shoulder, causing her to scream in terror, but it was only Theo DuMedd. She realized that the figures were, in fact, the other students who were staring at her. It was Hezekiah who broke the silence. "We'd better get out of here!" He glanced back over the balcony at the mess below, and took Agatha's other arm. "Now!"

Agatha shook herself free. "But I have to—"

A number of the others began to speak up, when a commanding voice cut through the babble. "*Move!* Or their deaths will be wasted!"

Everyone turned in surprise, and there, poised regally before them atop a canister, was Krosp. "Follow me," he ordered. "I can take you to the airship that the constructs used to get here.

Now *hurry!*" With that he leapt to the ground and strode off. Unhesitatingly, Agatha moved, and with the briefest of pauses, the rest quickly followed.

It was Z who felt he had to state the obvious. "It's a talking cat."

Theo shrugged. "Well, we're in a Heterodyne story now. These things happen." The others nodded.

"Hey, Theo," Nicodeamus realized, "she's your *cousin!*"

Theo stumbled. "Wow. I never had any family before." He considered this briefly. "I mean that wasn't dead, or missing, or a head in a jar or something."

Meanwhile at the front of the crowd, Agatha was trying to cope with the events of the last few minutes. "Lilith! She—"

"Focus!" Krosp roared over his shoulder.

Agatha swallowed and nodded. "I... I don't know how to fly an airship."

"Well, you're in luck. I do." He frowned. "I'll need something to *stand* on, though."

Agatha's brain gratefully seized the memory that bubbled up. "The airship manual—and the controls laid out on the floor. Those were yours?"

"Yes. I think I have everything memorized, so it wasn't that big a setback."

Agatha glanced back over her shoulder at the crowd following. Hezekiah puffed along behind her, a disbelieving grin on his face. Agatha dropped back slightly so she was running alongside him. "So what are you guys doing here?"

"We came to help you and Gil. We sure didn't expect this," he admitted. "You're a Heterodyne heir. Wow!"

Agatha shrugged. "Even if it's true, it doesn't change—"

"Don't be even more absurd," Zulenna interrupted. It was obvious from her face that the girl was almost as upset by the day's events as Agatha. "It changes everything. The Heterodynes saved my family's lands. Designed our defenses. When he incorporated our lands into the Empire, the Baron had to treat us with respect. We would have been another backwater former monarchy without their help." Zulenna sighed. "Whereas you yourself have done nothing; many of those who owe your family will feel obligated to support you. This could be a problem if you are not under the Baron's direct control. Arguably, to best preserve the stability of the Pax Transylvania, perhaps you *should*—"

"Naughty children!" The voice sent chills down their spines, and without conscious volition, the group stumbled to a halt. Filling the corridor behind them was the figure of Von Pinn, who glided forward. "Stop this at once," she hissed. "Bring me the Agatha girl."

The group was frozen until Zulenna suddenly stepped forward and, with a whisper, drew the rapier from the scabbard at her waist. Without looking back at the group she ordered them, "Go! I'll hold her off!"

Theo blinked. "Zulenna, what are you—"

"My family owes her family. Everything that I am dictates that I do this. Now GO!"

"Good luck," Krosp offered. "Now move!" With that the group reluctantly ran off. Seeing this, Von Pinn flowed forward impossibly fast, but found herself blocked in the narrow corridor by Zulenna's sword. She reared up. "Get out of my way, child."

Zulenna's hand shook slightly, but her voice remained firm. "You talk a good game, Madam, but you've never actually hurt any of us. Don't make me hurt you."

Vonn Pinn made a few lightning fast swipes at Zulenna's sword, but was unable to grab it. "You cannot hurt me, but I will hurt you in order to pass."

"Then that is what you will have to do."

Von Pinn screamed and lunged forward. Zulenna retreated slightly and slashed at Von Pinn's face. The construct flinched. "I am charged with your safety. I do not want to hurt you!" she muttered.

A friendly hand dropped onto her shoulder. Von Pinn spun and found Bangladesh at her side with a sympathetic look sitting incongruously on her face. "Kids, huh? What are you gonna do?" She patted the construct's leather-clad shoulder. "Let me take care of this."

"You must not—"

Bangladesh raised a hand in reassurance. "Relax. I ain't gonna hurt her. I'll just get her out of the way." With that she strode forward, a gleaming cutlass weaving idle figures in the air. "Hi, girlie, let's play!"

Zulenna brought her sword up, but clearly was unsure how to handle DuPree's casual advance. "I'm warning you—"

Bangladesh smiled. "Say, that's mighty nice of you." Her cutlass flicked out and Zulenna barely intercepted it in time. Bangladesh continued to walk forward, casually engaging the girl in a lightning fast series of moves. She spoke conversationally. "And really, a lot of people would consider you pretty good." With that, she brought her sword down from above. Zulenna raised her arm to block it, allowing Bangladesh to step forward and deftly sink a slim dagger into the girl's breast with her other hand.

Zulenna froze and stared at the spreading patch of red on her shirt. DuPree sighed and patted her shoulder. "But you know, I'm a Pirate Queen. I do this for a living. Adios, kid." With that, Zulenna's eyes rolled up into her head and she slumped to the ground. Bangladesh pirouetted around her as she fell, and grinned back at Von Pinn. "See? She never felt a thing. Now let's get the rest of them. This is fun!"

Von Pinn screamed and launched herself forward, claws extended.

For a fraction of a second, a look of surprise crossed Bangladesh's face, then she fell back laughing. "Oh yeah! Better and better!" Moving like a dancer, she swiveled and cut at the enraged construct as Von Pinn roared past her. The sword cut through the leather and a deep gash appeared. "So big and scary," DuPree taunted. "But you've got no teeth when it comes to the kids, hey? Well that'll make it even more fun when I catch 'em."

Von Pinn snarled in pain, spun to a halt and examined the wound. A tiny part of DuPree's brain offered up the observation that Von Pinn seemed more annoyed about the damage to her outfit than the large cut into her flesh. "Aw, does that hurt?"

Von Pinn swiveled her head towards Bangladesh, and the captain felt her smile falter. "Pain does not bother me." She slowly swayed forward and extended a hand toward Bangladesh. "I live with it."

Bangladesh raised her cutlass. Von Pinn continued to reach forward. She jabbed towards the construct's hand. With a sudden move, Von Pinn impaled her own hand upon the sword. DuPree was shocked and froze as Von Pinn drove her hand down the length of the sword until she could grasp the guard. "I use pain. Cultivate it." Effortlessly, she squeezed and the sword guard crumpled, trapping DuPree's hand within. "Shape it." Delicate bones snapped within DuPree's hand and she screamed. A leather-clad claw slapped over her nose and mouth, cutting off her breathing. She found herself face to face with a toothily grinning Von Pinn, who drew her close. "Ah-ah-ah—" she whispered. "Time for a lesson. A *final* lesson." She began to tighten the hand covering the struggling captain's face, and suddenly became aware of the slim dagger that DuPree was desperately trying to slide past the belts and buckles of her outfit and between her ribs. She grinned, but then both women were distracted by a small object arcing through the air and landing at their feet. They just had time to recognize the C-Gas canister for what it was when it went off, belching forth a cloud of thick gas that caused the two combatants to fall over unconscious.

The gas cleared quickly, and a shape loomed in the corridor. It was a combat clank. Its eyes broken by Adam's rivet attack. In its arms it carried Baron Wulfenbach, leg bandaged, and wearing a small facemask. A lapful of similar canisters clunked whenever the big clank moved. Klaus looked down at the three women and sighed in exasperation. "I'll deal with you idiots later." He addressed the clank carrying him. "Continue forward."

The machine continued down the corridor. Behind the Baron, he heard running footsteps and a Lackya appeared at his elbow. "Herr Baron!" he inquired. "Are you—"

Klaus interrupted him. "I am fine. Scout ahead and—" A thought struck him. "No—wait. Back there with Von Pinn and DuPree—There was someone else."

The Lackya nodded. "Ah. The Princess Zulenna. I checked them all, Herr Baron, and I regret to say that the princess appears to be dead."

Klaus pounded his fist on his leg. "Damnation!" he snarled. "You will take the princess to my medical lab and place her in the cold room."

The Lackya looked distressed. "You—The Baron would *revive* her? But she is—was a *Royal*. The Fifty Families expressly *forbid*—"

Klaus cut him off furiously. "The Fifty Families haven't got the authority or the power to forbid me from doing *anything*. Zulenna was under my protection, and I don't give a *damn* about their ridiculous games of succession."

"But Herr Baron—The princess *will*."

"That is her privilege. But she is the one who will choose her fate."

The Lackya opened his mouth, and Klaus roared, "GO! You're wasting time!"

The Lackya bowed, but could not resist adding, "I go, Herr Baron, but while the Royals have little *obvious* power, that which they do have, they use with deadly finesse. Beware." With that, he swiveled about and set off at great speed.

The Baron frowned. "The Lackya are getting… argumentative." He sighed and settled back into the arms of the clank. "It's always something."

"Herr Baron." Klaus raised his eyebrows in surprise as a group of students appeared from around the edge of a doorway where they had been hiding. Sleipnir stepped forward. "Thank you for taking care of Zulenna, sir."

Klaus looked uncomfortable. "Not a word about her

revivification. We shall talk about this later. Now stand aside. I have—"

"No, Herr Baron." It was Hezekiah who spoke up. He was sweating profusely, but stood tall. "You're trying to capture Agatha, yes?"

Sun Ming chimed in. "Please, just let her go."

Hezekiah nodded. "She's a good person, sir. She won't cause trouble."

"She didn't even know she was a Spark."

"Or a Heterodyne."

Z looked at the Baron's face. "But you aren't going to let her go. Why?"

Klaus sighed. "Because you hardly know her and still you rally to her side, even in defiance of me. If all of you—who have studied under me for so long, and have the best chance of understanding what it is that I have built and how terribly fragile it is—will do so, imagine what the populace at large will do?"

The group of students looked at each other uncertainly, which was when Klaus slipped the mask over his face and activated a new canister of C-Gas. They dropped to the floor and the great clank delicately stepped over them.

"I think it time you all returned home," he sighed. "Your use to me is ended. I can only hope you've learned your lessons."

Agatha and Theo followed Krosp. Theo suddenly called out, "This isn't the way to the docking bays! We've gotten turned around!"

Krosp paused. "No. I know where we are, but there's someone we have to bring with us!" Again he took off, leaving Agatha and Theo no choice but to follow. Everywhere there were signs that things were not going well aboard the great airship. In every corridor, lights were flashing orange, and swarms of people were rushing about in a surprisingly orderly fashion.

"Krosp," Agatha called out, "where are we going?"

"It's Monday! He'll be in the chemical locker," Krosp replied unhelpfully. They reached a large door marked "CHEMICAL STORAGE & DISPOSAL LOCKER 55." Krosp motioned to Theo. "Open it."

Theo did. Inside were racks and racks of metal shelves, holding endless canisters and glass tubes. Halfway down the second aisle, the large, hulking figure of Dr. Dim pushed a small cart and delicately wielded a feather duster.

"Papa!" Krosp cried as he ran up and leapt up onto Dim's cart. The man smiled at the sight of him, and patted his head.

"Hello, Krosp. Are you hungry?" He saw Agatha and DuMedd, and a guilty look crossed his face. "This is a good cat," he said defensively.

Krosp patted his hand. "It's all right, Papa. They're friends. They are here to help us. It's time for us to leave Castle Wulfenbach."

Dimitri looked confused. "Leave? I don't think we can do that."

"Yes we can. I have a ship, I have a crew, and the Baron is distracted. We have to take this opportunity to escape."

Dimitri took a step away from his cart and then stopped. Conflicting emotions played across his face. "But, I haven't finished dusting."

Krosp stared at him. "Forget the dusting, Papa. It's not important. We've got to—"

The man slammed a hand down on the cart. "You forget

yourself, cat." His face was filled with a cold arrogance that Agatha had seen on any number of Sparks when their knowledge or competence had been questioned. "I am Dr. Dimitri Vapnoople!"

At this declaration, DuMedd started, and looked from the large man to Krosp, and Agatha could see connections being made.

Vapnoople continued: "The Baron assured me that I would continue to do *important work*. Work worthy of my genius! And I have done my work and I have heard no complaint! The Baron's secretary saw me in the corridor last week, and do you know what he said to me? Do you? He said, 'You are doing a good job.' That's what he said! To me!" At this, Vapnoople hunched over, grinned, and whispered, "And he still does not know that I continue my real work! Here! In the very heart of his own castle!"

Krosp glanced at Agatha and DuMedd and looked distressed. "Yes, Papa, we know. But now we have to—"

"I have been constructing my armies! Here! Out of sight! And I have learned! I have learned from the Baron's own books and laboratories! I have improved my work! Each creature I build is better! Much better than the last!"

Throughout this tirade, DuMedd had gotten more and more nervous. "Dr. Vapnoople was famous for creating intelligent animals," he whispered to Agatha. "His armies of wolf/men controlled hundreds of square kilometers. It took the Baron almost three years to defeat him and capture them all."

"And Wulfenbach killed them!" Vapnoople roared. "He absorbs all sorts of half-finished trash into his service, but my creations he said weren't good enough! They had to die!"

"I believe, Herr Doctor," Theo said carefully, "that the Baron judged them as being... too good at what they did. Plus he was unable to break their loyalty to you. They couldn't accept a place in the Baron's forces."

A tear ran down Vapnoople's face. "Yes. I always did know how to build in the loyalty, eh Krosp?" He ruffled the top of Krosp's head. The cat's ears were flattened, but he still leaned into the big man's hand. "But I learned. Even at the beginning, when Wulfenbach was first engaging my glorious creations, I saw how it would go. I saw that I would have to do better the *next* time, and I *have*! BEHOLD!" With that he whipped open a small door in the cart and displayed a small patchwork bear made from rags. "My beautiful bears," he crooned. He picked it up, and holding its little paws, made slashing and growling noises before putting it back in the cart. "They will overrun Wulfenbach and send his oversized castle crashing to the ground! And you—" He patted a slumped Krosp on the head. "You will lead them to glory!" He pointed to Agatha. "I remember her. She said she would help."

Krosp and Agatha looked at each other.

Vapnoople picked up his duster. "And so you see why I cannot leave. Now, I must get back to my important work, so that the Baron does not suspect." So saying, he turned away and, cackling occasionally, returned to cleaning.

Agatha gently put a hand on Krosp's shoulder and whispered, "We have to go."

Krosp addressed Vapnoople's broad back. "I'll come back for you, Papa. I'll take you and... your bears and we'll go somewhere safe. I promise you."

Dr. Dimitri waved a hand without looking around. "I'll save you a fish."

* * *

Krosp was quiet. Several times DuMedd had to prod him to get him to tell them the correct turn to take, but quickly enough they opened a large door and found themselves in one of the hundreds of airship docks that peppered the sides of the vast dirigible. This one had bays for over a dozen mid-size ships, and from the debris that littered the deck, it was obvious that there had been a great deal of activity a short time ago. The only ship in evidence was a tiny two-engine pinnace. The three headed towards it, but stopped dead when they found a half-dozen Wulfenbach crewmen, unconscious and neatly lined up next to a fuel barrel. A faint whistling was heard, and to Agatha's amazement, a cheerful Othar straightened up from behind the ship where he was coiling some rope. He spotted them and his face broke into an easy grin. "Ah! Excellent! You made it!"

"Othar!" Agatha exclaimed. "You're alive!"

"As always!" he replied.

Theo's eyes widened. "That's really him? You know a talking cat AND Othar Tryggvassen?"

"But... he... Gilgamesh..."

Othar waved this off with obvious disdain. "I knew you'd choose the side of good in the end."

This snapped Agatha out of her confusion. "I'm not here for *you*—!"

She was cut short by Krosp shoving her towards Othar. "No time! Come *on*!"

"Yes!" Othar agreed. "Come on! It's time for adventure!"

Agatha looked at him levelly. "Get on the airship."

Othar looked surprised. "Don't you want to hear the exciting tale of my escape?"

Agatha was now on the ship and at Krosp's direction was untying ropes. Othar quickly clambered aboard. "Casting off!" she called out.

Theo came up. "Good luck."

Agatha looked surprised. "You're not coming?"

Theo shook his head. "I was, but now that I know you'll be traveling with Herr Tryggvassen, I know you'll be safe. I've got to see how the others are doing, I'll bet some of them will want to come along. We'll catch up to you in Mechanicsburg!"

Agatha looked panicked. "But—"

"That *is* where you'll be going, right?"

"Yes, but I don't want to travel alone."

Othar clapped her on the shoulder. "Silly girl, didn't you hear? You'll be under the protection of Othar Tryggvassen, Gentleman Adventurer!"

Krosp pulled her skirt. "And don't forget me."

Agatha looked at them and turned back to Theo. "No, really. You sure you don't want to come? There's room. Or I could stay with you."

Theo laughed. "Don't be silly."

Agatha sighed, "Well, you should know that Gil's got some kind of invisibility device."

Theo's eyes lit up. "Is that what that was? Interesting."

Agatha nodded. "It might help." With that, she reached out, drew his head towards her and placed a kiss upon his forehead. "Thank you for everything. And take care of yourself, cousin."

Theo grinned. "You too, cousin." With that he stepped back and helped shove the airship out of the docking cradle.

It floated beside the hanger bay until Krosp, standing atop a crate, activated the engines, and the tiny craft warped away from the side of the great airship. Suddenly Theo heard a rhythmic thudding from the corridor leading to the hanger. He ducked behind a gas tank just as Klaus' transport clanked through the doorway.

Klaus saw the airship pulling away and swore. He then directed the clank to the nearest signaling station. He picked up the handset and cranked the handle to activate the system. Suddenly an explosion gently rocked the deck, almost causing the clank carrying the Baron to fall. A cloud of smoke rolled out of one of the hanger doorways, and several coughing figures stumbled from it. They were revealed to be some of Castle Wulfenbach's fire-fighters. Most of them quickly recovered and rushed over to a water cistern and began refilling the pumper tanks they wore strapped to their backs. One of them saw the Baron and ran to him. "Herr Baron! You should get out of here! All of the experiments in the lower labs have either been let loose or activated, and three of the compartments are on fire."

Klaus stared at him, and with another oath, slammed the speaker phone back into place. "Assemble your men," he told the fire-fighter. "Have each of them grab one of those cylinders of Carbonic Acid Gas and then follow me!" He grabbed a cylinder himself, urged his clank forward, and the group ran back into the smoking doorway.

Agatha lowered the telescope she had been using. "And now they've gone back to fight the fire, I guess. The Baron looked pretty mad."

Othar laughed. "I imagine so. The little diversions I arranged before we left should keep him too busy to worry about us for a while."

Krosp nodded. "There's a lot of smoke, but I don't think the envelope is going to catch. It's looking bad enough that the support fleet is moving in to assist. They're not going to waste time on us. We need to put as much distance between us as we can." He turned back and spun the ship's wheel so that they were traveling in the opposite direction as the Castle.

"Normally I don't work with children or animals," Othar murmured, "but that is one amazing cat."

Agatha nodded. "Yes. I guess I'll have to get used to things like this now."

Othar grinned and clasped her shoulder. "Ah! So you're taking the sidekick job! Now it's strictly a profit-sharing situation, so—"

Agatha shrugged his hand off. "No. I'm not. I'm my own Spark, thank you. I'm going to have to get my own sidekicks."

Othar went still. "What?"

Agatha nodded and leaned on the railing. Below her the countryside sailed serenely past. "I'm a Spark. I'm afraid it's true: it explains so much."

Othar came up behind her. "I'm… very sorry to hear that."

Agatha rolled her eyes. "Yes, well, you don't have to make it sound like a death sentence."

"But it is."

The tone of Othar's voice brought Agatha around quickly. Othar's face was different. It was set in a grimace, and a small pistol was pointed unwaveringly at Agatha. "I'm really sorry about this," he muttered. "But you have to die."

Agatha realized that the comically jovial Othar she thought

she knew had vanished entirely. "Why?" she asked.

For a terrible moment she thought he wasn't going to answer. When he did, his voice was strained and intense. "What is the cause of everything wrong in the world today? Madboys. The Spark. They create monsters. Rip apart the cities with their constant fighting and terrorize the countryside... They can't help it. They're like mad dogs. They've almost completely destroyed civilization. Surely you can see that. For the good of the world, all Sparks have to die, and since you are one of them—"

"But you—You have the Spark."

Othar grimaced. "Yes! But I alone have the resolve to do what must be done! I must hunt down and destroy every Spark in existence! And then—" He threw his head up and screamed to the heavens, "And then I can finally kill myself! And rid the world of this scourge once and for all!"

He stood there panting and trembling while Agatha stared at him. "Well, why didn't you say so?" she exclaimed.

Othar paused. "I—what?"

Agatha nodded furiously. "Being a Spark has ruined my life! My parents were killed by some insane construct! I spent most of my life crippled by some mind-altering device! Everyone wants me dead or on an examining table!"

Othar raised his pistol. "You *do* understand."

Agatha stepped up to him and grabbed his sweater in both hands. "Of course! And now you say that I can work with you to destroy them all? Count me in!"

Othar's jaw dropped. Slowly a tentative smile, not the forced jocularity of his public face, but a genuine smile, blossomed upon his face. "At last." He whispered, "Do you really mean it?"

Agatha rolled her eyes and puffed out her cheeks in dismissal.

"No." And she shoved Othar over the side of the airship.

As he plummeted from sight, he called out, "Foul!" and snapped off a single shot from his pistol before he vanished into a cloud below.

Agatha and Krosp peered over the side for a moment. When nothing happened, Agatha slumped down and wearily rested her head in her hands. "I really owe Gil an apology," she muttered.

A faint sound caused Krosp to peer upwards. He frowned. "The idiot hit the envelope. But we should still be able to stay up for a few hours."

Agatha roused herself. "Perhaps they have a patch kit."

Krosp shrugged as he hauled himself back onto his crate. "Doubt it. Ship like this, they judge every gram. A minor repair like this would get fixed at a dock before it was a problem. Won't hurt to check though," he conceded. "We'll need to see what we have available anyway."

"Oh?"

"We've got to steer clear of civilization. Our best bet is the Wastelands."

Agatha shivered. She had heard stories about the Wastelands. Although the Empire of the Baron was extensive, there were whole territories that were still uncontrolled, wild expanses where entire towns had disappeared overnight. It was the perfect place to hide, but there was a distinct possibility that once in, they'd never return. Agatha felt a sense of desolation filling her. The future looked bleak.

Mad Othar may have been, but he certainly had a point. The last several hundred years had been filled with a distressingly long list of catastrophes, disasters, blights, monstrosities and terror directly attributable to a small handful of crazed geniuses.

"Why am I bothering?" she whispered.

Krosp shrugged. "What?"

"Why shouldn't I just turn myself over to the Baron? Why shouldn't I just throw myself over the side right now?"

Krosp scratched his chin and then jerked the steering wheel. The little airship lurched to the side. Agatha grabbed onto the railing and held on tightly. Krosp pointed to her hands. "Because you don't want to die."

"But Othar had a point. Sparks—"

"Not all Sparks," Krosp interrupted. "Most of them *are* dangerous," he conceded. "But what about the ones who fight the monsters, save the towns, build the machines that help people. It's not what you *are*, it's what you *do* with it."

"But so many of them are monsters!"

Krosp grinned. "That's because being a monster is easy. Doing good, making a positive difference: that's hard. But that's what your parents did." He considered her. "Unless you think the construct was lying about the Heterodynes being your parents."

Agatha didn't even have to think about that. "Lilith wouldn't lie to me. Not about that. Not then."

Krosp nodded. "I have to agree. It's not like she did you any favors acknowledging it."

"And everybody is making such a big deal about it. The Baron must discover new Sparks all the time."

Krosp glared at her. "Because you're not just a Spark. You're the last of the Heterodyne family. Surely you must understand how momentous that is. As long as you're around, the Baron and every other major power in Europa will want to control you, and everyone else will either want to follow you or kill you. You've got to understand that."

"But that's all... politics. I don't care about any of that."

"Well you'd better start to care. Because everyone's going to care about you."

"You mean they're all going to want something from me."

Krosp nodded. "That's right, and like it or not, you'll cause a lot of trouble just by existing."

Agatha thought about this and had to admit the logic of it. Her jaw tightened and she straightened up. "All right then," she declared. "Let's go cause some trouble."

ABOUT THE AUTHORS

PROFESSORESSA KAJA FOGLIO is the current head of the Department of Irrefutably True History at Transylvania Polygnostic University. She first became aware of the power of Creative History while listening to the excuses of her fellow students who had failed to produce their homework. Her doctoral work brought recognition to the long-hidden Canis operisphagus, or "homework-eating dog," which, as we now know, infests most of our major schools and universities. She first became interested in the history of the Heterodyne family during the infamous "Nymphenberg Pudding Incident" when she was mistaken for Agatha by an angry mob of dessert chefs, from whom she barely escaped. Her subsequent research has brought her the grudging acclaim and jealous rivalry of many of her academic colleagues. She enjoys airship racing, Hyrulian Electro-Mechanical Shadow Puppetry, and illustrated novels.

PROFESSOR PHIL FOGLIO spends most of his time in the field, collecting legends, folk songs, anecdotes, and gossip pertaining to Sparks and their effects on village society and "folk science." This is a bit odd, as he was originally hired by Transylvania Polygnostic University to teach Modern Dance. He first became interested in Heterodyne stories while doing research on simple automatons, and was actually present when the Lady Heterodyne unleashed her "Battle Circus" upon Baron Klaus Wulfenbach. Through subsequent research, bribery, and rampant speculation, the professor has managed to fill in a great many of the narrative gaps in the early life of Agatha Heterodyne. He enjoys botany, mechanical illustration, entomology, and—in moderation—modern dance.

The ongoing adventures of Agatha Heterodyne can be found online, where they are updated every Monday, Wednesday & Friday at www.girlgeniusonline.com.

BOOK TWO
AGATHA H AND THE CLOCKWORK PRINCESS
PHIL & KAJA FOGLIO

Intrigue! Subterfuge! Circus Folk! In a time when the
Industrial Revolution has escalated into all-out warfare, mad
science rules the world… with mixed success.

After escaping from the massive airship known as Castle
Wulfenbach, Agatha falls in with a travelling troupe of
performers, where she begins training under Zeetha,
swordmistress and princess of the lost city of Skifander. With
the ruthless Baron Wulfenbach on her trail, it's going to take
more than a spark of Mad Science for Agatha to traverse the
treacherous wasteland of war-torn Europa…

"This zany and playful gaslight fantasy is an immersive
yet lighthearted and delightful bit of adventurous fun."
Publishers Weekly

"Full of humour, skewed science, accidental adventure, and
perfectly awkward romance… As each page is turned, it is
increasingly hard to resist laughing out loud. This is how
steampunk is meant to be!" *Library Journal*

TITANBOOKS.COM

GLASS THORNS

MELANIE RAWN

TOUCHSTONE

Cayden Silversun is part Elven, part Fae, part human
Wizard—and all rebel. His aristocratic mother would have
him follow his father to the Royal Court, but Cade lives and
breathes for the theatre. With his company, he'll enter the
highest reaches of society and power, as an honoured artist—
or die trying.

ELSEWHENS

(February 2013)

Touchstone, the magical theatre troupe, continues to build
audiences. But Cayden is increasingly troubled by his
"elsewhens," the uncontrolled moments when he is plunged
into visions of the possible futures. He fears that his Fae gift
will forever taint his friendships, and his friends fear that his
increasing distance will destroy him.

"Rawn's storytelling mastery, ability to create unforgettable
characters, and fresh approaches to world building and
magic theory make this a must-read." *Library Journal*

"This strong, heartfelt performer's tale will appeal to fantasy
fans and theatre lovers alike." *Publishers Weekly*

LO'LIFE

JOANNE REAY

More weapon than woman, Lola hunts a predator like no other: the Tormenta. From their method comes their name: they torment their human prey into committing suicide. At the moment of death, they siphon their victim's unspent life span and live out the stolen years. If they're smart, they use their time to hone their fighting skills. Because all Tormenta know that there are Hunters out there, like Lola, devoted to bringing them down.

ROMEO SPIKES
BLACK ANTLERS
(coming soon)

"A powerful paranormal thriller that grips readers from start to finish." Alternative Worlds

"A fast paced, breath-of-fresh-air, scary, exciting, and rather unique, humdinger of a novel... I dare you not to get hooked at page one!" My Bookish Ways

"A great urban fantasy read... 5/5 stars." Fantasy Faction